A BRUTAL MUI
LAWYER, AND A R
THE FUTURE OF A NATIONAL FOREST
COMBINE IN A LETHAL MIX THAT
THREATENS TO DEVASTATE A SMALL
MONTANA COMMUNITY AND ANY
NUMBER OF LIVES ALONG WITH IT...

Kalispell, Montana Attorney Dave Matthews is on a downhill slide, blaming himself for the recent death of one of his closest friends. He's drinking heavily and generally avoiding his responsibilities when the brother of another close friend, a mill worker named Steve Helstrom, is charged with the murder of a prominent environmentalist. Dave reluctantly agrees to defend Helstrom and suddenly finds himself thrust into a case in which the evidence appears heavily stacked against his client. He's also finds himself thrown in the middle of a raging battle over the future of Montana's national forests, and before it's over Dave's own future will be very much on the line as well.

"Crossroads is a deep dive into the kind of deadly conflict that a vast and beautiful landscape can produce. There's treachery in Thane's Big Sky country, and battle-worn lawyer Dave Matthews is determined to peel back the layers to reveal the always-elusive truth. An engrossing read!"—*Gerry Boyle, author of Strawman and the Jack McMorrow mysteries.*

Praise for the Works of James L. Thane

"Fatal Blow is one of the best procedurals I've read in years. Packed with twists and turns and unexpected revelations, it's beautifully written and tautly plotted. Thane's finest yet!"

— *Christine Carbo, Award-winning author of The Wild Inside*

"Fatal Blow is a meticulous and engrossing procedural— from the perspective of both the dogged detective and the surprising, enterprising criminal."—**Lou Berney, Edgar Award winning author of** *The Long and Faraway Gone*

"Thane reads like Michael Connelly and his Phoenix is detailed." — *Paul French, CrimeReads*

"*No Place to Die* is a two-in-one treat, a convincing police procedural bolted to a nail-biter suspense novel. A good novel gives you real people in a real place, and James L. Thane delivers both with his skillfully drawn cops, victims and crooks in today's Phoenix." — *Sam Reaves, Author of Mean Town Blues*

"*No Place To Die* is an auspicious beginning to what I hope will become a series. Sean and Maggie make a great crime-solving team."— *Barbara D'Amato, Author of Death of a Thousand Cuts*

"An excellent debut..."— *The Poisoned Pen Booknews*

"An engaging police procedural that hooks the audience. ... Readers will relish James L. Thane's tense thriller."— *The Mystery Gazette*

"A fast action thriller"— *Suspense Magazine*

CROSSROADS

James L. Thane

Moonshine Cove Publishing, LLC
Abbeville, South Carolina U.S.A.
First Moonshine Cove edition August 2019

James L. Thane

ISBN: 978-1-945181-658
Library of Congress PCN: 2019908931
Copyright 2019 by James L. Thane

Dedication

This book is dedicated to the memory of my father who loved
Flathead Lake, as did his father before him

Other Works

No Place to Die

Until Death

Fatal Blow

CROSSROADS

1

Thursday, June sixteenth, nine fifty p.m. I was sitting in the Avalanche Saloon in Lakeside, drinking Jack Daniels straight up, trying to mind my own business and wishing desperately that the rest of the world would do the same.

Across the horseshoe-shaped bar, a petite woman with a strain of red hair unknown to nature smiled brightly every time I glanced in her direction. Although it was the middle of June, the NBA playoffs were still dragging on endlessly, and on the television set above the bar, the Lakers were thumping the Cleveland Cavaliers. For some reason, this frustrated the hell out of the guy sitting four stools to my right who was obviously the product of an excellent parochial school education. Every time the Lakers scored or the Cavs missed a shot, he exclaimed "Jesus, Mary and Joseph," most often slamming his fist onto the bar for added emphasis.

I wondered why somebody on the far western edge of Montana would care so passionately about the Cleveland Cavaliers, but I wasn't so curious that I wanted to start a conversation with the guy.

Behind me a tall busty blonde was setting up a Karaoke machine, which apparently constituted the rest of the evening's entertainment. Promptly at ten o'clock, she kicked off the festivities herself with a sultry rendition of "Summertime," which — surprisingly — wasn't half bad. She finished to a smattering of applause and called for volunteers to step up to the mike and take a turn.

I glanced around the room at the other six patrons. None of them seemed particularly excited about the prospect of taking the stage, but the redhead winked and flashed another smile as I looked her way. Just then Darrin Allan hit a three-pointer for the Lakers and the bar rocked again. "Jesus, Mary and Joseph!"

The blonde continued to plead her case, insisting it was time to "Party on!" Finally, a biker three stools to my left set down his beer, wandered over to the mike, and warbled a deeply emotional version of an old Kenny Rogers tune, "The Gambler," singing the entire song all in the same note.

I drained the last of my whiskey and signaled for a refill. Randy, the bartender, walked over, put his hand across the top of my glass and pulled the glass away. "That's enough for tonight, Dave," he said. "It's time for you to head on home and get some sleep."

"What do you mean? That's only my second drink of the night."

"Wrong, Counselor. That's only the second drink you've had in *here* tonight. That doesn't count all the ones you had up the road working your way down here."

"C'mon man, be a pal. I'm in good shape."

"Believe me, Dave, I *am* your pal. You might be in good enough shape to make it home in one piece if you leave right now. One more drink and you won't be in any shape at all. You're done in here for tonight."

With what little dignity I could still muster, I scooped up my change, leaving a five-dollar tip on the bar. As I slid off the stool, a dark-haired woman with the whitest complexion I'd ever seen followed the biker to the mike. Just as I reached the door, she began rocking from side to side and wailing at the top of her considerable lungs. I paused to listen for a moment and realized that she was attempting to sing "Chain of Fools." Shaking my head in disbelief, I stepped out into the cool night air knowing that somewhere in Motown, Aretha Franklin was turning over in her grave.

Jesus, Mary and Joseph.

***

I dug my keys out of my pocket, walked around to the parking lot on the north side of the building and settled into my car. I sat there for a moment, hoping that the fresh air would clear my head a bit, then started the engine, turned on the headlights and pulled carefully out of the parking spot.

I braked to a stop at the front of the lot and took a good long look up and down Highway 93, the north-south route that serves as Lakeside's principal artery. Seeing no traffic coming in either direction, I eased my way out onto the highway and headed south. Focusing as intently as I could, I managed to drive the next two miles without incident at a sedate fifty miles per hour and breathed a huge sigh of relief as I left the highway and turned east onto the blacktopped road that would take me the last three miles to my home on Angel Point. From here on at this time of night, there would be little likelihood of encountering any other traffic and zero chance of meeting up with the Montana State Highway Patrol.

I followed the twisting, hilly road at about twenty-five miles per hour, rolling slowly through the forest of lodge pole and ponderosa pines that towered over me like the spires of a medieval cathedral. Ten minutes later, I hit a button to open the gate at the head of my drive and another to open the garage door. I pulled into the garage, turned off the engine and the headlights, and pushed the appropriate buttons to close the gate and the garage door behind me.

I made my way through the garage and down the flight of stairs to the darkened house below. Turning on a light as I walked through the kitchen, I went to the bar in the living room and poured three fingers of Scotch into a heavy old-fashioned glass — my last drink of the evening. Then I crossed the living room, opened the sliding glass door, and stepped out onto the wide deck that fronted the upper level of the house.

Above me, millions of stars blazed across the clear night sky. Through the woods a hundred and fifty feet below the house, the lake lapped gently at the shore, and off in the distance, I heard the plaintive cry of a loon searching for its mate.

Ten months earlier, on a night very much like this one, my carelessness had caused the death of one of my best friends and had cost me the affection of his wife, Alice, who had once been my lover. The intervening months had, if anything, served only to intensify the guilt that had haunted my every moment in the days and nights since, and to further deepen the agonizing depression into which I had tumbled. For something like the ten thousandth time, I silently apologized to him. And to her. And then, staring off into the dark void across the lake, I tossed off a large portion of the whiskey, which would not be my last drink of the evening after all.

2

I was still dead to the world, lost in the melancholy of my haunted dreams, when the phone began ringing a few minutes after eight the next morning. Without opening my eyes, I reached an arm out from under the covers. Groping blindly, I snagged the phone, pulled it under the covers, and managed to mutter a weak "Hello?" through the bale of cotton that had taken up residence in my mouth.

"Dave? It's Bob. Sorry to bother you, but we've got a major crisis. I need to see you right away."

I pushed the covers away from my face, massaged my eyes, and pinched the bridge of my nose — like that would help dissipate a hangover that was registering somewhere around 9.5 on the Richter Scale — and said, "What's the problem?"

"It's Steve. Chris just showed up at his house and arrested him."

"Arrested him for what?"

"Murder."

"Bob, for God's sake, what do you mean, arrested him for murder? Whose murder?"

"Toby Martin, the attorney. He was found beaten to death last night on the lawn in front of his family's place outside of Creston and Chris is holding Steve on suspicion of the murder."

"Oh, Jesus, Bob, you can't be serious!"

"Unfortunately, I am."

"Where are you now?"

"I'm on my way to the sheriff's department. They're holding Steve there."

"Okay, I'm on my way. Give me forty-five minutes, depending on traffic."

"Thanks, Dave. But please hurry. I really need your help here."

I hung up the phone and crawled out of bed, willing the hangover out of my system. When that proved ineffective as it usually did, I fell back to plan B. I hurried into the kitchen, popped a couple of pieces of wheat bread into the toaster, and drank two full glasses of water. I followed the water with the toast, then shaved and showered as fast as my condition would allow.

Not knowing what the rest of the day might hold, I dressed in a dark blue blazer over a pair of gray slacks, a light blue shirt and black loafers. I grabbed a suitable tie in case I should need one, stuffed it into the pocket of the blazer and headed out the door. Fortunately, traffic between Lakeside and Kalispell was fairly light and thirty-five minutes after leaving home, I pushed through the doors of the Flathead County Justice Department where I found Bob Helstrom pacing anxiously back and forth in the lobby in front of the Sheriff's office.

Bob was born and raised in Bigfork, a small community directly across the lake from Angel Point. During the summer he runs a charter fishing boat service out of Somers at the head of the lake, and in the winter, he works as a ski instructor at the Big Mountain resort above Whitefish.

Given that we're about the same age and that we'd attended local schools at roughly the same time, we'd been generally aware of each other's existence for years. But several winters ago, we'd begun running into each other fairly routinely on the courts of the Glacier Tennis Club in Kalispell and had become close friends. We now played tennis and golf together on a regular basis, and another member of our usual foursome was Chris Williamson, the sheriff who'd just arrested Bob's brother on suspicion of murder.

Bob came over to greet me, looking like a man at the end of his wits — which, under the circumstances, was hardly surprising. He was wearing one of his older golf shirts over a pair of wrinkled chinos, and his thick dark hair was sticking out in every direction. His bluish-green eyes looked even worse than mine, and all in all, he gave the appearance of a frantic brother who'd just jumped out of bed, thrown on the first clothes he could find, and raced down to the sheriff's office.

"Dave, Jesus, thanks for coming so quickly. I don't know what the hell to do here."

"Tell me what happened."

He shook his head, ran his hand through his hair, and said, "I don't really know a helluva lot more than what I told you on the phone. Steve's wife, Karen, called me this morning and said that Chris and one of his deputies had come to the house a little before seven and asked for Steve.

"Karen said she went up to the bedroom where Steve was getting ready for work and asked him why Chris would be looking for him. Steve said that he had no idea. He told her that he'd been in a fight on Monday night, but that nobody'd been hurt too much, and that there hadn't been damage to any property. The only thing he could think of was that the guy he'd been fighting with wanted to give him grief by filing charges against him.

"Anyhow, Steve finished getting dressed and went downstairs. Before Chris would let Steve say anything, he read him his rights, emphasizing that Steve was entitled to ask for a lawyer and that the questioning would stop anytime Steve wanted it to.

"Steve said that he couldn't see why he'd need a lawyer and Chris asked him if he'd been in a fight on Monday night with Toby Martin. Steve said that he had but insisted that it didn't amount to anything at all. Then Chris asked if, during the course of the fight, Steve had threatened to kill Toby. At that point, Karen had sense enough to tell Steve not to answer the question and asked Chris what the hell was going on. Chris said that Toby was dead — that he'd been murdered — and that several people who witnessed the fight said they'd heard Steve threaten to kill him.

"Of course, Steve was shocked and insisted that he hadn't done it. He swore that he hadn't seen Martin since Monday night. Karen told him to shut the hell up and not to say another word without an attorney. Chris told Steve that was excellent advice. Then he said that he was very sorry, but that he had no choice in the matter — he had to arrest Steve on suspicion of murder.

"Steve told Karen to call and ask me to get in touch with you. Chris told her that they'd bring Steve into the department, put him a holding cell, and that no one would question him until you got here. They took the clothes Steve was wearing last night as evidence and they impounded his truck. When Karen called, I raced over and got here while they were fingerprinting and booking him."

"Jesus, Bob, I'm sorry. How's Karen holding up?"

"About like you'd expect — she's terrified. I told her to stay at home with the kids and that I'd call her as soon as there was any news."

"Okay," I said. "Let me go in and talk to Chris. Why don't you grab a seat over there and wait for me? It won't do you or Steve any good if you wear yourself out grinding down the linoleum."

***

I left Bob in the lobby, walked into the sheriff's department, and arched my eyebrows at Annie, the matronly receptionist. She shook her head slightly, gave me a sad smile, and said, "Go on in. He's waiting for you."

I found Chris leaning back in the chair behind his desk, wearing his usual law enforcement uniform — well-worn jeans, a long-sleeved blue oxford shirt, and a pair of Montrail hiking boots which were planted on the desk in front of him. At thirty-seven, he was two years older than I, a couple of inches taller than my five-eleven, and twenty-five pounds heavier than my one sixty-five. His hair, once the color of dense black coal, was now showing the first hints of silver, which complemented his slate-gray eyes and seemed to make him even more attractive to the large number of local women who'd been devastated when he married his long-time high school sweetheart. Looking thoroughly exhausted, he pointed me in the direction of a chair in front of the desk, and said, "Jesus H. Christ, can you believe this shit?"

"In a word, no."

"Me either. Going over to Steve's house this morning was one of the hardest things I've had to do since I took this goddamned job. But I figured I owed it to Bob to do it myself rather than sending Tony or someone else."

"You don't honestly believe that Steve killed Toby?"

"I sure as hell don't want to, but things are not lookin' good."

"How so?"

"For openers, we have a number of witnesses who saw the fight out at the Crossroads Monday night and who say they heard Steve swear that he was going to kill Martin. To make matters worse, we found the apparent murder weapon in the bed of Steve's pickup. It's an ax handle with blood all over the business end of it. The lab will run tests to see if the blood belongs to Martin."

"What about fingerprints?"

"Naturally, the lab will be checking for that as well, but I don't know yet if there are any usable prints on the thing, let alone who they might belong to."

I nodded my understanding. "When was Martin killed?"

"Sometime between seven and ten thirty last night. Witnesses confirm that he had dinner alone at Moroldo's in Bigfork and that he left there about seven o'clock. So far, we haven't found anyone who can tell us where he was between the time he left the restaurant and the time his brother Mike found the body on the lawn in front of the house at ten thirty. Mike called nine-one-one at ten thirty-seven, and the dispatcher rousted Tom and me. Uncle Gene examined the body on the scene and suggests that Toby was probably killed a lot closer to ten thirty than to seven. Gene's doing the autopsy as we speak, and he promised me a preliminary report

17

by noon. I'm hoping that he'll be able to pin down the time of death a little more closely by then.

"The killer left Toby's wallet in his pocket, an expensive watch on his wrist, and a hundred and eighty-seven bucks in his pocket, which suggests pretty clearly that robbery was not the motive. Naturally, we're still out interviewing witnesses and working the scene, and I'm hoping like hell that we'll come up with another explanation for what happened last night. But given what we've got at the moment, I had no choice but to bring Steve in, and I feel like hell about it."

"I understand. But it's not your fault. Given what you've got, you *didn't* have a choice."

"I know, but that doesn't make me feel any better about it. Why don't you go on down and see your client? He must be scared shitless."

***

I left Chris in his office and went back out into the bullpen where the deputies' desks were located. Tony Boyce, the deputy who'd accompanied Chris in making the arrest, got up from a desk where he was working and said, "Are you ready to see Steve now?"

I nodded, and he told me to wait in one of the interview rooms while he went back to get Steve.

The interview "room" was only a little larger than a small walk-in closet. A battered oak table sat in the middle of the floor with three matching straight-back chairs haphazardly arranged around it. Two ceiling-mounted fluorescent lights illuminated the dingy gray walls that looked like they'd last been painted sometime during the Truman administration. I knew the room well from the time I'd spent as the Assistant County Prosecutor, but back then I never could have imagined that one day I'd be waiting there to interview the brother of one of my best friends.

A couple of minutes later, Tony returned with Steve in tow. At forty, Steve was seven years older than Bob. He stood just under six feet, and like his brother, he'd inherited their mother's blue eyes and thick, darkish hair. He might have been a fairly handsome man, but he'd basically let himself go to seed, drinking too much beer, eating too much junk food, and refusing to do any exercise beyond that which he got working at the Krause Lumber Mill in Creston, a small town over on the east side of the valley, fifteen miles from the building in which he was now being held.

Generally speaking, Steve had a reputation as a hard worker, a dependable friend, a good family man, and a lousy drunk. He was one of those people who, for whatever reason, simply could not hold his liquor. This was not the first time he'd picked a fight in a bar — as often as not with the wrong person — and this in spite of the fact that he was not a particularly good barroom fighter. But, as is often the case with fights between drunks, he'd thus far never seriously injured anything other than his pride. He walked through the door of the interview room wearing a faded tee shirt hanging outside a pair of well-worn jeans, a couple days' worth of stubble, and a look of complete bewilderment on his face.

I stood, shook his hand, and said, "How are you doing, Steve?"

He shook his head in response. "Jesus, Dave, I have no idea why I'm here. They're saying that I killed Toby Martin. How could Chris possibly believe that?"

Tony interrupted to say, "I'll leave you two alone and wait outside at my desk. Let me know when you're finished, Dave."

I said that I would and motioned Steve to a chair as Tony left the room, closing the door behind him. I sat in the chair across from Steve's and said, "First of all, Steve, Chris doesn't want to believe that you're capable of this. Unfortunately, though, under the circumstances he had no choice other than to arrest you on suspicion. Believe me, he's sick about it."

"But I don't understand . . . I had a fight with the guy — that's all there was to it. I sure as hell didn't *kill* him."

"Why don't you take me through it from the beginning, starting on Monday night?"

He gave me a sheepish look and said, "Well, Monday night I was out at the Crossroads with Andy Barnett. We were having a couple of drinks, you know? Among other things, we were pissing and moaning about the state of the local economy and about how the damned environmentalists are making things even worse by trying to shut the loggers out of the national forests. We'd been in there for . . . I dunno . . . an hour or so maybe, when the door opens up and who the hell walks in but Ray Miller and that cocksucker Toby Martin, God rest his soul.

"Martin walked up to the bar, pretty as you please, as if he didn't care at all about the fact that he and his buddies are trying to put about half the town outa work. He sat down a couple of stools away from me and ordered a beer. So, I asked him if he was really fuckin' proud of himself or what? I reminded him that his family had been in this valley even longer than mine and said, didn't it bother him to side with the fuckin' enviros against the people he'd grown up with and known all his life?

"He gave me a smart-assed look and said that I was right. His family had been in the valley longer than mine, and that was probably why he cared for the valley more than I did and wanted to protect what was left of it. I called him a fuckin' tree-hugger and told him that thanks to him and his asshole friends, before long nobody in this valley would have a goddamned job.

"Well, one thing led to another, and before long we were both off our stools pushin' at each other. Then the bartender came over and told us to take it outside, so we did. A handful of people came out back with us to watch, and a couple of them were taking action on the outcome."

"How much had you had to drink up to that point?"

He paused for a moment, thinking about it, and then said, "four beers — no more than that. I had two at Moose's Saloon in

Kalispell, and I think I'd just finished my second at the Crossroads when all this started."

"Okay, Steve. What happened when you got outside?"

"Well, to be fair about it, once we got out there, he tried to let me off the hook. He told me I was too drunk to fight him, that he didn't want to fight me in the first place, and that we should just let it go. But he said he was tired of putting up with all the shit he'd been getting lately and that if I didn't want to let it go, he'd kick the crap out of me. I told him to go to hell and called him a chicken shit. I told him he couldn't kick the crap out of a girl scout. I said I'd fuckin' kill him."

"So, you *did* threaten to kill him?"

"No! . . . I mean, shit, not really. I didn't mean that I was *literally* going to kill him. I just meant like, you know, I was gonna kick the hell out of him in the fight."

"So, what happened?"

"Well, we danced around each other for a few seconds and I threw a punch at him but missed. I threw another one and he ducked inside it and smacked me in the nose. It started bleedin' pretty bad, and that really pissed me off. I charged him, and he wrapped me up. We swung at each other a few more times, but neither of us had enough leverage to do any damage. We dragged each other around the parking lot like that for another minute or so, and finally Andy and Miller stepped in and pulled us apart. Ray said something like, 'That's okay, leave it alone now.'

"We went back inside, and I went to the john and cleaned up. By the time I was finished, Toby and Ray were gone, and I never saw Toby again after that — I give you my word of honor, Dave. I sat down at the bar and had one more beer. By then it was about eleven o'clock. I left my truck in front of the Crossroads and Andy gave me a ride home. He picked me up yesterday morning and dropped me by my truck on our way out to the mill."

"Okay, Steve. What did you do yesterday and last night?"

He gave a small shrug. "I was at work from seven thirty to four thirty. On Tuesday nights, Karen works until nine at the fabric store, and so after work, I went over to Ed Ramsey's. We work together at the mill, and I was helping him put a new transmission in his truck. We worked on it until around eight fifteen."

"Was anyone else there?"

"No. Ed and Doris aren't gettin' along too well at the moment, and so last week she took the kids and went to her mom's over in Sandpoint."

"Were you and Ed drinking while you worked on the truck?"

"Yeah — mostly Ed, though. We took a six-pack out to the garage, and he drank four of them. I only had just the two beers between the time I got there and the time I left."

"What did you do after you left?"

"Well, I was driving home and as I passed the Crossroads, I decided to stop in for just one beer."

"What time did you get there?"

"I dunno — around eight thirty, I suppose."

"Okay, then what?"

Again, he gave me his sheepish look and said, "Well, I got there and ran into Bill Desmond who's up visiting his mom from Salt Lake. I hadn't seen Bill in forever and so we spent thirty minutes or so catching up over a couple of beers. Then about nine fifteen, I left to go home."

"Who else was in the bar?"

"Well, Lisa Jackson was tending bar. Then there was Bill. Chuck Wilson was just leaving when I got there, and there were two or three other people that I didn't know."

"So, you left the bar at nine fifteen. Then what?"

"I started drivin' home, but after a couple of beers at Ed's and then the two at the Crossroads, I wasn't really trackin' too good, and so I pulled over to the side of the road for a while to let my head clear a bit. I fell asleep in the truck and woke up about an hour later. I was feeling a little better by then, and so I drove on home as careful as I could. I got there about ten thirty or ten forty-five and went straight to bed. Then this morning, Chris showed up and arrested me."

"Okay," I said. "You're telling me that there are witnesses who can account for your time basically all day yesterday and into the evening except for the time it took you to get from Ed's house to the Crossroads and for the hour or so you spent napping in your truck on the way home?"

"Right."

"Okay, Steve, do you normally carry a spare ax handle in the bed of your pickup?

He gave me a look that appeared genuinely confused. "No. The only time I'd have one in the truck is if I also had an ax and was on my way somewhere to do some work with it."

"So, what do you have in the bed of your truck at the moment?"

Still looking confused, he thought about it for a moment, then said, "A tire, my jack, and the jack handle. I had a flat on the way to work Monday morning. I changed it as fast as I could and just threw the flat and the rest of that shit into the bed of the truck and raced off to the mill. I haven't had a chance to get the tire fixed yet, so it's still there."

"That's it? The tire, the jack, and the jack handle — no ax handle?"

"No. No ax handle. Why're you asking about an ax handle?"

"Well, Steve," I said, as sympathetically as I could, "that's the real crux of our problem here. Martin was beaten to death, apparently with an ax handle. And Chris and his deputy found a bloody ax handle in the bed of your truck this morning. That's the main reason why Chris had to hold you."

Helstrom's eyes widened; he shook his head, and said, "No fuckin' way. That can't possibly be true."

"I'm sorry, but I'm afraid it is."

He sat there looking totally bewildered and I said, "Where did you park your truck when you got home last night?"

"Right where I always do — in the driveway in front of my house."

"So, the truck was sitting out all night from the time you got home until the time Chris impounded it this morning?"

He nodded, then collapsed back into his chair and said in a bewildered voice, "I can't believe this. I fuckin' can't believe it. This has got to be some sorta nightmare."

"I know it is, and I'm sorry. Believe me, I'll do the best I can to figure out what happened here, and you know that Chris will too."

"What'll happen now?"

"Well, absent some miracle that would exonerate you in the next couple of hours, you'll be formally charged and arraigned sometime later today. We'll ask the court to set bail, but you need to prepare yourself for the fact that the judge will almost certainly not grant it in a case of this magnitude. In that event, you'll be held in jail until your trial."

Tears welled up in his eyes. "Jesus, Dave, I can't believe this. I didn't do it."

I squeezed his arm and said, "I'm sorry, Steve. I know that this is going to be hard as hell for you, but I promise that I'll work as quickly as I can to get you out of here. In the meantime, I'm your spokesman in this case. Don't talk to anyone about this — and I do mean *anyone* — unless I'm with you and tell you to do so, okay?"

He dropped his head to his chest, then nodded his understanding. I squeezed his arm again, then got up and went out to tell Tony that we were finished.

***

I walked back down the hall to Chris's office where I found him on the phone. He waved me back into the chair I'd vacated thirty minutes earlier and wrapped up his conversation. Then he hung up the phone, leaned back in his chair, and said, "Well?"

I waited while he settled himself, looked him squarely in the eye and said, "Steve didn't do it."

"And you know this how?"

"I know this because I know Steve. Admittedly, he's occasionally a belligerent drunk, but we both know that in over twenty years of picking fights in bars, he's never gone beyond throwing a few wild punches that almost always miss the mark. Killing somebody would be totally out of character for him. Beyond that, I've interviewed enough suspects and cross-examined enough witnesses over the years to know when someone's feeding me a line of crap. He's telling the truth."

"And the truth would be what?"

"As you know, he admits to the fight with Toby on Monday night, but swears that he didn't see him again after that. He was at work at the mill through the entire day yesterday. After leaving there at four thirty, he went directly to the house of a guy named Ed Ramsey. Steve works with Ramsey at the mill, and he was helping Ramsey work on his truck. He had a couple of beers while he was there and left about eight fifteen. Then there's a fifteen-minute gap while he was driving from Ramsey's house to the Crossroads, which certainly would not have given him enough time to kill Martin.

"Witnesses will place him in the Crossroads for the next hour or so until he left at around nine fifteen — he had a couple more beers there. And then we have a problem. He left the Crossroads and drove part of the way home. But he realized that he was in no condition to drive, so he pulled off to the side of the road and napped for an hour or so before he woke up and drove on home.

"Obviously, in that hour he would have had time to drive out to the Martin place, have another altercation with Toby, and whack him over the head with the ax handle. But again, it would be totally out of character. Steve's never attacked anybody with anything other than his fists. And — more important — you know as well as I do that after drinking four beers Steve wouldn't be capable of even driving out to Martin's, let alone getting into another scrap with him."

Chris shook his head, and said, "Well, you're right. You've got a problem — and it's a huge one. That hour would have given Steve *plenty* of time to get out to Martin's. What's more, that one unaccounted-for hour out of his evening is almost certainly the time that somebody was bashing Martin over the head. And not just once. He was beaten savagely, Dave. Somebody who must have been really pissed at Toby took after him with a vengeance. It wasn't a pretty sight, and jurors will not be in a forgiving frame of mind once they've seen the crime scene photos."

Shifting slightly in the chair, he said, "Admittedly, as you say, this would have been out of character for Steve. But as you know full well, emotions are running awfully high around here right now — especially among the folks in Creston who depend on that lumber mill for their economic livelihood. If the environmentalists manage to halt logging in the Kootenai National Forest, a lot of people are going to be in a world of hurt financially, Steve included. As much as I don't want to believe it, it's not beyond the realm of possibility that he got so pissed about the whole situation that he had a couple of beers, decided to have it out with Martin again, lost control of his emotions, and killed him in a fit of rage. And don't forget, of course, that Steve did threaten to kill Martin in the presence of a number of witnesses."

"But it wasn't a serious threat, and I doubt very much that any of the witnesses will swear that it was. He and Toby were just jawing at each other, pawing the ground before they started swinging. All Steve was threatening to do was to kick Toby's ass out there in the parking lot."

Chris fluttered his right hand. "Maybe, maybe not. But even if that were the case, there's still the minor matter of the ax handle to be considered, assuming that it does turn out to be the murder weapon."

"Well, yes and no. As you say, an awful lot of people will be adversely affected if this lawsuit succeeds; Steve certainly isn't the only one. Given that, *lots* of people might have been angry enough to attack Toby. For the record, Steve insists that there was no ax handle in his truck. And even if Martin was killed with an ax handle that you found there, that certainly doesn't prove that it belongs to Steve. His truck was parked all night right where you found it outside of his house this morning. Anybody could have killed Martin and pitched the ax handle into Steve's truck, setting Steve up as the fall guy."

"It's possible, but it's also not very likely." Ticking the points off on the fingers of his left hand, Chris said, "Steve had motive. He had opportunity. He threatened to kill Martin in front of a number of witnesses, and we found what appears to the murder weapon in his possession."

"But think about it. If Steve killed Toby, why wouldn't he just drop the murder weapon at the scene? At the very least, why wouldn't he pitch it out into the woods somewhere? Do you really think he'd be dumb enough to throw it back into his own truck so that you could conveniently find it there and hang him with it?"

"No, you wouldn't think that he'd do something that stupid. But, then, by his own admission, Steve was drunk last night. And there's no telling what he might have done under those circumstances.

"Hell, Dave, you know that we'll be chasing down every angle of this thing, and who knows — maybe it will turn out that the ax handle isn't the murder weapon after all. Or maybe it will turn out to have someone else's fingerprints on it. Maybe the autopsy will place the time of death earlier in the evening at a time when Steve has a solid alibi. God knows, I sure as hell hope it does. But failing that, I'd say you've got your work cut out for you, Pal."

"Don't I know it?" I said, rising to leave.

Chris shook his head, and then, indulging in the twisted variety of dark humor that can be permitted only after years of close friendship, he gave me a guilty smile and said, "I suppose this means that we won't be playing tennis tonight."

"I wouldn't think so," I said, returning his smile. "It looks like you and I will both be too busy, and I doubt very much that Bob will be in the mood. We're probably on hiatus until this business is resolved."

"I know." Shaking his head, he said, "Shit, this would have to happen just as we were getting back into a groove."

"Sorry about that. Let's just hope that we quickly discover that Steve couldn't have killed Martin, and then we can get back at it."

"Yeah, let's hope," he said, in a voice that didn't convey much confidence.

3

I walked back out into the lobby where I found Bob sitting on a bench. He listened attentively while I summarized my conversations with Steve and Chris. "You have to know that Chris feels like hell about this, but he really had no choice. Given the situation, especially given the fact that the apparent murder weapon was found in Steve's possession, Chris had to bring him in. But you also need to know that he'll be doing everything he can to get to the bottom of this as quickly as possible."

"I understand. And I don't hold this against Chris. He has a job to do, and I know that my damn brother can sometimes be his own worst enemy. But I also know that he isn't crazy enough to do something this stupid, no matter how drunk he might have been."

"I know that too," I said. "Now all we have to do is figure out what in the hell really did happen last night. I trust that you're going to go over and bring Karen and the kids up to date."

"Yeah, although I'm sure as hell not looking forward to it."

***

I left Bob to go deliver his bad news and drove the four blocks from the Justice Center to my office off of Main Street. After graduating from law school, I'd opened a solo practice in Kalispell. To help pay the bills while I was building up my client list, I'd also accepted a part-time position as assistant county prosecutor. However, I'd always loved to read and had long harbored the secret ambition of being a writer myself. And so, after several years, as a respite from prosecuting criminals and writing wills, pleadings, and real-estate closing agreements, I decided to try my hand at a novel featuring a prosecuting attorney named Randy Davis who had a much more exciting legal career than I did.

I knew there was only a slim chance that the book would ever find a publisher and an audience, but ultimately, I was much luckier than most aspiring authors. I was fortunate to find an agent who fell in love with my manuscript and sold it for an advance larger than I could ever have dreamed possible. The book was well received and did very well, although neither John Grisham nor Scott Turow had any reason to feel threatened by the competition. Two years and another book later, I gave up my part-time job with the county and began writing virtually full-time. I maintained an office and a small practice to go with it, but by then the law commanded an increasingly smaller amount of my time and attention — at least outside of the novels I was writing.

And then the disaster of last summer struck.

As a favor to Chris, I'd briefly gone back to work for the county to assist with a murder investigation, and the end result of my efforts were catastrophic. I'd helped produce a solution to the crime but at the cost of shattering several lives, my own included. In the aftermath, I withdrew from the world and retreated into a shell of isolation, rarely leaving the house except for business that I simply could not avoid and for the occasional solitary drinking spree when I could no longer stand even my own company.

Just in the last couple of months, I'd finally begun to emerge, somewhat gingerly, from my self-imposed exile and to reconnect with the friends that I'd abandoned. Most important among them were the other three men who constituted my Wednesday Night Tennis foursome, Chris, Bob, and Dick Walters, a local economist.

Until I'd deserted them, we'd been playing together regularly for several years, and getting back together with them had been a tentative first step toward reestablishing connections with the larger world as a whole. The last thing I wanted or needed at this point was another crisis — especially one that threatened to upset the normal patterns of a life that I was just beginning to renew. I especially dreaded the prospect of assuming a responsibility as daunting as a murder defense, and I seriously wondered if I was up to the job.

Given a choice, I would have immediately recommended that Steve find another lawyer. But I knew full well that he couldn't afford even to pay me, let alone any other attorney. If I didn't represent him, he'd be forced to rely on a public defender, and given the unfortunate realities of the system, even a reasonably talented P.D. would doubtless have only a minimal amount of time and even fewer resources to devote to Steve's defense.

Beyond that, I knew that even if I were able to duck the situation, my life was bound to be negatively affected by a murder investigation that placed two of my closest friends in an adversarial situation. And thus, as a practical matter, I had no choice. My only real chance of minimizing the damage was to take advantage of what legal skills I might still possess to try to get Steve out of this jam and get my own life back on the road to recovery as quickly as possible.

The question was, where to start? Admittedly, Steve might have had something of a motive to commit the crime; but, as I'd suggested to Chris, so did a large number of other local residents.

The victim, Toby Martin, was the elder son of one of the valley's leading families. In the 1930s, his grandfather, a wealthy banker from San Francisco, had purchased several hundred acres of prime land in the mountains and along the valley floor north of Creston, a tiny community fifteen miles east of Kalispell and about thirty miles south of Glacier National Park. Toby's grandfather built a cabin on the property and two generations of the family summered there through the 1940s, Fifties, and Sixties.

His son Robert — Toby's Father — married relatively late, and Toby was born three years later. Two years after that, Toby's mother died at the age of thirty-three while giving birth to his younger brother, Michael. Shattered by the loss of his wife, Toby's father gave up his life in San Francisco and bought controlling interest in a bank in Kalispell. He then built a new modern home on the family property near Creston and moved his two young sons to the Flathead Valley. Toby was a year ahead of me in high school and a year behind Chris.

Toby was an excellent student and an enthusiastic outdoorsman. He spent long hours in the mountains and along the lakes and rivers of the valley, hiking, hunting, fishing, and skiing. After graduating from Flathead High School, he returned to California to attend Stanford, the alma mater of both his father and grandfather. He graduated with honors and decided against a career in the family banking business. Instead, he remained at Stanford and enrolled in law school with an emphasis on environmental law. Degree in hand, he then returned to Montana and took a job as an attorney for the Northwestern Environmental Alliance in Missoula, a hundred and thirty miles south of Creston. He lived in Missoula but often drove up to spend weekends at the family place in the Flathead.

Earlier in the spring, Toby filed a lawsuit on behalf of the Alliance, challenging a group of timber sales in the Kootenai National Forest in the northwestern corner of the state. The Krause Lumber Mill in Creston, the town's principal employer, had won the right to log a portion of the land in question and had begun to harvest the timber. But Toby asked the district court to invalidate the sales and to halt the logging activity.

The judge was expected to rule on the request within the next couple of weeks. Were he to grant it, the mill would lose access to its principal source of timber and would be forced to drastically reduce operations, at least in the short term. This would result in the layoff of much of the mill's workforce and would also jeopardize the jobs of the loggers, truckers, and others who were employed in harvesting the timber from the lands in question and shipping it to area mills. Beyond that, of course, the negative effects of such a decision would ripple through the economy of the entire area.

Toby's action on behalf of the Alliance had further exacerbated the raging debate in northwestern Montana about the ways in which the area's natural resources should be managed and utilized. For several generations, the emphasis had been principally on the exploitation of those resources, particularly timber, with little regard for the environmental consequences of the logging and mining activity. And many Montanans continued to insist that the lands within the state's boundaries — national forest and range lands included — should be administered and developed in ways that would maximize the economic opportunities of the local population.

More recently though, growing numbers of people had moved to the area, attracted by its great scenic beauty and recreational opportunities. Additionally, an increasing number of valley residents now made their livings by providing goods and services to the two million tourists who visited the Flathead every year. Many of the newcomers supported much stricter environmental regulations that would preserve the forests and safeguard the many species of animals that lived there. Their views were shared, at least to some extent, by those in the tourism industry who were anxious to protect the natural attractions that brought visitors to the valley.

Each side insisted that it had the best interests of the valley and of the forests at heart, and extremists on both sides of the argument caricaturized their opponents in the most negative terms possible. The more radical environmentalists insisted, for example, that the timber interests were determined to clear-cut every last tree in the forest and to exterminate all of the animal species that depended on the forest habitat. Those on the opposing side insisted that the "enviros" were misinformed tree-hugging elitists who cared more about a handful of trees, birds, bears and fish than they did about the men, women, children and communities whose livelihoods depended upon the timber industry.

The voices of those moderates who favored something of a sensible middle approach were often lost in the cacophony of over-heated exaggerations that assaulted them from both sides of the argument. This had been especially true in the period since Toby filed the lawsuit, and feelings were running very high on both sides of the debate. Toby had been accumulating enemies left and right over the last few weeks, and realistically any one of them could have boiled over and killed him. Assuming that Steve was not the guilty party, there were any number of candidates. The challenge lay in reducing the list to a manageable size.

4

With a short break for lunch, I spent the rest of the morning and the early afternoon preparing for Steve's arraignment. Then, a little before two o'clock, I put on my tie, walked over to the Justice Center and up the stairs to the Flathead County Justice Court on the second floor. Promptly on the hour, Robert Gamble, the Justice of the Peace, took the bench and gaveled the proceedings to order. As I'd expected, he refused to set bail, and Steve was remanded to the county jail, pending trial on charges of deliberate homicide. By three o'clock, I was back in my office mapping out a strategy that I hoped would prevent his conviction on the charge.

I knew that Chris would be covering the ground thoroughly, but I still wanted to talk to most of the parties involved myself so that I could hear and evaluate their accounts firsthand. I decided that a good place to start would be with the staff of the victim's office, and so a few minutes after eight on Thursday morning, I cued up a Dave Alvin playlist on Spotify and rolled out of the garage.

Just under a million Montanans are sprinkled over the fourth-largest state in the union, and almost all of us are accustomed to spending a lot of time on the road. Work, school, shopping and recreational opportunities are often miles away from home, frequently by way of narrow, twisting two-lane roads and highways. My round trip to Missoula would be just over two hundred and forty miles, and native Montanans wouldn't even give it a second thought. We all grew up understanding that this was just the natural order of things.

The first thirty miles of the trip snaked along the west shore of Flathead Lake. It was a beautiful early summer morning, typical for this time of year, and the lake was coming to life under a bright blue sky. The sunlight sparkled off the water, which was swelling gently under a light breeze, and I sincerely envied the boaters, fishermen and others who were out enjoying the morning, probably without a care in the world.

From Polson at the foot of the lake, U.S. 93 took me through the Flathead Indian Reservation and a handful of small communities that were scattered through some of the most scenic landscapes in the country. The middle part of the route passed through the Mission Valley, a wide flat basin that had once been filled by Glacial Lake Missoula. When the lake's waters finally receded for the last time, about twelve thousand years ago, they left behind a very fertile bed of soil from which now sprouted a variety of crops. On the east side of the valley, the high peaks of the Mission Mountains stood sentinel over the activity below, as they had for thousands of years, mute testimony to the relative insignificance and impermanence of the changes that human beings had wrought upon the valley's landscape in the last two or three centuries.

Traffic was about average for this time on a weekday morning, and I rolled into Missoula just before ten. The Northwestern Environmental Alliance had its offices in an older two-story house on Spruce Street, on Missoula's north side. I parked on the street in front of the building and climbed the stairs to the front porch. A sign next to the door identified the house as the Alliance's offices and a bulletin board below the sign was papered with notices of various meetings and events related to environmental issues. Behind a screen door, the front door stood ajar and so I pulled open the screen door and stepped into a small foyer.

Immediately to my right was an open door with a plaque indicating that the office belonged to Toby Martin. Someone had taped a small black ribbon to the plaque, and in the office a young woman with her back to me was leaning over a desk sorting through some papers. I knocked softly on the door, startling the woman who'd obviously been sharply focused on the task in front of her. She jumped slightly and turned to face me.

She appeared to be somewhere in her middle twenties — a short, attractive brunette dressed in sandals, a pair of kaki cargo shorts, and a tee shirt with an image of the earth as seen from space along with the caution that, "It's the Only Planet We Happen to Have at the Moment."

Her hair was relatively short but styled in a way that nicely complemented her oval face. Four earrings in a variety of shapes were studded around the rim of her left ear; two more dangled from the right. Her light green eyes were bloodshot and ringed by dark circles as if she'd been crying heavily and not sleeping very well. She looked at me for a moment, gave a little sigh and said, "May I help you?"

"Forgive me," I said, digging out one of my cards. "I know that this is a difficult time for the people in your office, and I'm sorry to intrude. My name is Dave Matthews. I'm an attorney from Kalispell, and I was hoping that I could speak with some of the people who worked with Toby Martin."

Frowning, the woman took the card and looked at it for a second. Then she looked back to me and said, "Did you know Toby?"

"Yes, I did. Toby and I were in school in Kalispell at the same time. I knew him reasonably well then, but of course I didn't see hardly anything of him after he left to go to Stanford. Once he came back to Montana and took the job here, we ran into each other occasionally when he was up in the Flathead. Unfortunately, we weren't really close friends anymore, but I admired him. He was doing good work that he believed in, and I know that his death is a great tragedy for a large number of people, especially for those of you who worked closely with him. I'm very sorry for your loss."

"Thank you," she said, blinking back tears. "I just can't believe it."

"Did you work with Toby?"

"Yes," she said, extending her hand, "I'm Callie Buckner. I was his administrative assistant."

I shook her hand and said, "I regret meeting you under these circumstances, Ms. Buckner; again, I'm very sorry."

She nodded, sniffling lightly, and asked, "What was it you wanted to talk about?"

I looked at her, hoping that what I was about to tell her wouldn't cause her to have me thrown bodily out of the building, and said, "I'm trying to determine what led to Toby's death and who might have killed him. I know that a lot of people have been very angered by Toby's work here, especially by the lawsuit that he filed on the Alliance's behalf a few weeks ago. I wanted to get a more specific idea about the reaction to the work he'd been doing and to learn if any threats had been leveled against Toby as a result of it."

She backed away from me a couple of steps, folded her arms across her chest, and said in a hard voice, "Well, I don't understand what you mean. There doesn't seem to be any doubt about the fact that that asshole mill worker killed him. I hope that they hang the son of a bitch for it and that he rots in hell for the rest of eternity. What's your interest in all of this?"

"Well, Ms. Buckner," I said, "in the first place, it's not at all clear that the man who's been arrested for the crime is actually guilty of committing it. Obviously, there's some evidence that points in his direction or he wouldn't have been charged. But, of course, the standard of proof for conviction in such a case is obviously much higher than that required for an indictment on the charge. And in fact, this case is by no means open and shut. As you probably understand even better than I, an awful lot of people were very upset with Toby as a result of this lawsuit, and unfortunately, any number of them might have been angry enough to attack him. As it happens, I've been retained to defend Steve Helstrom, the man who's been charged, but I don't believe that he's guilty, and I'd very much like to know who really is."

Her faced reddened. She backed another step back away from me and said in a raised, agitated voice, "Wait a minute. You mean to tell me that you're representing the fucker who killed Toby and that you expect *us* to help you get him off the hook?"

"No, Ms. Buckner," I said quietly. "I'm not representing the fucker who killed Toby. I'm representing the man who's been accused of doing so, and again I don't believe that he's guilty. I assume that the people who worked with Toby would not want to see an innocent man convicted of the murder while the person or persons who actually committed the crime went free and were never punished."

"And just what in the hell makes you so sure that it wasn't your client who killed him?"

"A number of things, the most important of which is that I've known my client for several years, and I don't believe that he's capable, physically or emotionally, of committing such a crime. Also, I've heard his account of the events of the evening that Toby was killed. Believe me when I say that the prosecutor's case is not all that solid. Given the evidence that the state has at the moment, there's a good chance that my client will be acquitted on the charge. And if that should happen, enough time will have passed that it will be very difficult, if not impossible, to reopen the investigation and charge someone else with the crime. In that event, no one will ever be punished for Toby's death. I would think that possibility alone would motivate you and the others who worked with Toby, and who cared about him, to be sure that the authorities have charged the right person in the first place."

She paused, thinking about that for a moment, and then, obviously not convinced of my argument, said, "And what do you want from us?"

"Well, for openers I'd like to know if anyone had specifically threatened Toby as a result of this lawsuit or, for that matter, for any other reason."

She shook her head and flashed me a look of incredulity. "Again, you must be joking, right? If you live in the Flathead, you certainly know the climate that's been created up there by the militia types and the other right-wing wackos. We get letters and phone calls every day threatening violence against this office and against the members of the staff. It happens so regularly that we can't get the police to take any real interest in it. And frankly, it's become so routine that we're all virtually immune to it. We have a banker's box full of threatening letters in the closet upstairs."

"Were any of the more recent threats directed specifically against Toby?"

She gave me a small shrug and her tone softened a bit. "A few. As you said, his name has been prominently associated with the Kootenai lawsuit, and since we filed the suit, we've had a number of letters threatening retaliatory action of one kind or another. Some of them specifically mentioned Toby, but like virtually all of the hate mail we get here, the threats were unsigned and came with no return addresses."

"What about threatening phone calls?"

"We get a few. Again, it's a fairly regular thing."

"Do you have caller ID service here?"

"Yes, but those kinds of calls almost always show up as 'Unknown Caller' on the screen. What with all the crime shows on TV these days, hardly anyone is stupid enough to make an obscene or threatening call from his own home phone anymore."

I nodded. "So, as I understand the situation, you routinely file threatening letters in the banker's box you referred to. Do you keep any records of the phone calls?"

"Yes and no. We do keep the letters and we only make notes about phone calls in those rare instances when a number does show up on the caller ID."

"What about e-mails?"

"We do get e-mails fairly regularly from people regarding positions that we've taken. Some of them come from people who have obviously composed their own thoughts on some particular subject and who want to share them with us. A lot of e-mail messages, though, are form letters that people have been encouraged to send by some individual or group that supports or opposes a position that we've taken, and some of them are pretty angry. But we very rarely get e-mails that threaten violence against us."

"I gather from what you're telling me that Toby didn't appear to feel particularly threatened by any of the messages that he might have received lately?"

"No, I don't think so. And I'm sure he would have said something about it if he had." She smiled sadly and said, "Actually, Toby got a kick out of reading the crank letters that we get. Some of these people are pathetically illiterate. Some of them are just plain crazy, and a few of them are actually pretty funny. But he never took any of these people very seriously. He assumed that they were just venting."

"And none of these people ever showed up to vent in person?"

"Not as far as I know, although Toby did have a hellacious argument with Phil Krause, the mill owner, last week. But Toby certainly didn't seem worried about it after the fact."

"Tell me about the argument."

She leaned back against the desk and hooked a stray hair behind her ear. "Well, as you probably read in the paper, Krause organized a group of Creston citizens and brought them down here on a school bus to talk to our board about the lawsuit. The group included some of his employees from the sawmill, a few local business owners, and a couple of the Flathead County commissioners. He hoped that they could impress upon the board how important the mill was to the local economy up there and how they believed our lawsuit threatened the mill and the community.

"It was a fairly contentious meeting — very emotional as you might expect, especially on the part of the people in Krause's group. Frank Kane, our board president, did most of the talking for our side, but Toby was also there, as were most of the other board members. Frank tried to explain that we're not insensitive to the concerns of the people in Creston and in the other communities in that part of the state. He pointed out that the lumber industry in the northwest is suffering for a variety of reasons that have nothing to do with this lawsuit and told them that even if the Kootenai sales were allowed to go forward it would provide only temporary relief at best for the economy up there while causing serious, long-term damage to the forest itself.

"But, of course, Krause's people weren't having any of that. They aren't interested in the larger worldview. They're in trouble. They're looking for a scapegoat, and we're it. Basically, they made the same argument that they've been making for the last couple of months. They insisted that they're just as concerned about pre-serving the forest as we are and argued that if the loggers are barred from the Kootenai, it will ruin the economy of northwestern Montana and mark the end of a way of a way of life for the people up there. The meeting lasted for a couple of hours, with people basically just talking in circles until finally Frank thanked Krause and his group for coming down and told them that the board would take their arguments under consideration.

"When the meeting ended, the Creston people began filing out to their bus again and Toby came back down to the office. I stayed upstairs for a few minutes to gather up some things, and then as I came down the stairs, I heard Toby and Krause arguing in here. I didn't want to interrupt, so I waited outside until Krause left."

"What was the argument about?"

"Well, actually, I probably shouldn't have described it as an argument. Mostly it consisted of Krause shouting at Toby and asking him how he could care so little about the community where he'd lived most of his life. He said that Toby and his family had never been *real* Montanans — that they didn't understand the land or the people, and that they didn't care about anyone other than themselves.

"Toby tried to calm him down and insisted that he did care very much about the people in the valley. Again, he tried to point out that the problems of the timber industry in that area have much more to do with other, larger forces than they do with this lawsuit. And he told Krause that if anyone was to blame for his immediate problems it was Krause himself. He told Krause that his mill should not have relied so heavily on just one source of timber and that if he hadn't put all his eggs in one basket, his mill wouldn't have been running out of timber, lawsuit or no lawsuit.

"That really angered Krause and he told Toby that he'd be goddamned sorry that he ever got tangled up in this 'fucking environmental nonsense' quote, unquote. Then he stormed out the door, got on the bus, and went back up to Creston."

"Did you discuss the argument with Toby?"

"Yeah, but he just brushed it off. He said that Krause was basically a good man in a very difficult situation and that he was under a lot of strain. Toby said that he felt sorry for the guy — typical of Toby."

"I take it that you know of no one who might have been angry with Toby for any other reason — something that had nothing to do with his work, for example?"

"No, not at all. He was really a very kind and surprisingly gentle man. He was the person who was always trying to smooth over troubled waters, rather than roiling them up. The only people who disliked Toby were those who were unhappy about his work for the Alliance. No one who really knew him personally could have possibly disliked him."

I thanked the young woman for her help and again expressed my sympathy. She then showed me around the offices and introduced me to several other staff members, most of whom had the same initial reaction that she did when they learned who I was and what I wanted. A few of them ultimately relented and agreed to talk with me, but none of them was able to tell me anything more than what I'd learned from Buckner. I left the Alliance offices a little after noon and drove down Broadway to the Big Sky Drive-In where I got a hamburger and a Coke for lunch. Then I headed back up Highway 93 toward home.

5

An hour after leaving Missoula, I crossed over the Polson Moraine, passing from the Mission Valley back into the Flathead. At the bottom of the hill, I turned right onto Highway 35, which runs north through spectacularly beautiful country along the east side of the lake. For another thirty minutes, I made my way along the narrow, twisting two-lane road, which often seemed precariously balanced between the heavily forested mountains that rose sharply on my right and the lake that hugged the shoulder of the highway on my left. At Bigfork, I left the lake behind, and fifteen minutes later, the road bent to the west as it passed through the small community of Creston.

I rolled past the Creston Fish Hatchery and the MSU Agricultural Research station at the east end of town, then left the highway and followed Creston Road a mile and a half north to the Krause Mill. Hundreds of heavy logging trucks had preceded me over the road, leaving it seriously wash boarded and scarred with potholes, some of which appeared to be only slightly smaller than the Grand Canyon. I proceeded slowly and carefully, trying to circumvent the larger obstacles, but as my car bounced along over the gravel surface, it seemed that the wheels were airborne more often than they were in contact with the road itself.

Just as I reached the gates of the mill, an empty logging truck came roaring out and turned south down the road in my direction. I pulled over to the right, giving the driver as much room as possible, and waited as he shifted gears and accelerated past me. Then I turned through the gates and followed the signs to a cedar-sided office building. I parked in front of the building, climbed two stairs, and opened the door into a small reception area. A stout, middle-aged woman with bleached blonde hair sat at a desk, smoking a cigarette as she sorted through what appeared to be a stack of invoices. I handed her a card and asked if I could see Phil Krause.

She scrutinized the card carefully, holding it out in front of her practically at arm's length, and said, "Do you have an appointment?"

"No, Ma'am, I don't. And I'm sorry to barge in unannounced like this, but I was hoping that Mr. Krause might be able to spare me just a couple of minutes."

"And what shall I tell him you want to see him about?"

"Well actually, Miss, it's something of a personal matter."

She tilted her head a bit, looked at me skeptically, and said, "Well, just a minute then. I'll see if he's got time for you."

I thanked her and she put down the cigarette, pulled herself up out of the chair and headed slowly down a corridor to my left. A couple of minutes later she returned at an equally glacial pace and said, "Mr. Krause says that he can give you a couple of minutes. It's the second door on the right."

I thanked the woman and walked down the hallway to Krause's door, which was standing open. His desk sat at the far end of the large cluttered room, with two guest chairs facing it. At the other end of the room, opposite the desk, a tattered beige couch was flanked by two end tables. Both of the tables and about half of the couch itself were piled with books, magazines, maps and other materials that seemed to have been rather haphazardly deposited there. On the far wall, perpendicular to the desk and the couch, a large picture window looked out onto the activity in the main yard of the mill. Krause was sitting behind the desk, staring intently over the top of a pair of bifocals at something on his computer screen.

I tapped lightly on the door, and Krause looked up from the monitor and waved me into the office. He was a fairly large man,

46

a little over six feet tall, and pushing two hundred and thirty pounds, with thinning dark hair that was beginning to gray at the edges. I knew that he was somewhere in his middle fifties, but his careworn face looked more like it belonged to a man ten years older. Without rising from his chair, he picked up the card I'd given his receptionist, looked at it and said, "How can I help you, Mr. . . . Matthews?"

I walked over to the desk and extended my hand. He shook it warily, as he might have greeted an obnoxious salesman, and I said, "Well, sir, if you can spare me a couple of minutes, I'd like to talk to you about your relationship with Toby Martin."

"My relationship with Toby Martin? That's a good one. I *had* no relationship with Toby Martin. The guy was a major-league pain in the ass. I'm sorry he's dead, but that doesn't alter the fact that he caused enormous problems for me and for a lot of other people in this valley. Anyhow, just what the hell business is it of yours?"

"I'm defending Steve Helstrom, who, as I'm sure you know by now, has been charged with the killing."

Krause sighed, took off his bifocals, and invited me to sit in one of the chairs in front of the desk. I took a seat and in a voice that suddenly sounded very tired, he said, "I know Steve well. He's worked for us for nearly twenty years. He's a good man, and this whole thing is a goddamn shame. I feel sick about it."

"Having known Steve for twenty years, do you think he's capable of doing something like this?"

He shook his head. "Under normal circumstances, I'd say hell no. But then, these are hardly normal circumstances, are they? Right now, this mill and the jobs of a good number of people in this area are on the line. A lot of people, me included, are a judge's decision away from potentially losing everything we've worked for all our lives. And under those circumstances — when a man faces the prospect of losing his job, his home and what little

47

savings and security he might've been able to build up through the years — well, who the hell knows what any of us might be capable of doing?"

I nodded sympathetically. "I only know what I read in the papers, of course. Is the situation really that dire?"

He turned for a moment to look out the window into the mill yard, then picked up a letter opener with what looked like an especially fine-honed edge. Idly playing with the letter opener, he turned back to me. "Probably worse, actually. The truth of the matter is that small lumber mills like this one are more at risk than most of the damned critters on the endangered species list. Ten years ago, there were forty-five lumber mills in the state of Montana. Today there are twenty-two. Most of them are small operations struggling to survive just like we are, and of course, the situation is virtually the same in most of the other states here in the northwest.

"We're under assault from the damned Canadian mills as well as from mills in the southern U.S. The recession in Asia has killed the export market and the bottom has fallen out of timber prices. The economists and the other know-it-alls look at us like we're simple-minded children and tell us that there's too much lumber coming to market and too little demand for it. They say that we need to cut production to bring supply into line with demand. Well, as my son would say, No Shit! But that's a lot easier said than done.

"Like a lot of other mills, we've already cut production and our workforce fairly significantly over the last decade. But there's a limit to how much we can cut back and still remain a viable operation. And as I've been trying to explain to people, whether they want to listen or not, we're already there.

"This mill — and the people who depend on it — are basically hanging on by a thread as it is. And now, on top of all our other problems, we've got to contend with these damned tree-huggers who believe that the national forests should be off-limits for logging or for any other sort of human activity that might potentially offend the grizzlies, the salmon, or the goddamned Pileated Woodpeckers.

"In short, yeah — things really are that dire. I've had grown men in this office — men who've worked in this mill and in these woods all their lives — literally sobbing because they don't know how in the hell they'll be able to support their families if this mill closes. Would it surprise me if one of them boiled over and killed Martin? Not really, I guess."

I looked him squarely in the eye and said, "I understand that you had a pretty loud row with him yourself a couple of weeks ago."

"Oh, what — you think I killed him?" he said, with a harsh laugh.

"Did you?"

Shaking his head, he put down the letter opener, leaned forward and rested his arms on the desk. Then he looked up to meet my eyes and said, "No, Mr. Matthews, I did not. I'll confess that I've spent a lot of sleepless nights lately, lying in bed or pacing the floor in my living room, fantasizing about the various ways that I might have wanted to slowly torture Martin and the rest of his 'Alliance.' But it's not something I would've ever contemplated doing in real life. If you want to get Steve off the hook by finding 'The Real Killer,' you'll have to look elsewhere."

"Do you mind telling me about the argument?"

He shrugged and cleared his throat. "That's all it was, just an argument. There was nothing more to it. We'd gone down to Missoula, hat in hand, hoping that we might be able to prostrate ourselves before Martin's group and get them to appreciate the human cost of the action that they were proposing to take. We hoped, naively no doubt, that if we could get them to look into the faces of some of the people who would be directly affected, they might agree to drop the suit and work with us to find some compromise solution that would acknowledge the interests of both sides.

"It was a stupid idea, of course. Those people have no interest in us or in the fate of our communities up here. They're zealots, committed to their 'principles.' They're like religious fanatics who believe that they have a monopoly on truth and righteousness and that anyone who disagrees with them is in error and must be resisted and corrected.

"Anyhow, we went down there, and the two sides hollered at each other for a couple of hours without resolving anything. Then I followed Toby down to his office and he and I hollered at each other for another ten minutes or so. I told him that he, of all people, should realize the consequences of what he was doing. For God's sake, he spent most of his life in the Flathead Valley. He knew these people and their situation. He understood what this mill means to the community.

"Of course, he tried to tell me that he did care about the people and about the community but said that we couldn't continue to manage the forests for the short term — that we had to look to the long term as well. He insisted that the timber industry did whatever it wanted in the forests for well over a hundred years, and that the time had come to consider the interests of other people and of the forests themselves. He said he understood that the adjustment would be a painful one but that it had to happen sooner or later. He said he was truly sorry for the people who might be hurt."

"And what did you say to that?"

"I told him that he was basically full of shit. I said that it was easy for him to feel that way, having been born with a silver spoon in his mouth. I reminded him that the rest of the people in Creston hadn't been born with his advantages and said that he'd never been a *real* Montanan. Then I got the hell out of his office."

Holding his gaze with mine, I said, "I understand that during the course of the argument you warned Martin that he'd be sorry he'd gotten involved with the damned environmentalists."

Krause ran his hand through what was left of his hair and said in an exasperated voice, "Yeah, in the heat of the moment I guess I did say something to that effect. But I certainly didn't threaten him with physical harm — then or at any other time. I only meant to suggest that by siding with those lunatics he was making himself a pariah in his own hometown."

"Was that the last time you saw Toby?"

"No. The last time I saw him was the night he was killed. I was coming back to the office to do some work after dinner that night, and he was driving north out of town just as I was driving south into town. We passed each other on the highway just north of the volunteer fire department. He was driving that old beater pickup of his."

"What time was this?"

He shook his head. "I don't know — somewhere around seven fifteen or so, I guess."

"Do you mind telling me how you spent the rest of the evening?"

He shook his head. "And just why the hell should I?"

"You'll have to tell the sheriff's detectives anyhow. Why not humor me?"

Krause shrugged and said, "I worked here in the office — alone — until about nine thirty. Then I went home, clicked mindlessly around the television channels for an hour or so and went to bed. If the sheriff or his detectives want to talk to her, my wife will verify the time I got home."

"And I gather that, leaving Steve out of the equation, you have no idea who might have done this?"

"Mr. Matthews, I could give you a very long list of people who were mad as hell at Toby Martin. You might as well just open the local phone book and start with the letter A."

6

I left the mill, bumped my way along Creston Road back out to the highway, and headed south out of town. I skirted the north end of the lake, detoured briefly through the Blacktail market in Lakeside to pick up a few groceries, and continued on south to Angel Point Road.

Angel Point is a long promontory that juts out into the west side of the lake just south of the village of Lakeside. Over the years, the land has been repeatedly subdivided, and the entire point is now dotted with individual properties of varying size.

With my savings and the advance from my first book, I'd been able to afford the down payment on a beautiful piece of property that sloped gently from the county road some 400 feet down to the lake. It had a small house, built in the 1950s, which was in serious disrepair by the time I acquired the property. The seller was an elderly widow who then lived in Arizona and who had not visited the property in a good many years. Perhaps because of the dilapidated condition of the house, she set a very reasonable price on the property, especially considering its location and potential. She put it on the market in the middle of December, a time when hardly anyone is looking for property in the Flathead, and I made an offer two days later. She accepted it immediately, and I was convinced that I'd made the best real estate deal since the Louisiana Purchase of 1803.

Over the next year or so, I worked on plans for a new house to replace the one originally on the lot, and when the construction was finally completed, I sold my home in Kalispell and moved in. My neighbors included a mixture of families with modest homes who had owned their properties for a good number of years as well as a handful of fairly recent arrivals who'd built very lavish vacation homes on the point.

For many of the newcomers, their homes on the lake were merely places to spend a few pleasant weeks every summer away from their hectic and important lives in L.A., New York, or wherever. But for those of us who had been born and raised here, there was an attachment to Montana and especially to this valley that no one born outside of the state could ever truly understand. For me, as for so many others, the Flathead was in my blood, and I could never imagine living anywhere else.

Forty-five minutes after leaving Phil Krause's office, I pulled into my garage. I put away the groceries, grabbed my phone and speed-dialed Chris. Obviously seeing my name on his caller ID, he answered by saying, "I certainly hope that you have some bright ideas about this mess, because I sure as hell don't."

"Well, I'm sorry to say that I really don't either, but I wondered if you might want to get together over dinner and compare notes anyway."

He paused for a moment, apparently thinking about his schedule for the rest of the day, and then said, "Alfredo's, seven thirty?"

"I'll be waiting at the bar."

"See you then — and Dave? Don't get too much of a head start."

* * *

I sorted through the day's mail, thought about quickly mowing the lawn, then rejected the idea in favor of taking a swim. I changed into my trunks, grabbed a towel and a sweatshirt, and headed down the path to the lake. I draped the towel and the sweatshirt over a chaise lounge on the deck and continued on down to the dock, thirty feet beyond and below the deck. I stood at the edge of the dock for a moment, haunted by the spirits of Christmas past. Then, forcing the unbidden images from my mind, I dove into the chilly water.

Flathead Lake is the largest natural freshwater lake west of the Mississippi, twenty-eight miles long, and fifteen miles across at its maximum width. It's fed by cold spring rains and by the snowmelt from the mountains that surround it, and even at the height of the summer the water temperature rarely gets much higher than the low seventies. In the middle of June, it's still considerably colder than that, and the term "bracing" doesn't begin to accurately describe the experience of jumping into it.

I surfaced about twenty feet away, my body still reacting to the shock. I treaded water for a couple of minutes, adjusting to the temperature, and then swam a quick three laps between my neighbor's dock and my own. About thirty seconds before hypothermia set in, I dragged myself out of the water, hurried back up to the deck and toweled off. Then I pulled on the sweatshirt, stretched out on the lounge, and basically vegetated for the next thirty minutes or so, watching the early evening activity out on the lake in front of me.

Given that it was a weekday afternoon and that it was still pretty early in the season, there wasn't much to watch. There was barely any breeze, and the surface of the water was as calm and as flat as a sheet of glass. Seven miles across the lake, the Swan and Mission mountain ranges rose into the clear blue sky, and here and there a few gulls soared over the surface of the water.

A mile or so away, a couple of fishing boats trolled through the water, but the distance between us swallowed up the sound of their engines and the evening was blissfully silent and serene, save for the honking of a small flock of ducks who were paddling about fifty feet off the dock to my right.

High above the lake, I spotted an osprey soaring over the water in search of dinner. He made a couple of large circles and then dove, feet first, at incredible speed into the water, driving his talons into an unsuspecting fish that had wandered too close to the surface. Emerging from the water with a large trout thrashing helplessly in his grip, the graceful bird then wheeled off behind me, the evening meal in hand, presumably in the direction of his family's nest. Watching him fly off into the sunset, I decided it was about time to go in search of my own evening meal and so I gave up my reverie and went back up to the house.

**

At seven fifteen, I walked into Alfredo's restaurant on the beach in Lakeside and took my usual seat at the end of the bar. Alfredo waved a greeting from the other side of the half wall that separated the bar from the kitchen, and Johnnie Collins, the long, tall and very blonde bartender, dropped a cocktail napkin in front of me and raised her eyebrows in inquiry. In response, I said, "Club soda with a lime, please, Johnnie."

She gave me a quizzical look but said, "Good choice," as she scooped ice into an Old-Fashioned glass and set it on the napkin.

She squeezed the juice from a lime wedge over the ice, ran the wedge around the rim of the glass and dropped the lime on top of the ice. Then she cracked open a small bottle of club soda, filled the glass and set the bottle on the napkin next to the glass. "Not that I'm trying to discourage it," she said, "but why the change of pace?"

"Just seemed like a good idea."

She arched her eyebrows, nodded her agreement. "So, what are you up to tonight?"

"Not much. Chris and I are meeting for dinner. What's going on with you lately?"

"Oh, you know," she said, fluttering her hand. "Same old, same old."

A bus boy brought a rack of glasses fresh from the dishwasher and set them on a shelf behind the bar. Johnnie picked a glass out of the rack, began studiously polishing it and then said, as though it were an afterthought, "I got an email from Jenny yesterday."

I sighed and took a long pull on my drink, wishing fervently for a moment that it were something a lot stronger than club soda. Then I set the glass down on the bar, looked up at Johnnie, and said in a quiet voice, "How is she?"

She paused for a second, still contemplating the glass she was polishing, then gave me a small shrug. "Fine, I guess. She's finally found a job in a law office down there. She says that the work is challenging but very rewarding."

She hesitated for a moment while she set the glass on a shelf above the bar. Then, carefully looking away from me as she took another glass from the dish rack, she continued, "She says that she's begun dating a guy down there — a housing contractor, I guess."

I nodded, hesitated for a moment myself, then said, "I'm happy to hear it. I hope things work out for her."

Johnnie nodded her agreement and then moved up to the other end of the bar to fill an order for one of the waitresses, leaving me alone with my club soda and my memories.

"Jenny" was Jennifer Daniels, a vivacious, attractive, twenty-nine-year-old redhead who'd been my lover for several months before everything fell apart last September. She'd moved up to Lakeside from Colorado Springs early last year following her divorce and had taken a job waiting tables at Alfredo's while she looked for work as a legal assistant. We'd met soon after she arrived and began a relationship that had become increasingly serious as the summer progressed. She'd not been the love of my life, nor I of hers, but we'd forged a very comfortable rapport grounded in a growing affection and respect for each other, as well as a very strong sexual attraction.

In the end, though, I'd deserted her too, along with everyone else in my life. She waited patiently for a couple of months, hoping that the love I'd recently expressed for her would be strong enough — and important enough — to help coax me out of my depression.

But when that proved not to be the case, she packed her things into a small U-Haul trailer, gave up the house she'd been renting in Kalispell, and moved back to Colorado Springs. I knew that she was keeping in touch with Johnnie and with several of the other friends that she'd made up here, but I hadn't spoken to her or heard anything from her myself in seven months.

I sat there for several more minutes, lost in a tangled web of memories and regrets, until Chris walked through the door ten minutes late, at seven forty. I swallowed the last of my club soda and joined him at the hostess station.

***

A waitress who was doubling as the hostess for the evening, showed us to a table in front of the window that looked out over the marina and across the lake to the Swan Mountain Range in the distance. After listening to her description of the evening's specials, Chris ordered a breaded pork chop while I chose the Lasagna Bolognese. We agreed on a suitable bottle of wine, and as the waitress left with our orders, Chris took a drink of water and said, "So what have you discovered after a day and a half of sleuthing?"

"Well, in all fairness, after devoting most of yesterday afternoon to the arraignment, I really haven't had a full day and a half — more like three-quarters of today. And given all the manpower and other resources that the taxpayers have so generously provided you, I'm sure that you're considerably ahead of me in the sleuthing department."

"Jesus, I hope not. If that's the case, we're in deep shit here."

"Actually, what you really mean is that *Steve* is in deep shit here."

"Unfortunately, true. So, what have you discovered, if anything?"

I waited for a moment as the waitress returned with a plate of antipasti and set it on the table between us. Then I described my conversations with Callie Buckner and Phil Krause, concluding with the fact that Krause had seen Toby Martin driving north out of Creston at seven fifteen on the night of Martin's death.

Chris sat back in his chair, adjusted the napkin on his lap, and said, "Well, that *is* interesting. So far, we haven't been able to turn up anybody who saw Martin after he left Moroldo's at seven o'clock that night. And your visit to the Alliance office puts you a half a day ahead of us in that regard. Tom went down to interview the staff there this afternoon, but I haven't talked to him since he left. I assume he also heard about the argument with Krause and that he'll be talking to him shortly as well."

"So, what do you know?" I asked.

He shook his head and said, "I'm sorry to say that we haven't discovered anything yet that might be good news for your client. In fact, everything we've found since I talked to you yesterday only makes the case against him look stronger."

"How so?"

"Well, the worst news, I suppose, is that the lab has confirmed that Martin was killed with the ax handle that we found in the bed of Steve's truck. The only possible saving grace for you there is that the lab was not able to lift any usable prints from the ax handle.

"Otherwise, the autopsy report puts the time of death right around ten, with very little fudge factor either way. Since we knew exactly when Toby had eaten his last meal and what he'd had to eat, Uncle Gene was able to determine the time of death pretty precisely. And, as you well know, ten o'clock is the very time that Steve was allegedly sleeping it off in his truck with no one to vouch for him."

"But Krause has no one to vouch for him either for the virtually the entire period during which you can't trace Toby's movements that night. He claims that he was working alone in his office from seven thirty to nine thirty, but he has no one to verify it.

"Let's say, for the sake of argument, that he passes Toby on the road at seven fifteen, as he admits. And maybe he goes on to his office and sits there stewing about things for a while. Knowing that Toby was probably heading home, he grabs an ax handle and drives on out to the Martin place to confront him again. They have a row; Krause whacks Toby over the head, say around nine thirty, and goes straight home. Even if it doesn't take Toby several minutes to die, that's still close enough to fit comfortably with Gene's estimated time of death."

Chris shot me a skeptical look. "You're assuming, of course, that Krause knows about the fight between Steve and Toby and decides to make Steve the fall guy. So, he then slips out of bed in the middle of the night, drives over to Steve's house and drops the murder weapon into the bed of Steve's truck."

"Well, it's certainly possible. Stranger things have happened."

"That's going to be your defense?" He snorted. "Stranger things have happened? Jesus Christ, if that's the best you can do, your old boss is going to eat your lunch in court. But don't worry, we'll give Krause and his wife the third degree."

I ate an olive from the antipasti plate while I considered the improbability of the scenario I'd just suggested and said, "What else have you got?"

"Well, we've also continued to interview the witnesses to the fight on Monday night, all of whom insist that Steve did threaten to kill Martin. Steve will insist that he didn't mean it literally, but the jury's going to hear from five or six people who will swear that he did."

"What about the crime scene itself?"

Chris shrugged. "Not much there that will help or hurt Steve — or anybody else, for that matter. The evidence at the scene suggests that the killer caught Toby just as he was getting out of his truck in front of the house. There's a gravel road that runs in from the highway and loops around in front of the place. Mike Martin found the body lying right next to Toby's pickup. The driver's side door was standing open and Toby had fallen onto the lawn only a couple of feet off the driveway.

"Given the surface of the road and the dry conditions, we weren't able to identify tracks of any consequence, human or vehicular. A careful search of the scene turned up no evidence other than the body. As you know, the Martin place is very isolated, and so there aren't any neighbors who might have seen or heard anything. And as you also may know, Bob Martin, the boys' father, has been in the nursing home in Kalispell for most of the last year. And so, except for those times that Toby comes up — or came up — to visit, nobody except Mike Martin is currently living in the house."

"And where was Mike while all this was happening?"

"He took a date to dinner at Hops in Kalispell. The dinner lasted from seven until nine thirty, and then he drove the woman back to her home. The woman confirms this, as does the staff at the restaurant. Mike says that he left the woman's place in Kalispell a little after ten and drove straight home where he discovered his brother lying dead on the lawn."

"Of course you've interviewed Ed Ramsey by now?"

"Yeah, and he pretty much confirms Steve's story. He says that they were together from a little after five until Steve left around eight fifteen or eight thirty. He says that they spent a good portion of the evening commiserating with each other over the circumstances surrounding the mill and this lawsuit, and that they were both pretty pissed about Toby Martin's role in it. But Ramsey insists that it was all just talk — that Steve never indicated that he was thinking about going after Martin again."

I took a sip of wine. "What about Kevin McKinney and that crowd? McKinney's been going after Toby and the NEA pretty hard in that rag of his. Certainly, it's possible that one of his feeble-minded readers was inspired to go after Toby as a result."

"Of course it is. But which one of them? We have no evidence pointing in that direction, and as much as I might like to drag in for questioning anybody stupid enough to put fifty cents into a machine and buy a copy of McKinney's paper, I have no grounds for doing so. And hell, for all I know, Steve himself could be a charter subscriber."

I nodded my understanding, realizing full well that Chris was right, but not feeling any better about it.

While many people in the Flathead groused about environmentalists and believed them to be a threat to a long-established way of life, the vast majority northwestern Montanans were peaceful, law-abiding citizens who were willing to wage their battles in the legislature, in the courts, in letters to the editors of the regional newspapers, and in other such traditional and perfectly acceptable venues. Unfortunately, though, and for some un-fathomable reason, Montana had also attracted more than its share of radical extremists who were ready and willing to work outside of the system and who had no interest whatsoever in civil discussion.

Montana, of course, had been home to Ted Kaczynski, the infamous "Unabomber," who'd lived in a shack outside of Lincoln, about a hundred and twenty miles southeast of Kalispell. Then, shortly after Kaczynski's arrest, the nation had been treated to the bizarre spectacle of the long standoff between the "Montana Freemen" and state and federal authorities near Jordon in the eastern part of the state.

And unfortunately, in recent years, a small but dedicated group of militiamen and other extremists had found their way into Flathead County. Their numbers included white supremacists, anti-Semites, and devotees of fringe Christian fundamentalist groups. Some were anti-tax activists, while others were members of movements like Posse Comitatus, which denied the authority of any governmental body beyond the county level.

Earlier this spring, in another celebrated incident that had drawn national attention, Chris, working in concert with state and federal officials, had broken up a small militia cell that was apparently plotting to start a revolution by assassinating several Flathead County officials. The target list included Chris himself, the Kalispell police chief, a number of judges, and, for some reason that was never clearly articulated, the local dogcatcher.

The conspirators apparently assumed that in the wake of these assassinations, the governor would be forced to send in the National Guard to restore order. The group then planned to wipe out the National Guard, hoping that this would prompt the federal government to send NATO troops into the Flathead. They took it for granted that this, in turn, would cause the remaining citizens of the Flathead Valley to rise up in rebellion against the federal government and its international forces.

Unfortunately for the conspirators, the plan was exposed when the girlfriend of one the group's leaders was found sifting through a dumpster behind the Kalispell police station at two o'clock one morning, gathering "intelligence" in preparation for the revolution.

On the surface, the plot sounded like the screenplay for an implausible comedy, and all these developments provided a considerable amount of fodder for the late-night comedians. But when the scheme unraveled, Chris and a swat team raided the home of one of the conspirators. There they'd discovered plastic explosives, body armor, an extensive collection of weapons and over thirty thousand rounds of ammunition. Needless to say, no sensible person was laughing at that.

Many of these extremists were particularly hostile toward conservationists, arguing that environmental legislation was an especially egregious example of the federal government's effort to expand its powers and strip the people of their "natural right" to use the land in any way they saw fit. Heirs of the "Sagebrush Rebellion" of the 1980s, they argued that all federal lands should be turned over to the states and that county commissioners should have the ultimate authority to decide how the lands within their boundaries should be utilized.

In Montana, as in Nevada and some other western states, forest service and other federal employees had been subjected to harassment and intimidation. Some had been refused service in restaurants, or at motels and other business establishments because of their government employment. The flames of discontent were fanned by radio talk show hosts, Internet bloggers, some local politicians and others who kept up a steady drumbeat of criticism against the government's policies and against environmentalists in general.

In northwestern Montana, where environmental legislation obviously had a significant impact and where the timber economy had fallen on hard times, these arguments inevitably resonated with a fair number of citizens. While most Montanans would not support violence as an appropriate response to the environmental movement, and while most of them certainly opposed the radical solutions advocated by the militia cells and county supremacy advocates, many of them did accept the argument that environmental legislation was largely responsible for the region's economic difficulties. And many of them argued vehemently that the decisions about land use should be made locally, by the people closest to the land, and not by "addle-brained bureaucrats" in Washington who were far removed from the situation and who didn't understand or appreciate the needs of the people in Montana.

Locally, the anti-government, anti-environmental movement was stoked by a newspaper editor named Kevin McKinney. McKinney had first come to prominence as a leader of a land-use dispute that had pitted the federal government against the Elko County Commission in Nevada. In the wake of that controversy, McKinney moved to Kalispell and founded a newspaper, *The*

Flathead Valley Patriot, which, in a not entirely original vein, encouraged Montanans to "Live free or die."

McKinney's "newspaper," using the term very loosely, was a radical right-wing screed full of conspiracy theories arguing that either the Jews, or the U.N., or perhaps both were attempting to take over the United States and enslave the citizenry. In McKinney's view, gays and feminists were in collusion to emasculate America's white males and deprive them of their God-given place at the top of the social order. Christianity was under attack from activist judges and other liberals who refused to permit prayer in schools and who wanted to kick God out of the Pledge of Allegiance.

Worst of all were the dreaded environmentalists whom McKinney dubbed "Eco-Fascists," and upon whom he heaped the blame for virtually all the valley's problems. McKinney made no distinction between moderate conservationists and members of the radical Earth Liberation Front. He insisted that the "rights of all Americans" were under assault by "extremists posing as environmentalists" who were "waging war on the West" in order to implement "their Communistic views."

In an editorial condemning the lawsuit that the NEA filed, McKinney argued that the NEA and their "fellow Eco-Fascists will not rest until they've succeeded in sweeping the rural West free of all human beings." He was especially critical of Toby Martin whom he'd labeled a "traitor to his native state."

McKinney's paper, which appeared weekly, had a relatively small paid subscription list, although he refused to reveal the actual number of subscribers. Additionally, he sold a few copies from coin-operated newspaper racks that were scattered around the valley. He attracted support from a few steady advertisers, and each issue contained an appeal asking sympathetic readers to mail contributions in support of his efforts. Out of all of that, McKinney apparently cobbled together enough money to keep the paper alive, although it was rumored that he also received significant support from an unidentified backer who remained behind the scenes.

McKinney walked a fine line, calling his readers to action in defense of their "God-given rights and their way of life," without specifically advocating violence or other illegal activity. He insisted for the record that he always advised his readers to work within the law and that he was not responsible if the people who shared his views "sometimes got carried away in their enthusiasm for their righteous cause."

Thus, McKinney often published the home addresses and phone numbers of Forest Service employees or prominent environmentalists who angered him for one reason or another and then denied any responsibility for the threatening phone calls that his targets subsequently received or for the vandalism done to their homes or vehicles. On the Friday before Toby Martin's death, his address and phone number had appeared on the front page of the *Patriot*, and McKinney had urged his readers to be sure to let this "Eco-Fascist Turncoat" know how they felt about his "betrayal of the people of the Flathead."

It seemed perfectly logical to assume that someone reading McKinney's diatribe might have decided to take action beyond simply egging Martin's car or making threatening phone calls to him in the middle of the night. But, as Chris pointed out, there was no evidence to support such a contention, and even less to explain why such a person might have decided to lay the blame for the killing on Steve Helstrom.

Chris and I were sorting through all of this when the waitress appeared with our dinners. While we ate, we talked about a variety of things unrelated to the case and drank three-quarters of the bottle of wine we'd ordered. By nine o'clock, I'd finished eating and was absent-mindedly toying with my wine glass when Chris said, "So what are you thinking about now?"

I shook my head and gave him a thin smile. "Oh, shit, I don't know . . . I'm just not at all sure that I'm ready for this. I feel sort of like Al Pacino in *The Godfather III* — 'Just when I thought I was out, they pulled me back in.'"

Chris sat, watching me for a moment, then carefully folded his napkin and laid it on the table beside his plate. He sighed heavily, waited until I'd raised my eyes to meet his, and said in a soft voice, "Dave, for Christ's sake. If I've told you once, I've told you fifty times. You are not to blame for what happened last summer. It was not your fault. *You* did not betray your wife. *You* did not murder that poor girl, and *you* did not stick a gun in your mouth and take the easy way out. No one holds you responsible for any of that, other than you yourself."

I turned away for a moment then looked back and held his eyes for a full five seconds. Finally, Chris broke eye contact and shook his head. "Okay, *almost* no one."

***

We split the check, said our goodbyes to Alfredo and Johnnie, and walked out into the parking lot, promising that we'd check in with each other tomorrow. I got into my car and watched Chris turn north out of the parking lot in the direction of his wife and kids in Kalispell. I headed south, and a couple of blocks later drove slowly past the blue neon lights of the Avalanche Saloon, beckoning on my right. For a moment, I considered the notion of pulling in for one quick drink. Then, thinking better of the idea, I shifted into third, punched the accelerator, and hurried up the hill toward home.

7

It's a Friday evening, early in May. Alice and I are lying in bed, holding each other after making love.

The setting sun filters through the loosely woven curtains, casting a soft, muted light across the room, and the breeze lightly rustles the leaves on a tree outside the open window. On the CD player, Sade quietly sings "Is It a Crime?." Through the window, I can hear the laughter of two or three children playing in a yard down the street. Lying in the crook of my left arm, Alice slowly trails her fingers across my chest. In a soft, sad voice she says, "It's not going to work, is it?"

It feels like the weight of the universe is crushing my chest and I can hardly draw a breath. Everything I thought I'd ever want is in this room, right here, right now. And yet . . .

I swallow hard, squeeze her to me tightly, and say, "No, Babe, it isn't. I'm so sorry."

A tear trails slowly down her cheek and drops onto my chest. "Me too."

I pull her even closer and whisper, "I love you, Al. And you know I always will."

Crying softly, she says, "I know. And I love you too."

8

"Come on in, man, and please excuse the mess — I'm batching it at the moment."

Ed Ramsey stood aside, holding the door for me as I stepped gingerly into his small living room the following evening. Ramsey was somewhere in his middle thirties, a large man with dark hair, brown eyes, and a full, bushy beard. He was wearing a Brooks and Dunn tee shirt over faded Levi's, and even in his stocking feet, he had to go six-foot three or four. A long, tattooed snake slithered out from under the right sleeve of his tee shirt and down the arm toward a hand that was missing parts of two fingers — sacrificed, no doubt, to the rapacious blades of the sawmill where Ramsey worked.

His house looked — and smelled — like someone had been "batching" in it since a month and a half before Custer's Last Stand. What appeared to be a week's worth of dirty clothes had been pitched in the general direction of the dingy orange couch, and two pairs of boots had been kicked off and abandoned in the middle of the floor. On the wall above the couch, a replica of a Revolutionary War-era musket hung over a framed embroidered rendering of the Second Amendment.

A pizza box and the trays from two or three frozen dinners were piled precariously on a small table next to a faded green Barcalounger. On the other side of the chair an impressive number of Budweiser cans had been emptied and stacked into a large pyramid. Facing the recliner was a flat screen TV that seemed about three sizes too large for the room. Even with the windows cracked open, the house smelled like a bale of grimy gym socks had been mix-mastered together with a dozen pepperoni pizzas. I could only imagine what horrors might lie in the kitchen and the bathroom.

Ramsey closed the door, hustled over to the couch, scooped up a pile of clothes and dropped them unceremoniously on the floor. "Have a seat, Dave. Would you like a beer?"

I sat carefully on the space that he'd cleared on the couch and sank several inches into the sagging springs. "No thanks, Ed. I only have a few minutes and I don't want to intrude into your evening."

He settled into his recliner and threw up his hands. "Hey, man, no problem. I really don't have any plans for tonight beyond drinking a few brewskis and watchin' the tube. And if there's anything I can do to help Steve, you know I sure as hell want to."

"Thanks, Ed. I appreciate that, and you know that Steve does too."

"Yeah, well, I never heard such a fuckin' crock of shit in my entire life. I know damn good and well that Steve couldn't have killed that asshole. He would liked to at least have landed a couple of good punches on him the other night, but he sure as hell wouldn't never have gone after him with no ax handle."

"I wouldn't think so, either, but things are not looking good for him at the moment."

"What do you need from me?"

"Well, I know that you've already given a statement to the sheriff's detectives, but I'd like to hear first-hand your account of the time that you and Steve spent together on Tuesday night."

He snagged a can of beer off the top of his pyramid, took a long pull and said, "Sure."

He paused a moment, apparently collecting his thoughts, and then said, "Well, we got off from work at four thirty, and Steve followed me over here. Then we spent the evening wrestling a rebuilt tranny into my Ford. About six o'clock or so, I popped a frozen pizza into the oven, and we opened a couple of beers. We took the pizza out to the garage and ate it while we were working. We finished up about eight thirty or so, and Steve left to go home."

"How many beers did Steve have while he was here?"

Without even thinking, Ramsey answered, "Two. I put a six-pack into a cooler and we took it out to the garage with us. I had four and Steve had two."

"What was Steve's mood like that night?"

"Good — or at least as good as could be expected under the circumstances, what with the possibility that we both might be out of a job at any minute thanks to those tree-hugging, mother-fucking enviros."

Shaking his head, he took a swig of the beer and said, "God almighty, I cannot understand those assholes. What the hell do they expect guys like me and Steve to do for a living if they shut us out of the forests? And are those friggin' idiots really so dumb as to think that the trees won't grow back?"

"Tell me, Ed, when you were working on your truck that night, did Steve talk about his fight with Toby Martin?"

Ramsey grinned, toying with his beer can, and said, "Well, shit. Of course, I was ribbing him pretty hard about it. Hell, everybody was giving him crap about it all day at work on Tuesday, wondering why a big, strong lumberman like himself couldn't even land a punch on a goddamn little pansy-assed lawyer."

"I gather that the news of the fight on Monday night was pretty much common knowledge by Tuesday morning."

"Oh hell, yes. Bill Nielson and Hal Adams saw the fight. And even before Steve got to work on Tuesday morning, somebody'd painted a sign and stuck it in front of his saw that said, 'Welcome Mike Tyson — NOT!'"

"What was Steve's reaction to the kidding?"

"Oh, you know Steve. He took it in stride and tried to give it back as good as he was getting it. He called us a few choice names and said that at least he'd had guts enough to go after Martin while all the rest of us pussies were standing around afraid to get our skirts wrinkled."

"Do you think it's possible that somebody might have been listening to all of this and decided to go after Martin himself?"

"Well," he said, slowly contemplating his beer can, "I figure that's pretty much what had to've happened, don't you? I mean, I'd bet my last dollar that Steve didn't do it, so obviously that means somebody else did."

"Any ideas about who that somebody else might have been?

Still studying the beer can, he shook his head. "Nope . . . God knows Toby Martin made himself a shitload of enemies up here. Hell, it could have been any one of a hundred people. But I'd swear on my kid's life that it wasn't Steve."

"You said that Steve left here around eight fifteen or eight thirty that night?"

Ramsey studied me for a moment, then looked away and gave a small shrug. "About then, I guess. Of course, you understand that my memory isn't perfect. If it would help Steve to say that he left a little later than that, I might reconsider and decide that I was wrong when I told the sheriff's man that Steve left around eight thirty."

I leaned forward on the couch. "No, Ed, that wouldn't help Steve. His best defense is the truth. If he left at eight fifteen or eight thirty, that's what you need to say."

"Hey, man, whatever — you're the lawyer and all. I just don't want to see a good man get stuck for something that he probably didn't do — especially when the guy that got himself dead was sure as hell beggin' for it."

I pulled myself up and out of the couch and handed Ramsey one of my cards. "Thanks very much for your time, Ed. Needless to say, if you think of anything else, or if you hear anything that might be helpful, I'd appreciate it if you'd give me a call."

"Absolutely," he said, tucking the card into the pocket of his jeans. "I really appreciate what you're doin' for Steve. If there's anything I can do to help, you just holler."

We picked our way across the littered floor to the door, and Ramsey bid me good night. I wasn't sure if I'd learned anything useful, but it did occur to me that I needed to have another talk with my client.

9

I spent Monday morning working in my office and grabbed a quick bite of lunch in downtown Kalispell. Then I walked over to the Justice Center to talk with Steve. He was a man accustomed to spending a great deal of time outdoors, and it was evident that even five days of confinement had taken a heavy toll on him. He appeared ashen and pale, and dropped almost lifelessly into the chair across from me. "I'd ask you how you're holding up," I said, "but just looking at you it's pretty apparent."

He nodded and shook his head. "Being locked up in here is very nearly the hardest fucking thing I've ever had to do. Honest to God, Dave, I don't know how much more of this I can take. I can't imagine what'll happen if they convict me and I have to spend the rest of my life in prison. I swear I'd rather hang instead."

Trying to inject as much confidence into my voice as I could, I said, "Well, Steve, it's way too early to be thinking about anything like that. I know that it's easy for me to say, but you need to hold yourself together while this business gets sorted out. Things are not nearly as bad as they probably seem from your vantage point."

He gave me a sad smile. "I don't know, man. Right at the moment, things seem pretty fuckin' bleak. And it's not just that I'm sitting in here accused of a murder that I damn well didn't commit. Everyday I'm stuck in here is a day that I'm not workin'. Karen sure as hell can't support our family on the money she makes at the fabric store, and we don't have any savings to speak of. If this goes on much longer, we're gonna lose our house, our cars, and all the other shit that we're makin' payments on. Hell, even if I do get clear of this mess, we're gonna be totally fuckin' ruined."

He paused for a moment, looking down at the table rather than at me, and said, "Speakin' of which, we haven't talked yet about how much it's gonna cost to have you defend me, let alone when or how I might ever be able to actually pay you."

"Don't even think about it. That's the last thing you need to be worrying about now. We'll figure it out later."

He nodded his head slowly and said in an embarrassed voice, "Yeah, well, I want you to know, Dave, that I really appreciate what you're doin' for me, and so does Karen. And I promise that I will be good for your fee someday — assuming I ever get out of here."

"Well, getting you out of here is the *only* thing I'm worried about at the moment."

He nodded his thanks, and I said, "Let's talk about what happened on Tuesday at work. I understand from Ed Ramsey that by the time you got to the mill that morning, the news about your fight with Toby was fairly common knowledge and that some of your co-workers were giving you grief about it."

For the first time since his arrest, he flashed me a genuine smile and shook his head. "Those assholes. Yeah, I took a lot of crap about that all day long. Most of 'em told me I was a pretty goddamn piss-poor excuse of a man if I couldn't even beat up a fuckin' lawyer who was half my size."

"Did any of them suggest that they could have done a better job of it?"

"Oh, shit yeah. Hell, even a couple of the women bragged that *they* coulda beat the snot outa Martin."

"Did any of them suggest that they might take a shot at it themselves — maybe somebody who decided that instead of just joking around about it, they'd show you how to do things right?"

He thought about that for a few seconds and said, "Jesus, I dunno. Two or three guys said that next time I wanted to go out for a beer they'd come along to hold my hand and protect me in case

I ran into Martin again. A couple of people said that they wished they'd had the chance to swing on him themselves and that they damn well woulda connected. But again, most of it was just kidding around — you know, the sort of general bullshit you'd expect under the circumstances. I didn't hear anybody say they were actually gonna go lookin' for him."

I nodded, waited a moment, and said, "Tell me about Ed Ramsey."

"Ed? What about him?"

"Well, for openers, what's his situation? I gather that he and his wife are separated — what's going on there?"

Steve shrugged. "Oh, a lot of things, I guess. Even when they are together, Ed and Donna spend most of their time arguing about a lotta different things — money, Ed's drinkin,' shit like that. Things are pretty tight for them at the moment — not that they're all that great for anybody else I know. But Ed and Donna owe a lot of money to the finance and credit card companies. They're behind on the mortgage, and Donna got laid off from her job last month. Ed says that the credit union is on the verge of repossessing her old junker car, although I can't imagine why in the hell they'd bother.

"Anyhow, they had a huge dustup about two weeks ago. Ed'd been drinkin' and she started raggin' on him. One thing led to another, and I guess he popped her a couple of times. Anyhow, the next morning she piled the kids into the car and headed off to her mom's, tellin' Ed he could go blow himself on her way out the door."

"Had he ever hit her before?"

Again, Steve shrugged. "I dunno . . . I guess so. This isn't the first time she's taken off like this, but Ed's sort of thinkin' that maybe this time she won't be back."

"Does Ed have something of a mean streak generally, or does he just save it up for the wife and kids?"

"A bit, I guess. But usually only after he's had a few beers."

"What was his reaction to this whole business about the lawsuit?"

"The same as most everybody else's, I reckon. Ed thinks the enviros are about a thousand ants short of a picnic, and he's pretty pissed about the fact that they're trying to shut down the forest. Even more than most of us, he can't afford to lose his job. His money situation being what it is these days, unemployment checks aren't going to be much help."

"And what did he have to say about your fight with Toby?"

"Well of course he gave me shit about it all day, just like everybody else. Only he had a chance to keep on doin' it while we were workin' on his truck."

"Was he one of the people who said that he'd like to have a shot at Toby himself?"

He flashed me a look of incredulity. "Yeah, I guess. But surely you're not thinking that Ed mighta killed Toby, are you?"

"Well, *somebody* did, and I believe you when you say that it wasn't you. Certainly, Ed had at least as much reason to be angry at Toby as you did — probably more, given what you've told me about his financial circumstances. And, of course, he had just as much opportunity to kill Toby as you did. In fact, he had even more.

"You left his place at around eight thirty, which means that Ed has no one to vouch for his whereabouts for the rest of the evening. What would have prevented him from waiting until you left, going out to the Martin place, and attacking Toby himself? He could have then driven by your place, put the ax handle in the bed of your truck and gone on home."

Steve pushed his chair back a few inches, steeled his eyes on mine, and said, "You're suggesting that one of my best friends not only killed Martin, but that he set me up to take the blame for it?"

"No, I'm not suggesting that *is* what happened. But I am suggesting that something like that *could* have happened. Again, *somebody* killed Toby, and whoever it was obviously *did* set you up to take the blame. Maybe it wasn't Ed, but almost certainly it was somebody that you know. It had to be someone who'd heard about your fight with Toby and who knew where they could find your truck when they were ready to ditch the murder weapon."

Steve nodded slightly, obviously reluctant to believe that one of his friends might have betrayed him in such a fashion, but nonetheless forced to recognize the logic of the situation. "I don't know, man," he said in a soft, frustrated voice. "I just don't fuckin' know. I know that *I* didn't kill him, but it's hard for me to believe that one of my friends woulda done it and left me to take the blame."

"I know that it may be a hard thing to swallow, but it's hard to think of another explanation that puts the murder weapon in your truck. Is there anybody — say one of your fellow workers, in particular — who's mad at you for one reason or another and might have taken advantage of the situation both to strike out at Toby and to put you on the spot at the same time?"

He thought about it for a minute or so and then shook his head. "No, Dave, I really don't think so. We're all of us pretty much like a small family out there. We have our disagreements occasionally, but we all get along pretty well, and I can't think of anybody who really dislikes me — certainly not enough to put me in this kind of a fix."

"Okay, Steve," I said, rising to leave. "I'll keep plugging away at it, and you try to keep your spirits up as best you can."

He simply nodded his head, and I signaled the guard that we were through.

10

I was working in my office later that afternoon when I heard someone knocking on the outer door. I set down the brief I was reading, walked out and opened the door to discover the diminutive editor of the *Flathead Valley Patriot* standing in the hall. He stuck out his hand and said, "Dave? Kevin McKinney. Could I have a couple minutes of your time?"

I nodded, making very little effort to hide my reluctance, and said, "I guess so. Come on back."

I led him into my office and pointed him in the direction of one of the guest chairs in front of the desk. "What can I do for you, Mr. McKinney?"

He waited until I was back in my own chair behind the desk, then pushed his glasses up on his nose and said, "Well, sir, I know that you're representing Steve Helstrom. I also know that Steve doubtless can't afford the cost of a first-rate trial lawyer and that his family has got to be suffering financially while the local Gestapo has Steve sitting in a cell."

"And what business is any of that of yours?"

McKinney leaned forward in his chair. "It's the business of any patriotic American citizen when the government, doing the bidding of the eco-terrorists who are ruining this state, imprisons a man for no just cause."

I picked up a pen and tapped it a couple of times on the desk blotter. "I gather you believe that someone other than Steve killed Toby Martin. And you know this how?"

Vigorously shaking his head, McKinney said, "Whether Steve Helstrom actually killed that traitor is completely beside the point. Toby Martin got exactly the justice that was coming to him — no more, no less. Make no mistake about it, Mr. Matthews, we're in a war now — a new War for Independence, every bit as sacred and as vital as the first. And we're *all* combatants. We *all* have to decide which side we're on. Toby Martin was on the wrong side, and one day all Americans will understand the truth that some of us recognize right now, namely that Steve Helstrom — or whoever killed Martin — is a hero in that war."

I waited a beat, still toying with the pen, and said, "As I recall, Mr. Martin, you suggested in your newspaper not that long ago that the attacks of 9/11 on the Pentagon and the World Trade Center were actually instigated by environmentalists, internationalists, and others who calculated that the attacks would allow the government to greatly expand its regulatory authority."

"And it has! Just look at the Patriot Act and all the other legislation and regulations that have followed in the years since 9/11. Those attacks were deliberately calculated to produce a situation where the American people would willingly surrender more and more of their sacred freedoms in the name of increasing security against 'terrorists' quote, unquote. Well, at least some of us understand that the *real* terrorists aren't over there in Syria or Afghanistan or Iran. They're right here, living amongst us. Unfortunately, though, most Americans are too blind to see what's happening right in front of their eyes."

"And it's your job, I gather, to open their eyes and alert them to the danger?"

"You're damn right it is — along with others, of course."

"And what does all of this have to do with Steve Helstrom?"

Still leaning forward in the chair, McKinney pushed his glasses up again. "Just this: Even if Helstrom did kill Martin, it was clearly an act of self-defense."

I arched my eyebrows and said, "You're suggesting that Toby Martin attacked Steve first?"

"You're goddamn right he did. The lawsuit that Martin filed was a direct attack on the life and livelihood of Steve Helstrom and of virtually every other person in this valley. Helstrom, or whoever else it might have been who killed Martin, was acting to defend that way of life, and that should be your defense."

Arching my eyebrows, I said, "I may have forgotten, Mr. McKinney. Where did you get your law degree?"

"As you damn well know, I have no law degree. But I do have enough common sense to know the truth when I see it. And the truth of the matter is that there's no way a Flathead County jury is ever going to convict anyone for killing somebody like Toby Martin who was determined to destroy this valley. I came in here today to tell you that my paper is establishing a legal defense fund for Steve Helstrom. In our next edition we'll have an appeal to our readers to contribute to Steve's defense and for the support of his family while he's unjustly held in jail."

Shaking my head, I said, "Well, Mr. McKinney, I believe that Steve Helstrom is innocent of this crime, and I hope very much that if he does go to trial on the charge, a jury will agree with me. As to your contention that no jury in this county would ever convict *anyone* of killing Toby Martin, well, we'll just have to disagree about that, as I'm sure we'd disagree about a good many other things.

"If you want to raise money for the support of Steve's family, and if they want to take it, that's up to you and to them. As to the issue of contributing to Steve's defense fund, I'll say thanks, but no thanks."

McKinney leaned back and fixed me with what I imagined was his effort at a hard glare. "You're saying that you'd reject my assistance and that of my subscribers?"

"I'm saying exactly that, Mr. McKinney. I believe that you and your alleged 'newspaper' have poisoned the atmosphere in this valley and have made it even more difficult than it already was to forge a reasonable solution to the economic and environmental problems that we face here. I also believe that, for all your blustering about 'outsiders' trying to dictate the lives of Montanans, you are yourself an outsider who has no real stake in this argument other than to promote your own personal agenda and doubtless your own economic interests. You're preying on the fears of people who are caught up in the changes that are transforming the Flathead and playing to their basest emotions.

"In particular, I'm obviously aware of the fact that in your paper, you've made some particularly outrageous comments about Toby Martin in recent weeks. It may very well be that the person who did kill him was inspired to do so by one of your inflammatory editorials."

His face coloring, McKinney rose from the chair. "You'd better not be suggesting that I had anything to do with Martin's murder."

I shook my head and said, "Do I think that you might have been directly involved? No, I don't think so — at least not right now. And mainly because I'm quite sure that you'd never have the guts to go head-to-head with a man like Toby Martin, even with a weapon in your hands. I suspect that you're basically a coward, McKinney — the kind of guy who stands safely on the sidelines provoking others to take the risks and do the dirty work, without ever putting yourself on the line in any meaningful way.

"It remains to be seen whether you were indirectly involved in Martin's death because your diatribes convinced one of your readers to take the sort of direct action that you advocate but would never take yourself. But whatever the case, I think we'd all be a lot better off if you packed up your sorry act and took it somewhere else. And I'd much rather defend Steve Helstrom *pro bono* and pay the expenses out of my own pocket than accept a dime from you."

McKinney drew himself up to his full five-foot-six. "So basically, you're telling me that you agree with those freaking eco-fascists?"

"Part of your problem, McKinney, is that you make absolutely no distinction whatsoever between moderate conservationists and the small handful of people who *are* genuine eco-terrorists. More likely, I think, you deliberately choose not to do so. You simplemindedly lump them all together and rail about impending doom. I'm not an eco-terrorist and neither are the vast majority of conservationists. But if I haven't made it clear enough already, I detest not only your views about the environment but virtually everything else that you stand for as well."

"I'm very sorry to hear that. And it sounds to me like Steve would be much better off being represented by a lawyer who was more sympathetic to his situation."

"That, of course, is a decision for Steve to make. But in the meantime, I am his attorney and I have work to do. This interview is over."

McKinney waited a moment then nodded and leaned over the desk, closing the distance between us. "Your damn right it is. But you just remember what I said, smartass. This *is* a war, and like Toby Martin, you're on the wrong fucking side."

With that, he turned and stomped out of the office, slamming the outer door behind him.

11

Toby Martin's funeral was held at the Christ Episcopal Church in downtown Kalispell on the Tuesday morning following his death. It was a cloudy day with the temperature hovering in the middle fifties and the threat of rain in the air. I got there about ten minutes before the service was scheduled to begin and parked a couple of blocks east of the church on Second Street. Across the street from the church, about twenty protesters stood silently, holding hand-lettered signs claiming that Martin's life had been sacrificed for the cause of saving the forests and urging that the forests not be sacrificed along with him.

By the time the service started a few minutes after ten, the church was nearly full. The mayor and a number of other community leaders had turned out, reflecting the Martin family's stature in the county. The local business community was also well represented, as was the staff of the Northwestern Alliance, including a grieving Callie Buckner and three or four others that I'd met in Missoula on Thursday. I recognized a number of men and women who'd attended high school with Toby, some of whom still looked fairly fit and attractive as they advanced toward middle age, while others among them did not.

Robert Martin, looking dazed and extremely fragile, sat in the front pew on the right side of the church, flanked by his surviving son and by Toby's former wife, Amanda. A statuesque redhead, she'd dressed for the occasion in a black designer suit that showed her figure and her lustrous hair to excellent advantage and that obviously hadn't been purchased anywhere within five hundred miles of Kalispell, Montana.

I'd never met Amanda, and I knew the story of her relationship with Toby only from third- and fourth-hand sources. She was the daughter of a socially prominent San Francisco judge and had met Toby while he was a student at Stanford Law and she was an undergraduate there. They'd married the year after he completed his law degree. Amanda had then lived in Montana very briefly before deciding that the state was a bit too socially and culturally deprived for her taste. She returned to California, and when Toby refused to give up his life in Montana for her, they divorced after three years of marriage. Observing the way that the former Mrs. Martin fit into her widow's weeds, it struck me that Toby had been forced to make an excruciatingly difficult choice.

The service itself was mercifully short, and perhaps thirty percent of the mourners joined the procession from the church a few blocks east to the Conrad Memorial Cemetery. The tree-lined entrance passed through a somewhat-less-than-scenic mobile home park and then climbed a hill to the burial ground itself which was perched high on a bluff that dropped sharply to the woods below. Several varieties of pines were scattered through the grounds, along with some elms, birch, and a few Norway and silver maples. The hilltop location offered excellent views of the mountains off in the distance, and it struck me that, all things considered, if a person had to be buried somewhere, this was probably a better spot than most.

By the time we reached the cemetery at eleven fifteen, the skies had begun spitting a little rain, reinforcing the general gloom attendant to the occasion. A large canvass awning stretched across the gravesite, and many of the mourners who'd neglected to bring umbrellas crowded under the shelter in an effort to escape the cold drizzle. I took a position standing along the right-hand side of the casket, across from the elder Mr. Martin, Michael, and the widow who were seated on the left side.

The minister was a tall handsome man with craggy features and thinning gray hair who looked like he'd been summoned straight from Central Casting. He took his position at the head of the casket and intoned a prayer. As the rest of the crowd bowed their heads, I looked up to see Mary Jo Roth — now Mary Jo Watson — standing directly behind the family, weeping quietly. In contrast to the widow seated in front of her, Mary Jo was dressed in an ill-fitting black suit that was more than a couple of fashion seasons out of date and that no doubt *had* been purchased in Kalispell or somewhere very near.

Mary Jo had been Toby Martin's long-time high school girlfriend. She and I were in the same class together, and I'd known her fairly well as a fellow student. She and Toby had begun dating during our freshman year — his sophomore year — and the relationship had lasted even after he left for Stanford. Mary Jo had been — and for that matter still was — a very attractive woman. She'd been popular in school, genuinely liked by almost all of her peers. But she had hovered in the middle of our class academically, and her family would have been charitably described as lower middle class.

Which meant, unfortunately, that Mary Jo would not be following Toby to Stanford when she graduated from Flathead High a year behind him. Instead, the next fall semester found her majoring in fashion merchandising at Flathead Valley Community College in Kalispell. Inevitably of course, it proved impossible for the two of them to maintain a relationship, given the gulf — geographic and otherwise — that had opened between them. Surprisingly perhaps, the relationship did survive for eighteen months after Toby left for California, but by the time Mary Jo began her second semester at FVCC, the two of them had agreed that they were free to "see other people." Six months after that, they were no longer seeing each other at all.

On the rebound, Mary Jo had begun dating Don Watson, who, like Toby, had been in the class ahead of ours. I could easily understand the attraction from his perspective, but certainly not from hers. From the time I'd been a freshman in high school, Watson had impressed me as being a dimwitted, over-confident jerk.

He was at best an average student and a mediocre athlete. Certainly, he paled in every way when compared to Chris Williamson who was, in turn, a year ahead of him in school. Chris had been a genuine star in three sports as well as a bright student, and he ultimately became the starting quarterback at Michigan State in his junior and senior years there. On the football field and on the basketball court, Chris had made everyone who played around him look good — even Don Watson. But Watson believed that the light that radiated around him was exclusively his own, and he was constantly at pains to impress anyone who would listen with the obviously exaggerated tales of his exploits, both on and off the field.

Most of the students in our class tolerated Don, some of us more reluctantly than others. But none of the kids in my circle had been particularly distressed when he graduated and took his act down the road to Montana State University in Bozeman. Much to his chagrin, however, he failed even to make the football team there, let alone to win an athletic scholarship.

After three years in Bozeman as a business major, Don came home without graduating and joined his father in the family clothing store. He and Mary Jo married the following September and produced two children over the next four years. Don then inherited the family business upon his father's death, and the rumor around town was that he had little more talent as a businessman than he'd demonstrated as an offensive lineman.

I'd also heard speculation that he'd grown bored in his marriage and was seeking comfort elsewhere. I had no way of knowing if there was any truth to the rumor, but several weeks earlier I'd stumbled across him having dinner one night at the Beargrass Bistro in Lakeside with a young woman who I recognized as one of the clerks in his store. Not being in a position to cast the first stone myself, I'd adopted the charitable assumption that it was a business dinner and had never mentioned it to anyone.

Looking around the crowd, I noticed that Watson seemed to be conspicuously absent from the funeral, which was hardly surprising. In high school, he'd always appeared to be uncomfortable in the company of Toby Martin, perhaps because he recognized that Toby was the genuine article and knew deep inside that, for all his bravado, he himself was not. He'd appeared jealous of Toby, as he'd appeared jealous of Chris, and generally kept his distance, even though he and Toby were classmates. His feelings toward Toby were also doubtless influenced by the fact that, while we were all in school, he too had obviously lusted after Mary Jo, at a time when she'd had much better taste — or more accurately, perhaps, at a time when she'd had much better options.

I was still lost in these reminiscences when the minister led a final prayer and committed Toby's body to the ground. As the crowd dispersed, I watched Mary Jo slowly make her way across the damp, slippery grass toward her car. I wondered what she was thinking now about the choices she had made in life — and about the choices that life had made for her.

12

I got back to my office a little before two o'clock, and found Callie
Buckner standing in the hall in front of my door in the simple black
dress and low heels that she'd worn to the funeral. The collection
of earrings she'd been wearing when we first met had been
replaced by a single pair of small gold hoops, and the overall effect
suggested a much more sophisticated and attractive young woman
than the one that I'd met on Thursday. She smiled at me a bit shyly,
and said, "Hi. I knocked on the door, but didn't get an answer, so
I thought I'd hang around for a few minutes to see if you might be
coming back."

I returned the smile. "Sorry about that. I have a very small
practice — too small at the moment even to require a secretary.
Please come in."

I unlocked the door, opened it, and stood aside, allowing her to
precede me into the reception area where my secretary, when I'd
had one, had been positioned to greet visitors. I led her back into
my office and flipped on the lights. I walked her over to the leather
couch that sat opposite my desk and said, "Please sit down."

I took a chair opposite the couch, waited while she settled
herself, and said, "How can I help you, Ms. Buckner?"

Again, she showed me her timid smile and said, "Well, first of
all, you could call me Callie."

She hesitated a moment, then said, "Other than that, I was
feeling guilty when I saw you at the funeral today. I wanted to stop
by on my way out of town and apologize for the way I behaved the
other day."

I shook my head. "Really, Callie, you certainly don't owe me
an apology. If anything, just the reverse is true. I know that it was

a very difficult morning for you and for the other members of your staff, and I really wouldn't have bothered you if it hadn't been important."

She colored a bit. "I appreciate your saying that, even if it doesn't excuse my rude behavior. I just didn't know what to do with myself last week. Toby was such a bright and decent man, and he was so committed to the work that we're doing. He meant a great deal to me . . . to all of us. When I heard that he'd been murdered like that, I was both devastated and enraged — especially when I learned that the man who'd been arrested for killing him was a sawmill worker. I immediately jumped to the conclusion that he must be guilty — that he was angry about the lawsuit and that he'd killed Toby because of it."

"Well, under the circumstances it's a conclusion that a lot of people seem to have reached."

She shook her head and looked at me with pained eyes. "But Toby wouldn't have, and I shouldn't have either." She swallowed hard and continued. "Toby was the kind of lawyer ... he was the kind of person ... who would have immediately insisted that the man — Helstrom — was innocent until proven guilty. He would have given him the benefit of the doubt, and he would have been disappointed in me for not doing the same."

I leaned forward, closing the distance between us, and said, "I think you're being way too hard on yourself, Callie. And I knew Toby well enough, at least when we were in school together, to know that he would say the same thing."

She hooked her hair back behind her left ear, and said, "Do you really think your client is innocent?"

"Yes, I do. And not just because he's entitled to the presumption until proved guilty. As I told you last week, I've known Steve Helstrom for a long time. Getting drunk and picking a fight with Toby as he did was perfectly in character for Steve. But it would have been totally out of character for him even to have gone out looking for Toby the following night, let alone to have killed him. He says that he didn't do it, and I believe him."

She looked down into her lap where her hands were clasped tightly together and shook her head. "If he didn't do it, then who did?"

"I don't know. Assuming that the killer wasn't Steve Helstrom, it might very well have been another employee of the mill. But then, of course, it's also possible that Toby was killed for reasons that had nothing to do with this battle over the lawsuit."

She nodded, then looked at me and said, "And what about you, Mr. Matthews? Are you angry at the 'enviros' too?" she said, forming quotation marks with her fingers.

"Dave, please. And no, I'm not. My own personal sympathies are much more with the environmentalists than with their opponents. I believe that we do have an obligation as a society to manage the forests and all of our natural resources in an intelligent manner and to conserve them for future generations.

"That said, I've lived in this valley all my life, and I understand the pain and frustration that many people up here are feeling. Many of these families have been employed in the woods and in the mills for two or three generations. It's not only been their livelihood; it's been their way of life. I understand that they feel threatened. I understand that they don't want to give up this way of life. And while I don't necessarily agree with them, I do feel sympathy for them."

"And so do we. We don't want to put people out of work. We don't want to destroy these communities. And we aren't even suggesting that these people have to give up their jobs in the woods. A rational approach to managing and conserving the forests would still provide jobs in the woods and timber for the mills.

"There's plenty of work to be done, thinning forests to protect homes and the urban interface, and processing the trees and underbrush that are removed in the process. But most of the people up here don't seem to want to hear that, and neither does the Forest Service, for that matter. All of them, or most all of them anyway, just want to continue business as usual.

"When they do talk about their alleged interest in 'conserving' the forests and reducing the threat of fires, it's almost always just a smokescreen. What they want to do is 'thin' the forests by logging the largest and most profitable trees and leaving everything else. That's not conservation, that's raping the land. And it leaves groups like ours with no real choice. They force us to use the courts in order to protect the environment and then claim that *we're* the obstructionists who are trying to destroy their communities."

She paused for a moment, apparently chagrined over her outburst. Then she shrugged and flashed me a weak smile. "Sorry I got on my soapbox. I should get out of here and let you get to work. Again, I just wanted to stop by and apologize."

We stood, and I said, "Again, there's no reason to apologize, and again, I really am very sorry about Toby's death."

"Thank you."

I escorted her back to the door, once again expressing my sympathy. As I watched her walk down the hall to the head of the stairs, I wondered if her obvious regard for Toby Martin had been anything more than professional. I also found myself wondering why the only three females who'd displayed any obvious distress over his death were his administrative assistant, his former wife, and his high school girlfriend.

13

"It's a good thing we're not playing tennis this week," Chris said, "cause I would whip your ass but good. I went out and hit with Doug last night, and he only managed to win two games."

"That's the way you build your son's confidence," I replied, "by mopping up the court with the poor kid? And what sort of telephone greeting is that? Suppose that instead of me it would have been one of the county commissioners with the response to your budget request for next year?"

"Well, in the first place, my 'poor son' is twelve years old and he's already too damned cocky as it is. In the second place, in another couple of years, he'll be mopping up the court with me. I need to beat up on him while I still can. And in the third place, I doubt very much that any of the county commissioners could even find your office, let alone that one of them might drop by to use the phone. What's on your mind?"

"Toby Martin's love life."

"What about it?"

"My question exactly. Trained criminal investigator that you are, I'm sure you noticed that the only three women who seemed to be unusually distressed by Toby's passing were Callie Buckner, Amanda Martin, and Mary Jo Watson."

"Buckner was his administrative assistant, right? I gather that she was the young brunette with the short hair and long legs. I haven't met her myself. Tom interviewed her down in Missoula."

"Yeah, that was her. I was just wondering, did Tom suggest that she and Toby might have had a relationship outside of the office?"

"No. He did say that Buckner seemed particularly upset about Toby's death — more so than any of the other staff that he interviewed. But he attributed that to the fact that she'd worked more closely with Toby than any of the others. He didn't pick up any hint that they might have been more intimately involved than that."

"Who was Toby dating at the moment?"

"No one that we know of. There was no sign of any female presence either in his room at the family place up here or at his house in Missoula, save for a studio photo of the very delectable Amanda that was on his dresser down there."

"So, what are you saying? Do you think that he was still pining away for her and that he wasn't seeing other women, even after this much time had passed?"

"Hey, you saw her in that outfit at the funeral this morning. Wouldn't you still be pining away?"

"Yeah, that thought occurred to me. Still, it has been a long time."

"Well, it's been a long time for Mary Jo too, but to look at her this morning, you wouldn't think that she'd gotten over losing Toby yet."

"Yeah," I said, nodding my agreement even though Chris obviously couldn't see it. "Poor Mary Jo. She loses the love of her life and then gets stuck with that jerkoff Watson."

"The term 'jerkoff' doesn't begin to adequately describe him. That boy is a total fucking train wreck. How Mary Jo Roth ever got hooked up with him will forever be the great mystery of our generation."

I hesitated a couple of seconds while a thought percolated to the surface and said, "Have you heard anything about Don maybe playing around on her?"

Chris laughed. "He'd be a complete idiot if he was. But then, of course, he *is* a complete idiot. Why? Do you know something?"

"I don't *know* anything. But I did see him having dinner up at the Beargrass Bistro one night a few weeks ago with one of his salesclerks, and I was just wondering about it. But I guess what I was really wondering about was Mary Jo's love life."

"How do you mean?"

"Oh, I don't know. It just strikes me that she and Toby were together for a long time and that neither of them ever even dated anyone else, except for the people that they ultimately married. It also strikes me that Don Watson has become an even bigger ass, both literally and figuratively, as an adult than he was in high school. Even if he isn't playing around on her, I find it hard to imagine that Mary Jo could be especially happy in her marriage. Further, I find it curious that Toby doesn't seem to have had a serious relationship since his divorce. And it strikes me that for a guy who lives and works in Missoula, he seems to have spent an awful lot of time visiting the family homestead up here."

Chris paused for a couple of beats and then said, "You're suggesting that perhaps his love of the Flathead wasn't the only thing that kept him coming back home?"

"I have no reason on earth to suggest any such thing, but the thought occurs to me."

I could hear Chris exhale heavily on the other end of the phone. "That would be a very delicate interview."

"Yeah, I suppose it would be."

"Would you be willing to do it?"

"Would *I* be willing to do it?"

"Look Dave, you and Mary Jo were pals in school. Your girlfriend was her best friend."

"Well, in case it's slipped your mind, you might also recall that my girlfriend, who *was* Mary Jo's best friend, also happened to be *your* sister. You don't think that Mary Jo would be comfortable talking to you?"

"Probably not as comfortable as she would be talking to you. In spite of the fact that Angie was her best friend, I really didn't know Mary Jo very well. And the truth is that, outside of Toby and Angie and a few of Mary Jo's other girlfriends, you knew her as well as anybody did. You'd doubtless stand a much better chance of getting her to open up, especially on a subject like this, than Tom or I would. It *is* an interesting notion, and since it was your idea to begin with, you could do us all a favor by following up."

Ducking the issue for a moment, I said, "Have you discovered yet where Toby spent the time from seven fifteen to ten thirty the night he was killed?"

"Nope. We haven't had any legitimate responses to the appeal for information that we made in the media. It looks like he just dropped off the edge of the world for that three-hour period.... Kind of makes you wonder, doesn't it?"

I paused again for a few seconds and then said, "Okay, I'll give her a couple of days and then see if she'd be willing to talk to me. I'll let you know what she has to say."

14

I hung up the phone and decided to call it a day. Given that the evening rush hour had begun in earnest, it took me an agonizing four or five minutes to get from my office in the center of Kalispell to the south end of the town where the speed limit rises to sixty-five miles per hour. Fourteen miles and thirteen minutes later, I turned left off of Highway 93 onto Angel Point Road. I made my way slowly down the road, passing a couple of people who were out for late afternoon walks, and stopping long enough to let a black bear cub amble slowly across the road in the direction of the lake. Three hundred yards from my own driveway, I slowed and stopped in front of the road that led down to the West Shore Inn.

As had been the case for the last eight months, the gates at the head of the driveway were chained and locked, and a large "For Sale" sign remained wired to the right-hand gate. Seventy-five feet down the drive, I could see the northwest corner of the house and three windows, tightly shuttered.

The inn had belonged to my friends, Alice and Bill Johnson. Alice was a life-long Montanan who'd grown up spending summers at her parents' cabin on the property where the small inn now stood. Her husband, Bill, had been an English professor at the University of Montana in Missoula. They built the inn when Alice inherited the property from her mother and booked guests from the first of May to the end of September each year. In the off-season they lived in a small home in Missoula where Alice worked part-time, organizing conventions and other events for a local hotel while Bill taught his classes at the University.

For Alice particularly, the inn had been a labor of love — a dream that exploded in horror on a late summer night at the end of the season last year. In the aftermath, she remained only long enough to close the inn and put it on the market. She'd then sold her house in Missoula and left for parts unknown — or, more accurately, for parts unknown to me. I'd neither seen nor heard anything of her since a week after Bill's death. In the middle of my testimony at the inquest, I'd looked away from the coroner for a moment to see Alice pressing forward in her seat, watching me intently, her bright blue eyes brimming with tears.

I remember losing my train of thought and pausing in my answer to the coroner's question. For several long seconds her eyes continued to bore into mine, searching — desperately it seemed — for an answer I was powerless to give her. Then she'd risen from her seat, turned and walked slowly out of the room and out of my life.

15

It's a warm evening, late in June. Although it's nearly nine o'clock, dusk is just beginning to settle over the valley, the bright blue sky fading first to purple and then to gray as the sun drops slowly behind the mountains to the west. Alice and I are eating dinner outside at the Edgewater Inn on the Clark Fork River in Missoula. On the table between us a candle flickers in a hurricane lamp.

Fifty yards away, the river rushes over its rocky bed and the sound of the roiling water merges with that of a few birds who are chirping at each other and with that of the light breeze that whispers through the cottonwoods along the riverbank. Out in the middle of the stream, a fisherman in chest-high waders patiently casts his fly back and forth over the water, hoping that a fish will rise.

I'm waiting patiently too. For the last hour I've been watching Alice push the food around on her plate, listening as she nervously tries to make idle small talk. I'm fairly certain I know why she wanted to have dinner together tonight and why she's so uncharacteristically anxious. I'm waiting to hear the words and wondering what I'll feel when she says them.

She's dressed for the occasion in a sleeveless blue shell that matches the color of her eyes, a white linen skirt, and a pair of sandals with medium heels. Her golden blonde hair is gathered back into a ponytail that hangs to her shoulder blades, revealing the blue sapphire earrings that I gave her for her twenty-fourth birthday. On her right arm, a trio of gold bracelets clangs lightly together as she idly watches a couple walking hand-in-hand along the river and gestures with her fork to make a point.

Finally, I lean forward, reach across the table and slip the fork from her fingers. I rest the fork on the plate, then take her hand. She turns back from watching the river and slowly lifts her eyes to meet mine. I give her a faint smile, cock my head an inch or two to the left, and say, "Enough already, Al. Why did you call this meeting?"

She squeezes my hand and holds my eyes with hers for a good ten or fifteen seconds. Then, in a voice so soft I can barely hear it, she whispers, "Bill has asked me to marry him. I told him that I would."

16

I got up at six thirty the next morning and went for a long run. After cooling down for ten minutes while I skimmed through the morning paper, I showered, shaved, and ate a light breakfast. By nine o'clock, I was out on the road, headed for Kalispell, hoping to talk to Mike Martin, Toby's brother.

Mike was two years younger than Toby, and I hardly knew him at all. I remembered him as a detached, skinny kid, a year behind me in school, who'd had a reputation for preferring booze and drugs to academics. Unlike some of his cohorts, though, he had managed to graduate, albeit without distinction, and had lasted two or three semesters before flunking out of the University of Montana. He'd come home to Kalispell and his father had eventually staked him to half ownership in a used car lot out on Highway 2, near the eastern city limits. I gathered that he was making a living out of the enterprise, but I didn't know how successfully.

I pulled into the lot about nine forty-five. Pennants fluttered in the breeze along lines that had been strung from a post mounted on top of the small sales building out to the light poles at the edge of the lot. A sign on one side of the building promised "EASY CREDIT!!!" On the other side, a banner urged prospective customers to "BUY HERE/ PAY HERE — WE TOTE THE NOTE!"

I got out of my car and was greeted immediately by a florid, overweight salesman who appeared to be somewhere in his middle forties and who could have served as the poster boy for the archetypal image of the used car salesman. He approached me with an outstretched hand, a wide toothy grin, and the overwhelming scent of some cheap aftershave lotion. "Dan Ballard," he announced in his best hearty, salesman's voice. "And what can I do for you this morning?"

Without introducing myself I shook his hand and said, "Well, Mr. Ballard, I was actually looking for Mike Martin. Is he in today?"

Ballard looked over my shoulder, apparently making a quick appraisal of my BMW, and perhaps wondering what he might have on the lot that I would possibly be interested in trading for. Then he established eye contact again, made a small clucking sound and gave me what was apparently his best effort at a sad but sincere smile. "I'm afraid that there's been a tragedy in the family," he said. "Mike won't be in this week. Perhaps I can help you?"

I shook my head. "Thanks just the same, Mr. Ballard, but I wanted to see Mike on a personal matter. I'll try him some other time."

"Certainly," he replied. And then, perhaps constitutionally unable to prevent himself from doing so, he gave me a card and another hearty smile. "If you're ever interested in trading out of the Bimmer, I could make you a really sweet deal."

I took the card, stuck it in my pocket and said, "I'll certainly bear that in mind, Mr. Ballard. Thanks for your time."

Then, before he could press the matter any further, I jumped back in my car, fired up the engine, and left as quickly as I could.

***

I assumed that since Martin was not at his lot, he was most likely at home. Given that I was already on the east side of town, I decided that I might as well drive on out and see if I could catch him there. I followed Highway 2 east to its intersection with Highway 35, the location of the Crossroads Bar where Toby Martin and Steve Helstrom had fought the night before Toby's murder. Even at ten fifteen on a Wednesday morning, two pickups and an ancient Pontiac Grand Prix sat parked in front of the place, their owners no doubt inside doing brunch.

I continued east on 35, and a few minutes later the highway curved south toward Creston, rolling through fields of wheat, alfalfa and hay that shimmered in the bright morning sun. To the east, the Swan Mountain range climbed out of the valley floor to peaks that were still dusted with snow. Two miles north of Creston, a mailbox and an open gate marked the entrance to the Martin family property.

I turned left off the highway and followed the gravel road straight across the valley floor for quarter of a mile or so. The road then curved slightly to the north and up a small rise to the spot where Robert Martin had built an imposing log home with breathtaking views of the valley below the house and of the mountains behind it. A late model Lincoln Town Car was parked in front of the house, right where I imagined that Toby Martin might have parked on the last night of his life.

I pulled up behind the Lincoln, and just as I got out of my car, I saw Mike Martin coming down the steps with Denny Graham, a local realtor. Graham was dressed for business in a sport coat and tie. Martin, who'd had the gaunt, wasted look of a perpetual doper in high school, had gained a considerable amount of weight in the years since. Still, at six feet or so, he carried the additional pounds fairly well. He was sporting a pair of black designer jeans, a black tee shirt, and an unbuttoned white dress shirt with the tail hanging out over the jeans. He'd pulled his longish dark blond hair back into a short ponytail which seemed to exaggerate his large, hawk-like nose.

We met at the bottom of the steps where I shook hands with each of them and expressed my condolences to Martin. He nodded warily. "I saw you at the funeral yesterday. Thanks for coming."

At that point, Graham interrupted to say that he was late for another meeting and needed to be on his way. Turning from me to

Martin, he said, "Nice seeing you as always, Dave. Mike, Thanks for the update. I'll get back to you ASAP."

Martin and I both nodded our goodbyes and watched as Graham got into his car and headed back down the drive. As the Lincoln disappeared around a bend in the road, Martin turned to me, crossed his arms over his chest, and said in a chilly voice, "What brings you out here this morning, Dave?"

He remained standing on the steps above me, perhaps attempting to maintain some sort of psychological advantage. Looking up at him, I said, "I was hoping that I might talk to you for a few minutes about Toby."

He grunted, gave me a disgusted look and said, "And why in the hell would I be willing to talk to you of all people about my brother?"

I climbed the first two steps toward the porch, neutralizing his height advantage, leaned back against the railing, and said, "Why wouldn't you be willing to talk to me?"

Martin shook his head. "You've got to be joking, right? You're representing the motherfucker who killed Toby and you want help from *me*?"

"Well, actually," I said in a measured tone, "I don't believe that Steve killed Toby, and I'd like to know who did. I'd think you would want to know that too."

"Who the fuck do you think you are — Perry Mason?"

"Not hardly. But I understand enough about this case already to know that I should easily be able to raise enough reasonable doubt in the minds of jurors to win an acquittal for Steve. In that event, the person who really killed your brother will very likely never be caught and punished. Certainly, you don't want that."

He stiffened. In a bitter voice, he said, "Bullshit! The asshole who killed my brother is sitting in the county jail right now, and the murder weapon was found in his goddamn truck. Reasonable doubt, my ass. I'll be in court to see that sonofabitch convicted, and I'm looking forward to sitting behind the glass in Deer Lodge when they give him the needle. In the meantime, why don't you just get the hell back in your car and off my property?"

I was tempted to remind him that, at least as far as I knew, the property still belonged to his father. But there was no point in antagonizing the guy any further, so I simply nodded a goodbye, got the hell back in my car as he'd requested, and made my way back to town.

17

Driving back to Kalispell, I couldn't help but wonder what sort of business Mike Martin and Denny Graham might have been contemplating together. My authority for all things automotive is Rusty Nelson, the local Chevy dealer who's also the Official Substitute for Wednesday Night Tennis. I decided to stop by his office on the way back to mine to see what he could tell me about Mike Martin.

Quite in contrast to Martin's rather shabby used car lot, everything about Rusty's dealership suggested a carefully organized and precision run business operation. The showroom and the shop were cleaner than most operating rooms; the stock was polished and gleaming, and the sales force dressed and behaved in a professional manner. I made my way across the showroom floor and found Rusty in his office talking to someone on the phone. He held up a finger to indicate that he'd be just a moment longer and motioned me to a chair in front of the desk.

Rusty was six years my senior. He was about my height and carried ten more pounds than I, but none of it ran to fat. He'd always been very active and was in great physical shape. In particular, he had excellent stamina, and the key to his success on the tennis court was his ability to wear down opponents much younger than he — an advantage that more than compensated for his lousy second serve.

On the court he wore a single contact lens; otherwise he preferred the tortoiseshell-framed glasses that now fronted his light blue eyes. His brown hair was turning to gray and cut to a medium length, and this morning he was wearing a heavily starched white shirt over the pants from a dark blue suit and a maroon tie with a muted pattern. He wrapped up his conversation, hung up the phone, and said, "So, what — you guys are so desperate that you're now reduced to begging for substitutes in person?"

Laughing, I said, "Well, it hasn't quite come to that yet, but the way things are going these days, we may not be far from it. Actually, I wanted to talk to you about one of your esteemed competitors."

Rusty leaned back in his chair and clasped his hands behind his head. "Which competitor did you have in mind?"

"Mike Martin."

"*Oh*, you fooled me there for a minute. I thought you said one of my *esteemed* competitors. I don't think that most other dealers in town would think of Mike quite that generously."

I arched my eyebrows and waited for him to elaborate.

He exhaled and said, "Mike and Ted have a very small operation that they're running on a shoestring. They might move a handful of cars in any given month, and only to customers who don't know their reputation. They cater to people with bad credit, who are willing to pay exorbitant interest rates in order to buy a ride — only they usually don't have the ride for very long. Mike and Ted have a cozy relationship with a couple of lenders of last resort. As soon as a buyer misses a payment — and virtually all of them do — the repo man pays them a visit in the dead of night, and faster than you can say 'Gone in 60 Seconds,' the vehicle is back on Mike's lot."

"So basically, you're telling me that Mike and Ted don't usually get invited to the local dealer association lunches."

"Not usually."

"But they are making money?"

"A little, as I understand it, but not enough to support themselves in the lifestyles to which they'd like to become accustomed. The rumor mill suggests that they're both living beyond their means, and juggling credit cards and paying their bills late in order to stay afloat."

"Do you know if Mike has other economic ambitions? I ask because when I saw him this morning, he was meeting with Denny Graham."

Rusty nodded, took off his glasses, and began absentmindedly chewing on one of the earpieces. "I heard an interesting rumor, but I don't know if there's anything to it."

"And the rumor would be?"

"Well, I was playing tennis with Mark Adamson a couple of weeks ago, and while we were taking a break, he started ribbing me about how one of my 'colleagues' was going to be taking a big step up in the world. I asked him who and how, and he told me that Mike had approached him about developing part of the family property in Creston."

"You've got to be kidding!"

"Yeah, well, that was my reaction. But Mark's development group is about halfway through with the subdivision that they're doing up in Whitefish, and they're looking for property for their next project. Mike apparently caught wind of this and made an appointment to meet with Mark. He had some grand scheme worked out in which he and Mark's group would form a partnership and go in on this deal together. Mike proposed to put up two hundred acres of prime land along the front of the Swan Range as his entrée into the deal. He figured that Mark and his group would front the initial development costs and that they could subdivide the land, sell it in five or ten-acre parcels and make a fortune."

Shaking my head in disbelief, I said, "And how did Mark respond to that?"

"Well, you know Mark — he's nobody's fool. He knows damned good and well that neither Bob nor Toby Martin would ever consider selling any part of that land, let alone allow a subdivision to be built on it. So, he thanked Mike for his time and told him that it was a very interesting idea, but that he and his partners were close to being locked into another piece of land that would keep them busy for the foreseeable future."

"So, we can assume that Mike is trying to sell the idea elsewhere — to Denny Graham, perhaps."

"That's what I would assume. Denny's a very ambitious guy. He'd love to be a player on the same level as Mark."

"But could he put together a deal of this magnitude?"

Rusty shrugged. "Who knows? With the land as collateral, he and Mike could no doubt raise enough money to begin the development. If they could bring in a partner or two with deep pockets, it would probably be very doable. But, of course, even with Toby's death, they'd still have to get Bob Martin's signature on the dotted line, and you know as well as I do that no matter how long the old man sits out there in that nursing home, he'll never be *that* old and senile."

***

I left Rusty's office thinking, perhaps uncharitably, that Toby's death had been very convenient for his brother's grand designs and wondering about the physical health and mental well-being of their father. I knew that Mike had always been considered the black sheep of the family and wondered what sort of relationship he'd had with Toby. The whole Cain and Abel business notwithstanding, I couldn't believe that Mike might have murdered his own brother as a means of advancing his plans to develop the family property. Still, Mike had appeared on the scene within minutes of Toby's murder; it certainly wasn't beyond the realm of possibility that he could have gotten there a few minutes earlier.

I could only imagine the argument that would have ensued if Toby had gotten wind of his brother's scheme. But if he had, and if they had quarreled over it, perhaps Mike could have boiled over and killed Toby in a fit of rage. The only problem with my hypothesis, of course, was the not inconsequential fact that the murder weapon had been found in the possession of my client and not in that of Mike Martin.

I knew of only one person outside of their father who probably understood the relationship between the Martin brothers better than anyone else, and I decided that I'd probably better go see her sooner rather than later.

18

Mary Jo Roth — for some reason, I would never be able to think of her as Mary Jo Watson — greeted me at her front door wearing a Glacier Park tee shirt over a pair of khaki shorts and running shoes. Her thick black hair was long and full, blow-dried and styled in a look that had been in vogue perhaps five or ten years ago, but which still looked very appealing on her. Even in the athletic shoes, she probably would have had to stretch to reach a full five foot-two, but she had a figure which, as the personal ads would say, was "proportionate to her height," and which would have never betrayed the fact that she'd given birth to two children. In fact, standing there in the door, even without any makeup, she still looked awfully damn good, save for the dark circles that rimmed her hazel eyes, and the bloodshot eyes themselves.

She pushed open the screen door, gave me a quick hug, and said, "Hey, Dave, it's been a long time."

With my arms still circling her tiny waist, I pulled back a bit, looked down at her and said, "Too long, Mary Jo. How are you doing?"

She nodded and bit her lower lip. "To be honest, not all that great. I've been bawling my eyes out for the last week. My kids can't figure out what the hell is going on, and my husband isn't speaking to me. Other than that, life is peachy keen as usual. And how are you?"

"All right, I guess." I pulled her close again for a moment and said, "I'm so sorry about Toby."

She nodded her head, squeezed me tightly again for a second, and then released me. She dug a Kleenex out of her pocket, sniffled and wiped at her eyes. "I'm making such an idiot of myself," she said in a soft voice, "and I can't seem to stop it." Then she touched my arm and forced a sad smile. "But this hasn't exactly been a banner few months for you either, has it? I'm very sorry for all you've been through."

I nodded my thanks, waited a moment, and then said, "Mary Jo, I know that this is doubtless a bad time, and I feel like hell even asking, but are you up to talking with me for a few minutes?"

She hesitated for a couple of seconds, then nodded and said, "Sure, why not? Jesus, I sure need to talk to *somebody.*"

She led me into a small living room that had been carefully furnished, obviously some time ago, by someone with a good eye. The pieces, though well chosen, were showing their age, as was the remainder of the house — or at least what I could see of it. Someone — Mary Jo, I assumed — was making a gallant effort to keep the yard well-trimmed and the interior of the house clean and tidy, but it appeared to be an uphill battle waged with perhaps insufficient resources. I'd heard rumors to the effect that Mary Jo and Don were keeping up a brave front while struggling to make ends meet, and the condition of the house seemed to support that contention.

We sat opposite each other at the ends of a long couch, and she said, "Would you like something to drink — some coffee or a Coke?"

"No thanks, Mary Jo. I'm fine."

She nodded her head and said, "Okay. Let me know if you change your mind. She shifted a bit in her seat, and said, "So what did you want to talk to me about?"

"I was hoping you could tell me something about the relationship between Toby and Mike."

She furrowed her brow, gave me a confused look, and said, "I don't understand."

"Well," I replied, "As you've doubtless heard, I'm representing Steve Helstrom."

She pursed her lips, nodded, and said in a distinctly chillier voice, "I know that, Dave. To be honest, I wish you weren't, but I understand that somebody has to."

I leaned toward her and said, "Listen, Mary Jo. I know that virtually everybody in the state assumes that Steve is guilty of this crime, mostly because of the fact that he's been arrested for it. And, certainly, there is some evidence against him. But I honestly don't believe that he did it."

She looked at me skeptically then lowered her eyes. "If he didn't kill Toby, then who did?"

"I don't know yet."

Looking up again, she said, "Certainly you're not suggesting that it might have been Mike?"

"No, of course not. At this point I'm making no suggestion at all in that regard."

"So why do you want to know about their relationship?"

"I'm simply attempting to understand as best I can what was going on in Toby's life during the last couple of months. Obviously, I'm hoping that I can discover some thread that will lead to the person who actually did commit the crime."

"Isn't that Chris's job?"

"Yes, of course. But I have a responsibility too, and I don't feel that I can simply sit back and base my defense on whatever evidence Chris and his detectives might uncover."

"And how does Mike figure into all of this?"

"I honestly don't know. Maybe he doesn't figure into it at all. But there's a rumor around town that Mike is attempting to put together a partnership to develop a portion of the family land. I assume that Toby would have strongly opposed any such plan, and I'm just trying to get a sense of what their relationship was like."

Mary Jo nodded her agreement and said, somewhat tentatively, "Well, certainly, if Toby had gotten wind of anything like that, he would have been furious. Do you know if he'd heard the rumors?"

"No, I don't."

She turned to look out the window behind the couch. "Well, of course, I hadn't seen Toby recently enough to know if he'd heard anything about it, but I certainly knew him well enough to know that he'd never allow anything like that to happen."

"When was the last time you did see him?"

Still looking out the window rather than at me, she blinked back tears and said, "About three weeks ago. Don and I were having dinner at the MacKenzie River Pizza Co., and Toby came in with one of the people from his office down in Missoula. He came over to the table for a minute to say hello, but that was about it — just 'Hi, how're things?'" She sniffled, gave me a smile, and said, "As you well know, Toby and Don were never the best of friends. They weren't ever all that eager to catch up with one another."

I waited for a moment while she looked down at the tissue she was kneading in her lap. Then she gave me a sheepish look and said, "I know that everybody thinks that I was a complete idiot to have married Don. When we were in school, you all thought that he was a pompous blowhard, and nobody could ever understand what I might have seen in him. But the truth is that all that bluster was masking a huge inferiority complex. Deep down, Don had — and still has — very little self-confidence. He's always felt intimidated by people he believed were smarter than he was or who were better athletes, or whatever — Toby most of all.

"But after Toby went off to Stanford, and after . . . well, you know . . . after he and I broke up, Don showed me a different side of himself — the person he never let any of the rest of you see. He was soft and tender. . . I could talk to him and he would listen to me at a time when virtually everybody else was keeping their distance, save for you and Angie. It was like people figured they had to tiptoe around me or avoid me altogether — like they assumed that I would be destroyed because Toby had broken up with me and they didn't dare intrude into my grief.

"Well," she laughed bitterly, "of course, I *was* destroyed. And you were probably all right — I doubtless did fall for Don on the rebound. Still, there was a time there when I knew and thought I loved a Don Watson that no one else ever saw or understood. But then, who knows?" she said, exhaling heavily. "Maybe I was kidding myself and it was all just a mirage. God knows, that Don Watson disappeared a long time ago."

"I'm sorry, Mary Jo."

"Yeah, well," she said, shaking her head slowly, "we all make our own beds, so to speak." She looked at me with a sad smile and said, "Did you know that he's screwing one of his salesgirls?"

I gave her what I hoped was a sympathetic look. She smiled ruefully and said, "Don't answer that. I'm sorry. I didn't mean to put you on the spot. It's just that he's been so blatant about it that I assume that everybody in a three-state area must have heard the rumors by now."

"What are you going to do?"

She shook her head. "I really don't know. Hell, right now I don't even care. I'll worry about that tomorrow, Miss Scarlett."

I nodded, and she reached out and squeezed my hand. "But enough of that crap. You wanted to talk about Toby and Mike and instead I'm dragging you through my tale of woe. I'm sorry."

I waved off her apology, and she shifted again, tucking her legs up under her on the couch. "Toby and Mike — what can I say? Mike has always been the family problem child of course, but when Toby and I were dating, I always felt very sorry for Mike. It was bad enough that the poor kid had to grow up without a mother, but what was even worse, of course, was the fact that he had to grow up knowing that his mother had died giving him life. And his father certainly didn't help matters much."

"Are you suggesting that Mike's father blamed him for his mother's death?"

"Oh no, I don't mean that — at least he didn't consciously blame him. But Mike's father is, and always was, a man of his own generation. He was very reserved, very taciturn. He didn't ever demonstrate much affection. He kept his feelings to himself and didn't reveal much of himself to anyone, his sons included. I have the sense that he probably withdrew even more within himself when his wife died. And then, of course, he brought his sons out here, away from their extended family, and basically left them to be raised by their nanny-slash-housekeeper while he threw himself into his work.

"It was easier for Toby, I think, because he was older. At least he had memories of his mother to sustain him, and he didn't have the psychological baggage that Mike had to bear in that regard. And, for whatever reason, Toby was always his father's favorite son, which was clear to Mike as well as to everybody else. When their father did have time to spare for his sons, Toby got the lion's share of his attention while Mike sat on the sidelines wondering why he always seemed to be an afterthought in his father's eyes.

"Hell," she said, shaking her head, "given all that, it's no wonder that the poor kid turned into a loner who abused every substance he could get his hands on. The miracle is that he didn't turn into the Son of the Son of Sam."

"And how did Toby react to all of that?"

She thought about it for a moment, again looking out the window at nothing in particular. "When they were boys, Toby and Mike were close. You remember from when we were in school that Toby was always mature for his age, and he understood, at least to some extent, what Mike was going through. Toby sympathized with Mike's situation and tried to take him under his wing. He tried to be Mike's friend as well as his brother. You remember how he always defended Mike with the teachers and with the other kids, even when Mike had done something that was basically indefensible."

I nodded, remembering a couple of celebrated incidents in which Toby had come to his brother's rescue, while Mary Jo continued. "Unfortunately, though, and no matter how hard he might have tried, Toby couldn't make up for the fact that his brother had no mother and that, as a practical matter, he had no father either. Then, when Toby went off to Stanford, Mike was left completely on his own.

"While Toby was out in California, setting the world on fire and making the old man proud, Mike was getting busted for drugs and for drinking under age, and was flunking out of school. Naturally, Mike felt the weight of the comparisons that his father and everybody else made between himself and Toby, and of course that just made matters worse for Mike.

"Inevitably, I suppose, Mike became very resentful of Toby. It was like he came to believe that Toby was succeeding simply to spite him. Meanwhile, like their father, Toby became increasingly disappointed in Mike and impatient with his repeated failures. In the end, then, I would say that, by the time Toby graduated from law school, the two brothers neither knew nor liked each other very well at all."

She hesitated for a few seconds, then met my eyes. "Fate played a very cruel trick on Mike, and all things considered, I still find it difficult to blame him for the man that he's become."

Still kneading the tissue in her lap, she said, "You know, it strikes me that in many ways, Mike and Don are a lot alike. They both resent and feel threatened by the success of others. They're both constantly struggling to prove themselves and usually falling short of the mark, and they've both become bitter, angry men with little regard or concern for anyone other than themselves. The difference between the two of them, I guess, is that Mike, at least, had a legitimate reason for feeling and acting that way. Still, having said all of that, I really can't believe for a moment that he could have killed Toby."

"I understand, and you certainly don't need to apologize for believing that. Again, I don't mean to imply for an instant that I think he did. I was just looking for some insight into the relationship between the two of them, and I appreciate your help."

"Well, I don't know how much help it was, but you're welcome to it, and I appreciate the fact that you came by, even if it was only for that. Seeing you always reminds me of much better times."

I nodded my understanding and she walked me back to the door. I took her hand and said, "I wish I knew what to say about all of this, Mary Jo. Hell, I wish I knew what to say about any of it. But again, I am sorry about Toby."

She nodded, again blinking back tears. Then she rose up on the tips of her toes, gave me a quick peck on the cheek, and said goodbye.

19

I grabbed a late lunch on the way back to the office where I found a voice-mail message from Bob Helstrom saying that he'd like a chance to talk about his brother's case. The message indicated that he'd be out on a charter for most of the afternoon but would be back at his dock in Somers by four. I called and left a message for him, telling him I'd stop by on my way home.

A little after five o'clock I parked my car in the public lot across from the Montana Grill in Somers and walked over to the dock. I found Bob on his boat, stowing the gear from his afternoon charter and getting ready for another first thing in the morning. It was a beautiful afternoon, with the temperature somewhere in the high seventies. A number of people were down on the beach enjoying the day, and a mile or so out on the lake, a large sailboat tacked slowly to the east, propelled by only the slightest of winds.

Bob waved as I approached the boat and then finished wiping down the bench seat on the port side of the vessel. As I stepped aboard, he pitched the rag into a bucket and said, "Your timing is perfect. Would you like a beer?"

"You read my mind."

I took a seat in the stern looking out at the lake, kicked off my shoes, and propped my feet up on the engine cover. Bob pulled two Trout Slayer Ales out of the ice chest, popped the tops, and dropped the caps into a small garbage bag. He handed me one of the beers, dropped into the seat next to mine, and said, "Thanks for stopping by."

"No problem," I said, saluting him with the bottle. "It's right on the way home, and as you know full well, I'm always happy to drop in and drink your beer. I just wish I were doing so at a better time."

Bob took a pull on his beer and we watched a small boy pitch a stick out into the lake for his dog. The dog splashed out into the water, retrieved the stick, brought it back to the shore and dropped it at the boy's feet. Then the dog vigorously shook the water off his coat, showering both the little boy and a woman I assumed to be the boy's mother. The child squealed with delight while the woman laughed and screamed, "Barney! Stop it! Yuck!"

We watched as the boy pitched the stick out into the lake again, and I turned to Bob. "So, I assume you're looking for a progress report?"

He nodded. "Well, that's one of the reasons why I wanted to see you. How do things look at this point?

I took a pull on my own beer and said, "Well, there's some good news, but sadly not very much of it. It seems pretty clear that an awful lot of people were angry with Toby Martin, and theoretically any one of them might have attacked and killed him. Unfortunately, we're stuck with the fact that Steve had threatened to kill Toby. You and I both know that Steve didn't mean the threat literally, but apparently there are witnesses who will testify that he sounded as though he did. And, also unfortunately, although a lot of other people were pissed at Toby, as far as we know, no one else threatened to kill him.

"The second problem, of course, is the murder weapon. We can argue that any number of people had the opportunity to pitch it into the bed of Steve's truck, but at least at the moment, we have no way of proving that somebody did."

"So, where does that leave us?"

I shrugged. "The honest truth is that I don't know. On the basis of the evidence as it now stands, I'm afraid that the best we can hope for at the moment is that we can raise enough reasonable doubt in the minds of jurors to win an acquittal. But we're still a

120

long way from going to trial with this case, and anything can happen. That's doubtless not as optimistic an appraisal as you'd like to hear, but I know you want me to be straight with you."

"Yeah, I do. It's just that this business is so damned hard on Karen and the kids as well as on Steve. I wish I could give them some more encouraging news."

"I know, I wish you could too."

Bob sat for a moment, passing his beer back and forth from one hand to the other. "I talked to Steve yesterday. He said he discussed your fee with you."

"He mentioned it. But as I told him, that's the furthest thing from my mind at the moment."

"I appreciate that, Dave, and of course Steve and Karen do too. But you've already put in a lot of time and effort on Steve's behalf, and we both know that this is only the beginning. Obviously, we've got to make some sort of an arrangement here."

"No, Bob, we don't. I . . ."

He held up his hand to cut me off and said, "Yeah, we do. It's one thing for me to go out on a limb here. Steve's my brother. But we can't ask you to devote yourself to defending Steve simply because you and I are friends. I've been talking to George Froleich over at my bank. I'm going to take out a second mortgage on my house and use the proceeds to make a down payment on your fee. Then once this business is behind us, we'll work out a schedule to pay you the rest of it."

I got up, walked over to the cooler and snagged another couple of beers. I popped the tops and handed one to Bob. "Like hell you will. The only reason I agreed to take this case is because you and I *are* friends, and this is the kind of thing that friends do for each other. I know damned good and well that if the situation were reversed, you'd do the same for me — or for Chris or Dick.

"Besides which, it's not like I had a really full schedule right at the moment. In fact, if anything, you're probably the one doing me the favor. I can think of a few saloon owners who doubtless aren't very happy about it, but I'm probably already money ahead as a result of this case. And if I'm not, I can always take out my fee in beer, fish and firewood."

Shaking his head, Bob smiled. "Christ, Dave, don't even joke about it. In the end, you just might have to."

We sat for a couple of minutes looking out over the lake and he said, "What do you suppose you might have ended up doing if you hadn't been interested enough to go to college, or if for some reason you hadn't been able to go?"

I watched as a speedboat swung by and dropped off an attractive blonde water skier who slalomed parallel to the dock and then deftly stepped out of her ski and onto the dock without even getting her ankles wet.

"Jesus, Bob, I don't know. To be honest, the thought never crossed my mind. During the summers while I was in high school and college, I always had jobs that required a lot of hard, physical labor and that didn't pay a hell of a lot of money. I always found those summer jobs to be a very good incentive to get back to school, hit the books, and work as hard as I could to make sure that I didn't wind up working in one of them for the rest of my life. How about you?"

Admiring the view as the blonde leaned over to retrieve her ski from the water, he said, "The same I guess, although my accounting degree isn't doing me an awful lot of good at the moment. I really always thought of it as my safety net in case the charter business didn't work out. God knows I'd be making a lot more money working as an accountant, but I just can't imagine a life other than the one I have right now. I love being out on the lake in the summer and up on the slopes in the winter. I wouldn't be cooped up in an office somewhere for ten times the money — even here in Montana, let alone somewhere out of state."

I smiled and said, "No life in the mill for you, huh?"

"Oh, Jesus Christ, no. Don't get me wrong. Steve's my brother and I love him, but I've always been a bit disappointed in him because he settled so readily for that life. Beneath that good ol' boy facade he puts up for the people he hangs out with, Steve's actually a very bright guy. He could have gone to college and made something more of himself. At the very least he could have given himself some options instead of painting himself into a corner. But he figured that the mill was good enough for the Old Man and so it was good enough for him. And look where it got him. Leaving this current mess aside, what's his future — what's he going to do if that mill closes?"

I shook my head. "Damned if I know. But he's certainly not the only one in this valley who's facing that dilemma."

"I understand that," he replied, absent-mindedly peeling the label off his beer bottle. "But just between you and me, this whole logging controversy really pisses me off. I know I sound like a traitor to my family — I mean, that mill provided jobs for my Dad, for my Uncle Mike and now for Steve. It paid the bills in our house while I was growing up. But in spite of all that, I love this country up here just the way it is."

Gesturing toward the mountains behind us, he said, "This land — these mountains especially — are in my blood, and I don't want people gashing the mountainsides with a network of logging roads. I don't want them cutting down the trees, and otherwise fucking up the countryside more than they already have."

I smiled and said, "I'll bet those sentiments are warmly received at family gatherings."

Returning the laugh, he shrugged. "Yeah, well, on those occasions I usually just keep my opinions to myself and my damned mouth shut. To his credit, because I'm his brother, I suppose, Steve respects my right to disagree with him on this subject and so he doesn't bait me about it. He might punch out Toby Martin for wanting to protect the forests, but he hasn't swung on me since I was twelve years old and questioned the virtue of some skanky girl he was dating."

I smiled at the thought. "So, how's the charter business?"

"Good," he said in a much brighter voice. "In fact, so far, it's been my best year yet. I've got a lot of reservations booked and I've been doing a lot of repeat business, which means that I've actually had a few customers who could manage their own lines. It's still early in the summer, but so far, the weather's been great and the fishing's been excellent. The clients are happy and so am I."

Looking out over the lake, he shook his head sadly and said, "If it wasn't for this business with Steve, life would be just about perfect."

20

Banner headlines in Thursday morning's paper announced that a District Court Judge in Missoula had issued an order temporarily banning all logging activity in the Kootenai National Forest. In his decision, the judge supported the argument made by the Northwestern Environmental Alliance to the effect that the U.S. Forest Service had violated its own rules for maintaining the forest and monitoring the health of the wildlife that inhabited it.

The judge ruled, as Toby Martin had argued before the court, that the forest's management plan "clearly and unequivocally" required that at least ten percent of the forest below fifty-five hundred feet be preserved as old-growth habitat. The judge noted, however, that the Kootenai forest managers had not actually known how much old-growth habitat existed in the forest when they had approved a series of timber sales a year earlier. The managers' "best guess" was that about 8.9 percent of the forest was then protected as old-growth.

The judge thus ruled that the Forest Service was in clear violation of its own management plan and prohibited any additional timber sales in the forest until Forest Service officials could prove that there was at least ten percent of old-growth habitat and until they could adequately document the population of several species of wildlife dependent upon the old-growth trees. The article indicated that the practical effect of the decision would be to immediately halt all logging activity in the forest.

The paper quoted a spokesman for the Northwestern Environmental Alliance who said that the judge's decision vindicated the group's decision to file the suit and was a major victory in the struggle to preserve the national forests. "It's critically important to remember," the spokesman said, "that in this case we are not talking about privately-owned timber stands. These are national forests. They belong to all of the people of the United States, and they must be managed in a way that protects the interests of the people as a whole and of the wildlife species who depend upon these forests for their continued survival."

The spokesman insisted that the Alliance "was not insensitive to the interests of the people and communities who are dependent on the forest for their livelihoods. We would very much like to work with them on restoration and other projects that would both promote truly healthy forests and provide jobs for the people of northwestern Montana. But we can no longer allow our national forests to be carelessly exploited for the short-term economic advantage of a few special interests."

The Alliance spokesman concluded by noting that the judge's decision was a fitting tribute to the work of Toby Martin who had died, the spokesman said, "serving the cause that had been his life's work."

In a separate article, the paper quoted mill owner Phil Krause as saying that it was a "dark day" for the people of Creston. He indicated that he had bid successfully on two of the five sales in question and that his mill had already begun logging timber from one of them. However, Forest Service officials told him that he would have to cease the work immediately. Krause noted that the mill had only a four or five-day supply of logs in the yard and had been relying on timber from the Kootenai sales.

"I don't know where in the hell we're going to get replacement logs," he was quoted as saying, "especially on such short notice. But until we can find some, we'll have no choice other than to basically shut down our operation." Krause indicated that this would directly impact the eighty people employed by his mill and that it would also jeopardize the jobs of nearly a hundred and twenty-five other workers in the Creston area who were employed by companies using byproducts from the mill. That, in turn, would have a negative effect on the economy of the entire community.

"As I understand the judge's ruling," Krause continued, "it could be years before we see any more timber coming out of the Kootenai, and that just make me furious. This makes no damned sense to me at all. I just can't understand how one judge and a bunch of wild-eyed environmental radicals down in Missoula should be able to cause such a catastrophe for the average, hard-working, tax-paying people who've lived up here all their lives."

**

I knew, of course, that the judge's decision was bound to infuriate a lot of people in addition to Phil Krause and that it would certainly further inflame the tensions that already existed between people on opposite sides of the environmental divide. On a more personal level, I couldn't help but speculate about the effect that the decision might have on the effort to impanel a fair and impartial jury in the event that Steve Helstrom should be brought to trial for the murder of Toby Martin.

I still hoped, of course, that Steve would not have to stand trial on the charge, and to that end, I'd made an appointment with Mark Adamson, hoping to gain some additional insight into Mike Martin's development plans. Mark was a Seattle native who'd moved to the Flathead in the late 1990s and was the major partner in an investment group that had developed two exclusive subdivisions in the valley, one near Bigfork and the other in the mountains overlooking Whitefish.

I knew Mark slightly, mostly from the tennis courts, although we occasionally ran into each other in area restaurants or at various local social events. He'd earned a reputation as a bright, energetic entrepreneur, with a good eye for property and the ability to bring his projects in on time and under budget.

Area natives were divided in their opinion of Mark and his efforts. Some were grateful for the jobs his projects generated and for the money they brought into the valley. Others, though, opposed what they described as the growing "Californication" of Montana in general and of the Flathead Valley in particular. They resented the growing number of celebrities and other wealthy flatlanders who built lavish, multi-million-dollar homes along the lakes and in developments like Mark's, and then visited those homes for only a few weeks every year. In part as a result of this trend, housing prices and property taxes were spiraling upward in the valley and growing numbers of locals maintained that before long, a "real Montanan" wouldn't be able to afford to live in the Flathead Valley.

Like a lot of natives, I was of two minds on the subject. I understood that the growth and expansion of the valley was inevitable, and I also understood the importance of the activity for the local economy. At a time when jobs in the mills, forests, and other extractive industries were in decline, the new jobs that were being created in health care, in construction, in technology, and in the service sector were vitally important to the people who lived here, natives and newcomers alike.

Still, it all seemed to be happening so quickly — and, unfortunately, without nearly as much care and thought to the long-term future of the valley as I would have liked. The population of Flathead County was now growing faster than that of any virtually other county in Montana. In response, developers, many of whom were not as responsible as Mark Adamson, were throwing up subdivisions and strip malls helter-skelter all over the valley, and the combination of all these forces was overwhelming the local transportation network, schools and other public services.

The social problems and other pathologies that once seemed to be the exclusive concern of people who lived in big cities far away from the Flathead had inevitably landed on our doorstep as well, and sometimes, sitting in a traffic jam or looking down from the mountains onto another ugly, ill-designed, cookie-cutter subdivision, I was not at all certain that the benefits of all this growth were enough to offset the costs.

I arrived at Adamson's offices in Whitefish a few minutes before my ten o'clock appointment. His receptionist, a lithe young woman in her early thirties, greeted me and buzzed Mark to tell him that I had arrived. She then led me down a short hallway to an office where her boss was working at a large desk.

The room was tastefully furnished with wood and glass furniture pieces that sat on what appeared to be an expensive wool carpet. Photos of Mark's projects in various stages of development lined the off-white walls, and brochures and other materials advertising his latest project were arranged on a coffee table in front of a green leather couch in a seating area opposite the desk. Mark smiled and rose to greet me, dressed in a pair of boots, crisp jeans, and a crew-neck sweater that he was wearing over a polo shirt. "Hey, Dave. Come on in."

He walked around the desk, gave me a firm handshake, and led me toward the couch.

I declined an offer of coffee and Adamson turned to the receptionist who was waiting near the door. "Thanks, Abby, that'll be all. Please hold my calls."

She smiled, nodded, and then closed the door as she left. I took a seat on the couch and as Adamson sank into an upholstered chair opposite me, I thanked him for seeing me.

"No problem," he said smiling. "Although I'd rather see you on the tennis courts or on the golf course — unless, of course, you came in because you're interested in buying a lot up in Eagle's Peak."

I returned the smile. "No, I'm pretty happy right where I am. But from what I understand, I'd have to stand in line to buy property up there anyhow."

"Well, that's not quite true, but it's doing very well for us. Virtually all the lots are spoken for, and we've started construction on several of the homes. It's keeping us busy, but naturally that's the way we like it. So, what can I do for you?"

"Well, as you no doubt know, I'm defending Steve Helstrom. I'm working the background of the case and wanted to talk to you about it."

Mark nodded, sat back in his chair and said, "What a goddamn shame. I barely knew Toby Martin, but he seemed like a nice guy with a very good head on his shoulders. And even though some people up here might not agree, especially after seeing this morning's paper, his killing is a tragedy for this valley."

"I gather that you and your partners had no problem with his efforts on behalf of the Northwestern Alliance?"

"Oh, hell no. We're strongly supportive of their efforts. The type of customer that we're appealing to wants the forests preserved and the wildlife left unmolested. Some of the more extreme environmentalists believe that every mountain and every forest should be left untouched and so they oppose even the type of projects that we're doing, but Martin wasn't in that camp. He understood that some development was not only inevitable but that it was also important to the valley's economic future. His concern was that it be done in an environmentally sensitive manner, which is exactly what we're determined to do.

"I know there are some locals who believe that the houses we build and the people who can afford to buy them don't really belong up here. They'd like to fence off the Flathead and keep it exactly the way it was thirty years ago. But, obviously, that's not going to happen. This valley is going to continue to grow and the sensible thing to do is to try to control the growth and channel it in a responsible and ecologically sensitive way. Toby understood that. Obviously, he was concerned about some of the developments that are being thrown up haphazardly around here, but at least as far as I know, he had no such concerns about either of our projects."

"But he *did* object to the idea that your next project might be on his family's land?"

"Oh, Jesus, you heard about that, did you?"

I nodded. "I heard through the grapevine that Mike Martin approached you with the idea."

Mark shifted in his chair, crossed his legs and said, "Yeah, he came in with a half-baked plan in which we'd go partners with him to develop a part of the property. I listened politely and then told him that we were occupied elsewhere and wouldn't be interested. As to the question of whether Toby objected to the idea, I can't help you. I certainly didn't hear from him on the subject, and as far as I know, he wasn't even aware of his brother's grand plans."

"I gather you didn't think the plan was viable?"

"Not necessarily. In fact, the land in question would be a beautiful spot for the type of small, exclusive residential community that we build. But I know full well that neither Bob nor Toby Martin would have ever agreed to such a development."

"Did you ask Mike if he'd run the idea by his father and brother?"

"No. He inferred that he was trying to get the deal in place before approaching them, but I didn't ask him directly — there wasn't any point. Even if he had come to me with the blessing of his father and brother, I'd have still turned him down. If Toby had brought the idea to me, I'd have jumped at the chance to work with him. But I'd never get tangled up in a project with Mike. He doesn't possess enough business sense even to run a used car lot very well. And, just between you and me, the guy's too slippery for my taste. In a partnership with him, I'd feel that I had to be watching him constantly, and I have no interest in that sort of a business relationship."

"I understand that Mike has approached Denny Graham with the idea."

Adamson nodded and picked a piece of lint off his sweater. "That wouldn't surprise me. Mike and Denny are birds of a feather and Denny is particularly anxious to move up in the world. Personally, I'd argue that he's found his ideal role in life as a small-time real estate agent, but I guess everybody's entitled to his dreams."

"Do you think the two of them could pull it off, assuming that they had Bob's consent?"

"Oh, I'm sure they could cobble something together. Neither one of them has a pot to piss in financially, and I find it hard to imagine that they could convince anyone who's intelligent enough to have serious money to go in with them. But if they were able to use the land as collateral, they might be able to borrow enough money to at least do some rough development. Knowing the two of them, though, the project would be designed to squeeze the maximum profit out of the land without concern for anything else, and in the end, it would probably be a major disaster aesthetically and environmentally. But, if you don't mind my asking, what does all this have to do with your defense of Steve Helstrom?"

"Probably nothing. I'm just trying to get a handle on what was going on in Toby's life lately to see who else, if anyone, might have been angry enough to go after him."

"Well, as upset as a lot of people are over this lawsuit, I'd think you'd probably have to rent a pretty large hall to accommodate all the likely suspects."

"People keep reminding me of that. But I'd feel a lot better about it if I could narrow the list a bit."

"Well, I sure as hell don't know anything about criminal law, but it strikes me that just the opposite would be true. All you have to do is raise enough reasonable doubt in the minds of the jurors and your guy is off the hook. I would think that the longer the list of alternate suspects, the better your chances would be."

132

I nodded. "In one sense, of course, you're absolutely correct. And, certainly, getting Steve acquitted on grounds of reasonable doubt is preferable to having him convicted for a murder that he didn't commit. But obviously it would be a lot better for Steve and for the cause of justice if the person who really killed Toby were caught and convicted. After all this is over, Steve still has to live in this valley. And it would be difficult to do so if, for the rest of his life, he was marked as the man who committed murder and got off on a technicality."

Mark uncrossed his legs and leaned forward in his chair. "I understand your logic and I wish you luck — unless of course, your client is actually guilty. In that case, I hope you'll pardon me if I say that I hope he gets everything he's got coming to him. As I said, Toby Martin was a good man who didn't deserve to come to that end."

"On that, we're agreed," I said, rising. "Thanks for your time, Mark."

"No problem," he said rising with me. "But once this business is resolved and you have the time, let's make it a point to play some tennis."

"I'll look forward to it."

21

Adamson walked me back out to the door and we bid each other goodbye, again promising that we'd get together soon for golf or tennis. By then it was eleven thirty, and I decided to see if I could catch Denny Graham before lunch. I retrieved my car and drove out to the aging strip mall on the south end of town where he had a small, one-man agency. I had no trouble finding a parking spot right in front of the office, which was sandwiched between a nail parlor and a pet supply shop.

The place suggested an air of quiet desperation, not unlike Mike Martin's used car lot. Taped to the windows facing the parking lot were photos and descriptions of several properties listed with Graham's agency, including a few sad-looking retail estab-lishments, several older houses, and a fair selection of mobile homes. Apparently, there were no multi-million-dollar lakeshore or mountain properties for sale here — at least not yet.

I found Graham working at his desk, his tie loosened, and his sport coat draped over the back of his chair. He was a medium-sized man, somewhere on the wrong side of forty with light brown hair that he'd strategically arranged in a largely unsuccessful effort to disguise the bald spot that was spreading from the center of the top of his head. As I walked through the door, he looked up from the papers on his desk and showed an amazing number of teeth through what must have been a well-practiced smile. When he recognized me, the smile faded for an instant, but then reappeared, looking even more insincere than it had a second earlier. He stubbed out a cigarette in an ashtray, stood and said, "Morning, Dave. I didn't expect to see you again quite this quickly."

We shook hands and I said, "Sorry to interrupt you Denny, but I was hoping that you might be able to spare me a couple of minutes."

"I suppose so. Have a seat."

I took a chair in front of the desk as Graham settled back into his own chair and said, "How can I help you, Dave?"

"Well, I know that you're doubtless very busy and I don't want to take up too much of your time here, so I'll get right to the point. I've heard from several sources that you and Mike are planning to develop part of the Martin family property."

He hesitated for a moment, then took a package of Winstons from his shirt pocket. Moving very deliberately, he shook a cigarette from the package, picked up a silver Zippo lighter from the desktop and fired up the cigarette. He inhaled deeply then slowly exhaled the smoke and said, "Well, Dave, I don't know who these 'sources' are, and I don't think I should probably make any comment on these rumors you might have heard at this point."

I leaned back in my chair and attempted a disarming smile. "I don't understand. As I said, I've heard the story from several different people. You know as well as I do that this is a very small town. A project this significant to the economy of the valley is hardly going to stay a secret very long. And why should it?"

He tapped the ash off the end of the Winston and gave me what I imagined was supposed to be a conspiratorial grin. "Well, certainly as a lawyer you can appreciate the fact that *if* Mike and I were planning something like this, we wouldn't want to go public with it until the plans were fairly well set and all the necessary paperwork was in place."

"I gather, then, that all of the paperwork is not yet in place?"

"Not quite."

"What did Toby think of the project?"

Again, he paused long enough to take a drag on the cigarette and to get his thoughts in order. "That's a question that you should really direct to Mike. Naturally, getting his father and his brother on board was his responsibility."

"And were they on board?"

Graham nodded vigorously. "Mike had every confidence that they would be. What we're proposing is a first-class development that would make excellent use of the land and which would also make a lot of money for the Martin family. Given the way the Flathead is growing, there's a real opportunity here. That land can't stay vacant forever, and I'm sure that ultimately Toby and Bob would have agreed that ours is a sensible approach to its development."

"But, reading between the lines of what you're saying, apparently they hadn't agreed yet."

Graham exhaled and carefully balanced the cigarette on the edge of the ashtray. "Let's not kid each other here. You and I both know that the Martins — Mike included — have always had a very strong attachment to that land. Certainly, you can understand that Mike would have to be very sensitive in the way that he raised the subject with Toby and with their father. He'd been waiting for the right moment to broach the subject with Toby and then once he had Toby's blessing, he was going to approach their dad. But Toby'd been very busy lately, and Mike felt that the time really wasn't right. He told me the other morning that Toby was killed before he had a chance to discuss the issue with him."

"So, where does that leave you?"

"Well, as you can understand, Mike is devastated by his brother's death, and business is the last thing on his mind at the moment. So, we're on hold for the time being. After an appropriate amount of time has passed and Mike is ready to climb back into the saddle, he'll approach his father with the idea and we'll go from there."

"Okay," I said, rising from the chair. I extended my hand and said, "Thanks for your help, Denny. I appreciate your taking the time to talk to me."

He rose, gave me a firm handshake, and said, "My pleasure, Dave. Naturally, though, I'll ask you to keep our conversation to yourself. Even though the rumors are apparently beginning to make their way around town, we really would like to keep this project under wraps until the time is right."

"I understand completely. Thanks again for your time."

22

I hadn't talked to Chris in a couple of days and so, following lunch, I wandered over to the Justice Center. I found him sitting at his desk, every square inch of which seemed to be a foot and a half deep in paper. The rest of the office mirrored the character of the desk, with books, files and loose papers scattered everywhere. Behind Chris's chair, a window afforded him a view of the traffic moving through the middle of Kalispell on Highway 93. On one side of the window was a poster of the Michigan State Spartans from his senior year, his second year as starting quarterback. Below that was an eight-by-ten photo of his Montana State High School Championship team.

I was always amused by the juxtaposition of the football poster and the picture. While Chris was a local football legend, there were still any number of western Montanans who had never forgiven him for selecting Michigan State over the University of Montana. They knew that the Grizzlies would have been a much more formidable football power during his college years if he'd chosen to go to school in Missoula and play in state, and I always assumed that the display in his office was as much a declaration of his own independent spirit as it was a reminder of his glory days on the gridiron. As I walked through the door, he looked up from a report he was reading and said, "I was just thinking about you."

I dropped into a chair in front of his desk. "Something nice, I'm sure."

"Naturally," he said, laughing.

He leaned back in his chair, propped his feet up on the desk. "So, what's new on your end of things?"

"A couple of items you might find interesting, that is if you're not already aware of them. First of all, Mike Martin is apparently making plans with Denny Graham to develop a portion of the Martin family property."

"In his dreams, maybe."

"Actually, he seems serious about the idea. He approached Mark Adamson with it, but Mark turned him down. So now Mike's joining forces with Graham. I talked to Graham this morning and he says that Mike was waiting for the right moment to approach Toby with the idea, but that he hadn't done so before Toby was killed."

Chris sat quietly for a moment, digesting the information, and then said, "And the second item?"

"I also talked to Mary Jo. She says that she hadn't seen Toby in about three weeks. She and Don ran into him one evening at MacKenzie River Pizza."

"You believe her?"

"I don't know. She's obviously taking Toby's death very hard, but that certainly doesn't mean that they'd been seeing each other again, and it didn't seem like the right moment to press the issue. I gather that you still can't account for Toby's time in the three hours before he was killed."

"No, we can't. And we've been busting our balls trying to trace his movements. We know where he was practically every minute of the day from eight o'clock that morning up until the time that Phil Krause passed him on the highway at seven fifteen that evening, but the period from seven fifteen to ten thirty is still a giant goddamn black hole.

"When Krause passed him, Toby was headed north in the direction of home, but it sure as hell wouldn't have taken him over three hours to drive that three or four miles. We've had people calling the tip line, claiming to have seen his pickup all over the friggin' county that night, but so far none of the tips has panned out. At the moment, we have absolutely no idea where in the hell he might have gone during that period."

"Is there any good news?"

Chris re-crossed his legs on the desk and said, "Not really. We took a closer look at your pal Ed Ramsey but didn't come up with much. In the last two years, he's had a couple of speeding tickets and pled out on a DUI. Dispatch also sent a deputy to answer a domestic disturbance call at Ramsey's house back in March.

"Of course, as often happens in these cases, when the deputy got there, Ramsey and his wife immediately turned their antagonism on the deputy and on the neighbor who called it in. They insisted that their marital problems were none of the deputy's fucking business and that he should just leave them the hell alone to settle things between themselves. Since neither of them was interested in making a complaint, there wasn't much the deputy could do except to threaten them with arrest for disturbing the peace if they didn't quiet down and quit annoying the neighbors. Then he left.

"Ramsey is apparently active in local gun circles and may be on the fringes of the militia movement, but we have no reason to think that he might be involved in any illegal activities in those areas. Tom did talk to him again, under the guise of reconfirming some of the information from the original interview. Ramsey claims that after Steve left at about eight thirty on the night of the murder, he went back in the house and cleaned up. He says that from nine to ten thirty, he watched a soft-core porn flick on Cinemax — something called *Desire and Deception*, probably starring Sir Laurence Olivier and two or three of the Barrymores."

"No doubt." I laughed.

"Yeah, well, Ramsey gave Tom a surprisingly complete summary of the plot of the movie. Tom looked it up and it seems pretty clear that Ramsey saw it. The problem is that it was on the satellite again, on the west coast Cinemax channel, three hours later."

"So, there's no way of proving that Ed was planted in his recliner watching this Academy-Award-winning epic at the time that Martin was killed."

"No, there isn't. But, of course, there's also absolutely no evidence whatsoever to suggest that he was out at the Martin place smashing Toby's skull with an ax handle, either. It's pretty clear that Ramsey has a giant chip on his shoulder. Clearly, he'd be a lot happier if all the environmentalists, judges, Forest Service lackeys, and other government scum would just clear out of Montana and leave him to his own devices. But that in and of itself isn't a crime, and it certainly doesn't mean that he's a killer."

"And I suppose you're going to tell me that Mrs. Krause provided a solid alibi for her husband?"

Chris fluttered his hand. "More or less. I interviewed her myself. She says that she spent the evening reading a book and doing some sewing. She didn't look at the clock when her husband got home, although she's sure he was there by nine thirty as he claims."

"But . . ."

"But nothing, probably. It's just that she seemed extraordinarily nervous for some reason. She impressed me as a fairly quiet, traditional housewife who would have been right at home living next door to Ozzie and Harriet back in the 1950s. I'm sure that this is the first time she's ever been interviewed in the course of a criminal investigation, and that's probably why she was so unsettled."

"And I don't suppose you'd consider dragging her in and trying out the thumb screws on her to see if she changes her story?"

"I don't think so, not unless we come up with some good reason to doubt her husband's story. But I'll keep the thought in mind, just in case."

I rose to leave, and Chris said, "Totally changing the subject, I haven't had a day off in two weeks. I was thinking about playing hooky tomorrow morning and investigating the golf course for a change. You interested?"

"What'd you have in mind?"

"Well, Dick is out of town at a conference, and it might be a little tricky asking Bob to play right now. I was thinking that maybe you and I could play Buffalo Hill by ourselves, say eight thirty?"

"Sounds fine to me."

"Good," he said. "I'll reserve a tee time. Bring lots of money."

23

It had turned into a beautiful day, with clear blue skies and the temperature in the high sixties, and so when I got home a little after three, I decided to get some exercise. I changed into my running gear, locked up the house, and headed north up Angel Point Road. Passing the West Shore Inn, I was reminded, as always, of the scores of times that Alice and I had run along this same road together.

We met in a history class at the University of Montana when she was a junior and I a senior. Descended from Swedish immigrants who'd settled on the plains of northeastern Montana during the First World War, she was a natural blonde with bright blue eyes and a tall, thin frame. Even more intelligent than she was beautiful, she'd attracted my attention immediately, along with that of every other male in the class.

On the second day of the course, she'd raised her hand and corrected the instructor who'd mistakenly identified the World War II traitor Vidkun Quisling as a Swede rather than a Norwegian, a gaffe that any Swede would have naturally resented. As we were leaving the room at the end of the hour, I took advantage of the opportunity to introduce myself and to congratulate her for being brave enough to challenge a professor whose reputation suggested that he did not suffer criticism lightly.

She shook her head, flashed me a beautiful smile, and said, "Oh, crap. I'm a sociology major. This is only the second history course I've taken here, and I hadn't heard anything about this guy. I guess I just totally screwed my chances for getting a decent grade in his class."

I assured her that her action probably hadn't been fatal and asked if she'd like to get a Coke or some coffee in the Student Union. "I would like that," she replied, still smiling. "But unfortunately, I don't have time today. I'm due at track practice in thirty minutes and I've barely got time to get over to the gym, change, and get out on the field."

I asked if she had track practice every afternoon.

She turned to watch a dog that was chasing a Frisbee on the lawn below the steps where we were standing, and said, "Yes, I do." She paused a moment, then turned back to me. "But I'm almost always finished by five thirty."

"In that case," I'd said, "if you don't already have plans, would you like to get together after practice on Friday? Maybe we could get something to eat and see a movie?"

She slipped her book bag over her left shoulder and hooked her long hair back behind her ear. "I hate to sound so coy about it, but I may be tied up on Friday night. If not, a movie sounds like fun. Could we talk about it again after class on Thursday?"

"No problem," I'd said. "I'll see you in class on Thursday."

Only after we'd been seeing each other for four months did she confess that she'd already had a date for that Friday night but had broken it so that she could go to the movies with me. By that time, I was already madly in love with her, and couldn't bring myself to feel even remotely sorry for the guy she'd jilted that night.

For the next two years, we were virtually inseparable. After finishing my undergraduate degree in history and political science, I was accepted into the University's Law School, and when Alice graduated a year after me, she went to work at the Edgewater Inn as an assistant manager. During that period, she continued to live with her widowed mother on Missoula's south side while I remained in my student apartment near the University campus. We ran together on a regular basis; we spent most evenings together, and with increasing frequency, Alice spent the night in my apartment. Her mother, Eileen, grew increasingly fond of me and appeared untroubled by this arrangement.

After Alice and I had been dating for several months, my parents drove down from Kalispell to meet Eileen, and although no one was ready to make a formal announcement of the fact, all five of us took it for granted that in the not-too-distant future we would all be formally related. But, for reasons that neither Alice nor I could ever articulate very well, that never came to pass.

In many ways, we were very much alike — in the end, perhaps too much so. We were both strong-willed and very independent. I'd once told a subsequent lover that in the relationship between Alice and me, there'd been too much yang and not enough yin, and that as a result, we could not have had a successful marriage. Alice had once explained the end of our romance by arguing that we loved each other too much to spoil our friendship by getting married. And in the end, hers was the rationale that I clung to.

Whatever the case, we'd ultimately agreed that we were better matched as friends than as lovers, and so after being together for twenty-five months, we agreed to end our love affair in order to preserve our relationship. After a few more weeks of false starts at this new order of things, we finally stopped sleeping together, and a couple of months after that, we both began dating other people, albeit very tentatively at first. In the years after, we'd each remained the other's closest friend and confidant, and had encouraged, supported and consoled each other through a variety of triumphs and tragedies, romantic and otherwise.

Alice had ultimately married Bill Johnson, the English professor that she'd met while helping to arrange a convention that his department was hosting at the Edgewater. Meanwhile, I'd drifted through a succession of relationships of varying duration. I'd been extremely fond of a number of the women with whom I'd been involved but had never again been moved to consider the prospect of matrimony.

For his part, Bill had accepted without difficulty my continuing friendship with Alice and had become one of my closest friends himself. Four years older than I, he was an outgoing and very engaging man, widely read and conversant on any number of topics. He was genuinely interested in other people and had a natural gift for making friends easily and quickly.

It was Bill who'd alerted me to the fact that the property two doors down from their inn was going on the market, eighteen months after they'd completed construction. Given his own recent experience, he'd been an excellent source of good advice when I bought the property and constructed my own home.

Once we'd become practically next-door neighbors at least for half of the year, we'd become even closer friends, often having dinner together and freely dropping in on one another. Alice, Bill and I frequently went hiking together, often accompanied by the woman I was dating at the moment. Bill and I played golf regularly, and Alice and I continued to run together a couple of times a week.

Our proximity also allowed Alice to keep an even closer eye on my love life. As she had ever since we'd decided to be "just friends," she freely critiqued the women I was dating, some of whom she liked a lot and others of whom she didn't like at all. She'd grown particularly fond of Jenny and had decided late last summer that it was time for me to settle down permanently with Jenny — or with someone very much like her — before I became an embittered and lonely old man. Three nights after she'd offered this sage advice, our idyllic world had been shattered.

***

I was still reminiscing about all of this two and a half miles later when I reached Highway 93. I made the turn, forced myself to concentrate on the exercise, picked up the pace and ran back home. I spent the next couple of hours catching up on the housework and laundry I'd been neglecting for the last week and then decided to reward myself with dinner at Alfredo's.

It was Thursday, which meant that there would be live music starting at eight o'clock, and so I timed my arrival to coincide with the beginning of the first set. The restaurant was about three-quarters full at that point, but I managed to get a table near the window across from the bandstand and ordered a glass of Rams Head Pinot Noir while I mulled over the evening's specials. I decided on the mostocolli forno, and as I set the menu down, I looked up to see Phil Krause watching me from a table across the room. He rose and said something to the woman he was with and whom I presumed to be Mrs. Krause. Then he laid his napkin on the chair behind him and headed toward my table. I stood, and he said, "May I join you for a moment?"

"Sure. Have a seat."

He pulled out a chair next to mine, sat down, and said, "I hear that Kevin McKinney is organizing a defense fund for Steve."

"That's what he says. I told him I wasn't interested in taking money from him."

Krause nodded. "Would you take it from me?"

I arched my eyebrows, and he continued. "Look, Mr. Matthews. As you doubtless know, I don't have much enthusiasm for most environmentalists — at least not for the sort that we've been seeing in the last ten years or so. I think that most of them, at best, are simple-minded idealists who don't really understand the complexities of the situation that we face up here. And at worst, some of them *are* radical extremists who, for whatever reason, are bent on a course of action that would do grave damage to the people and to the economy of this region. More than that, I honestly believe that the policies they advocate would ultimately wind up doing more harm than good to the forests that they allegedly want to 'protect.'

147

"That said, I'm not about to jump into bed with Kevin McKinney and that crowd of extremists that he caters to. Those guys are just plain nuts. They do more harm than good for those people who want a sensible forest policy, and that includes me."

He leaned forward in his chair and said, "I grew up in this valley just like Toby Martin did, and I love it at least as much, if not more, than he did. And no matter what he and the people at the Northwestern Environmental Alliance might think, I'm not about to see it destroyed just to feather my own nest. I'm a conservationist too, but in the old-fashioned sense — the one that believed, and still believes, that the forests can be managed in a way that accommodates a variety of different interests and still preserves the forests for the generations to come. I have children and grandchildren too, and I want them to know and love and be able to enjoy this land just as much as I do."

I nodded my understanding. "I appreciate all of that but what does it have to do with Steve?"

Krause sighed. "As I told you the other day, I've known Steve for the better part of twenty years. He's a part of our family out there. I honestly don't know if he killed Toby Martin or not. If he did, I want to believe that he did so in a moment of insanity when all this business just boiled over and he impulsively did something that he never would have done if he were thinking rationally.

"And whichever the case, I want to see that he gets his day in court and that he gets a good defense when that day comes. I heard through the grapevine that you'd refused to take money from McKinney, and I applaud you for that." Smiling slightly, he said, "I have to confess that the fact that you turned him down raised my opinion of lawyers more than a couple of notches."

I returned the smile, and he continued. "The people at the mill have put together a little money to help Karen pay the bills and otherwise help the family get by while Steve is in jail. And if you'd take it, I'd like to make a contribution to his defense fund.

Unfortunately, given the current state of affairs, it won't be much, but I'd appreciate it if you'd accept it."

I nodded. "Thank you, Mr. Krause. I appreciate it, and I know that Steve will too. If you wanted to make a contribution, I'd be pleased to take it and use it to help pay some of the expenses that I'll inevitably incur in preparing Steve's defense. And, of course, I'll be happy to give you an accounting so that you know exactly where your money went and what it was used for."

Krause rose from the chair, smiled, and extended his hand. "Thanks, but that won't be necessary. I'm quite sure that you'll spend the money wisely."

I stood, shook his hand and thanked him again. He gave me a slight wave and said, "Enjoy the rest of your evening."

The waitress watched Krause return to his wife. Then she came over, set a basket of rolls on the table and said, "I didn't want to interrupt your conversation. Are you ready to order?"

I indicated that I was and ordered the pasta along with another glass of wine. Then I grabbed a hot roll from the basket and settled back to listen to the music while I waited for the rest of my dinner.

This week's band was a blues group, consisting of keyboards, guitar, drums, and a female vocalist. Like most local musicians, the band members all had day jobs, and played basically because they enjoyed it and not because they ever expected to make any money out of their music. Indeed, Alfredo had once observed that most of the musicians who played in the local bars and restaurants usually wound up owing the house money at the end of the gig because their bar bills exceeded the paltry sums that they were being paid to play. That notwithstanding, the groups that Alfredo booked played with enthusiasm, and most of the band members were genuinely talented. That was particularly true of tonight's group, Billie and the Blue Genes, who covered a variety of classic Blues tunes and played a few of their own as well.

By nine thirty, I'd finished my dinner and was slowly sipping another glass of the Pinot Noir, when Johnnie, the bartender, walked over to the table, carrying the wine bottle and an empty glass. She gave me a smile that seemed surprisingly shy coming from a woman who was anything but, and said, "I'm finished for the evening and Sherry is now officially on duty at the bar. Do you mind if I join you for a few minutes?"

I started to rise from my chair and said, "Of course not."

She waved me back into my seat, set the bottle and the glass on the table, and pulled out the chair next to mine. She settled into the chair with a sigh and a look that said she was glad to be off her feet. Then she reached over, pulled the cork from the bottle, and arched her eyebrows at me. I nodded and said, "Just a little, please."

She poured a couple of ounces of the purple liquid into my glass and then filled her own glass a third of the way. She raised the glass and said, "Here's to crime." Then she took a sip, leaned back in her chair toying with the glass, and said, "Mmm, that tastes especially good tonight."

"Long night?"

Looking at the glass rather than at me, she tossed her hair back and said. "They've all been long lately."

I said nothing, waiting for her to continue. She took another sip of the wine, raised her eyes to mine, and gave a small shrug. "Larry and I broke up again last week — for good this time. I'm adjusting to the single life again."

"I'm sorry, Johnnie."

She shook her head and grinned broadly. "No, you're not — no more than any of my other friends. Everybody thought that my getting involved with Larry was a major mistake. The only difference is that you didn't think it necessary to lecture me about it repeatedly, and you're not the type to gloat and say, 'I told you so.'"

I returned her smile. "Well, I'm sure he had his good points, even though it was hard for some of us to appreciate just exactly what they might have been."

"Yeah, he did. Believe me, with Larry, there was never a dull moment."

"But?"

"But . . . Oh, I dunno. In the end, I guess he was just too jealous, too possessive, and way too high maintenance. It must be a sign of old age or something, but I think I'm about at the end of the 'Bad Boy' phase of my existence."

I leaned back and gave her a look of mock appraisal. She was wearing a white sleeveless blouse over a black skirt that stopped a good five inches above her knees. Both the skirt and the blouse showed off her excellent figure, and I noticed that since I'd first said hello to her ninety minutes earlier, a second button at the top of the blouse had come undone. Her long ash blonde hair fell straight to the middle of her back, framing a very attractive face highlighted by high cheekbones and a pair of deep green eyes.

Shaking my head, I reached over and patted the top of her hand. "Well Johnnie, given that you're still only twenty-seven, I wouldn't be too worried about old age at the moment. I doubt very much that the AARP recruiters have you locked in their sights just yet."

"Jesus, I hope not. I've already decided that the day I get my first letter from those bastards is going to be the day I check myself off the planet."

By that point, the restaurant was about half full, and the crowd consisted mostly of people who had finished eating and who were now listening to the music over dessert, coffee and drinks. With things in the kitchen apparently under control, Alfredo emerged, having hung up his apron for the evening, and made his way to the bandstand. As Billie and the band segued into a slow, bluesy version of "Stormy Monday," Alfredo plugged in his bass and began picking out a line behind the guitar and keyboards. Billie flashed him a smile, then closed her eyes and lost herself in the lyrics. Johnnie watched Alfredo settle in with the band, then turned and said, "I love the way these guys do this song. Will you dance with me?"

"Sure," I said, rising from my chair.

I followed her out onto the small dance floor, took her right hand in my left and circled her narrow waist with my other arm. We began moving slowly around the dance floor, somewhat tentatively at first, neither of us exactly sure of where this was leading, or of where we might want it to go. Then, as the band moved into an extended bridge of the song, Johnnie closed the little distance between us and molded her upper body to mine. At five-nine, she was only a couple of inches shorter than I and fit very comfortably into my embrace. She laid her head on my shoulder and I surrendered to the moment, closing down my consciousness to any other thoughts or memories.

We danced for another thirty minutes or so, sitting out a couple of times to finish our wine. Finally, the band closed out the evening with an extended version of "The Thrill Is Gone," and I paid my check. Johnnie and I said goodbye to Alfredo and the band members who had gathered at the bar for a nightcap, and I walked her out to her car.

She gave me her keys and I unlocked the driver's side door for her as she hugged herself against the chill night air. I pulled the door open and handed her the keys. She slipped her arms around my neck, and said, "Thank you. I enjoyed that."

Putting my hands on her waist I said, "I did too."

She closed her eyes, pulled me close, and gave me a sweet, lingering kiss. Still holding me, she slowly broke the kiss, laid her forehead on my shoulder and said in a quiet voice, "Would you like to follow me home?"

I hesitated for a long moment, squeezed her tightly to me, and then released her a bit, opening a few inches between us. As she lifted her eyes to meet mine, I said, "Johnnie, I . . ."

She put a finger on my lips and shook her head slightly. "It's okay. You don't have to explain. It was just a thought."

Still holding her, I said, "Johnnie, you know that I like you very much, and you also know that I think you're an enormously attractive woman. But believe me, I'm the last guy in the world you'd want to get tangled up with at this point."

She squeezed me tightly for a second and said in a sad voice, "Actually, Dave, no you're not — not by a long shot. But I understand where you're coming from, and I'm sorry. As I said, it was just a thought."

"There's nothing to be sorry for, Johnnie. . . In another time and place. . ."

"I understand," she said, once again putting her finger to my lips.

She hugged me close for a couple of seconds, gave me another, more abbreviated kiss, and then settled into her car. I watched as she drove out of the parking lot, turning in the direction of Kalispell, then got into my own car and headed slowly south toward home.

24

At eight o'clock the next morning, I was hitting my five-iron on the driving range at the Buffalo Hill Golf Club in Kalispell. It had been cloudy earlier in the morning, but the sun was now out, and the temperature had climbed into the middle sixties. A light carpet of dew glistened on the fairways, and several foursomes were already out on the course when Chris appeared and set his clubs down next to mine. I bid him a good morning as he pulled a wedge from his bag. He grimaced and shook his head. "Like hell it is."

"What's the matter?"

He dropped a yellow range ball on the plastic mat, set up to the ball and took a smooth easy swing with the wedge, lifting the ball on a high arc to a soft landing about seventy-five yards out onto the range. "Early yesterday afternoon, a group calling itself 'Citizens for a Responsible Forest Policy' announced that it would be holding a march and rally in Creston tomorrow afternoon to protest the court's decision closing the Kootenai Forest to logging.

"Three hours later, the Northwestern Environmental Alliance announced that they would hold a rally in Creston on Sunday afternoon in support of the decision. This morning, Kevin McKinney printed an editorial in that fuckin' rag of his, urging all Montana 'patriots' to join the march tomorrow and to show up again on Sunday to let the 'eco-Fascists' know that no one in Flathead County supported their 'radical, socialistic and communistic' policies."

"Ouch."

He hit another shot with the wedge. "Believe me, 'Ouch' doesn't begin to cover it. Each side is naturally insisting on its constitutionally protected rights to free speech, freedom of assembly and so forth, and all I can do is assign every deputy I can spare to try to keep things orderly. But I greatly fear that the weekend is going to turn into one gigantic clusterfuck."

I again expressed my sympathy, and for the next ten minutes we continued to loosen up on the range. Then we carried our clubs over to the practice green adjacent to the first tee and spent a few minutes putting while waiting for the starter to call us to the tee. A couple of minutes after eight thirty, he did, and we were relieved to discover that we would be able to go out alone and would not be forced to play with another twosome.

It's not that we're necessarily anti-social, but more often than not we find ourselves paired up with a husband and wife or with a couple of old retired farts who are riding carts, who seem to have a great deal of difficulty finding their balls even when they're in the fairway, and who then take even longer to hit them — usually several times a hole. This inevitably slows our play and breaks the rhythm of our game. Worst of all, it inhibits our colorful language.

Given that the group ahead of us was playing at a fairly steady pace, we moved quickly through the round. I was playing reasonably well, but Chris's game was decidedly out of synch. He had trouble finding the fairway off the tee and couldn't make a putt to save his life. He rallied a bit on the back nine, but in the end, it was too little, too late.

After changing our shoes and stowing our clubs in our cars, we went back to the clubhouse and ordered burgers and beer for lunch. While we waited for our food, Chris counted out the twelve dollars he owed me. "I think that's a season record," I said, grinning as I pocketed the money. "I don't think that either of us has lost that much to the other yet this year."

"I think you're right. But you played unusually well today. In fact, I can't remember a day when you *ever* birdied both seventeen and eighteen."

"I can't either. Even so, I wouldn't have beaten you nearly as handily if you'd been concentrating the way you normally do."

"Yeah, well, I just couldn't get my head in the game. For the life of me, I can't figure out why those idiots at the NEA want to hold this march on Sunday. The people protesting the decision, I can understand. But the judge has ruled in favor of the Alliance. They've won, for Christ's sake. What do they figure they have to gain by coming up here and rubbing peoples' noses in it?"

"I don't understand it either. I'm sure that it wouldn't do the slightest bit of good, but I could call Callie Buckner and see what their thinking is."

"I'd appreciate that. As you say, it probably won't do a damned bit of good, but it can't hurt."

***

We finished lunch, showered and changed, and said our goodbyes in the parking lot. I drove the few blocks from the golf club to my office and called Callie Buckner at the NEA office in Missoula. She answered on the third ring, sounding short of breath.

"Hi, Callie. It's Dave Matthews. How are you today?"

"Hi!" she said. "So-so, I guess. It's been a pretty rough couple of weeks and, as you may have heard, we're organizing a rally in Creston on Sunday, and so things are pretty frantic around here at the moment."

"I had heard about the rally. Actually, that's what I was calling about."

"Oh?"

"Yeah, well, to be honest, I was curious about the thinking behind the decision."

She paused for a moment, and in the background I could hear the sound of several people who were apparently conversing as they worked. Then she said, "I assume you've also heard that the pro-logging people are holding a rally in Creston tomorrow afternoon to protest the judge's decision in the Kootenai lawsuit."

"Yes, I know that."

"Well, to be honest, a lot of us who worked with Toby were very angry when we heard about it. I mean, it hasn't even been a week since Toby's funeral. For those people to hold a rally in his hometown protesting the decision that he worked so hard to achieve . . . it's like they were spitting on his grave. We decided that we should hold a rally of our own to show our respect for Toby's memory and our support for the judge's decision."

I hesitated for a moment myself, and then said, "I really don't think that their intention is to dishonor Toby's memory. These people are angry and afraid for their futures. They're rallying in support of their jobs. Certainly, they're not marching in celebration of Toby's murder."

"Maybe not directly, but that's certainly what it amounts to. And it's also important that we not let their condemnation of the court decision go unanswered. People need to know that there's a lot of support for this decision and for the idea of protecting the forests generally."

"I don't disagree with the sentiment, but are you sure that this is a wise decision, tactically? Feelings are running pretty high over there at the moment. You're almost certainly asking for trouble."

"We think it's absolutely the right decision," she said, sounding somewhat defensive.

"So, what are your plans?"

"Well, this is still a work in progress. We understand that the pro-logging event tomorrow will be held in and around the grounds of the elementary school. We plan to gather at the south end of Creston about two o'clock on Sunday and march quietly through town to the same site. Frank Kane and a few others will speak in support of the judge's decision, and also memorialize Toby."

"I'm not sure what to say, Callie," I said, staring out the window behind me. "As I said the other day, I'm generally in support of your position on this issue, but I'm not at all sure that this is the best way to defend it. The judge has decided in your favor and logging in the forest has ended, at least for the time being. You've won this round. If you hold a rally in Creston, a lot of people will feel like you're rubbing salt in their wounds. It will doubtless create an adverse reaction, even among many of those people who generally agree with your views. Frankly, I think you're bound to do your cause more harm than good."

I listened to a few seconds of silence from the other end of the line, and then Buckner said, "Well, I'm sorry you feel that way about it, but we all feel that it's important to show our support for a vital cause and our respect for Toby's memory."

"I have no quarrel with you on either score. I just think that this is the wrong time and place to do it."

"Okay, I guess we'll just have to agree to disagree on the issue. In the meantime, I have a lot of work to do here, and so I really can't talk any longer."

She disconnected before I could respond.

25

Sunday morning's paper reported that nearly five hundred people had crowded into Creston on Saturday afternoon to protest the decision prohibiting logging in the Kootenai. The crowd had been orderly, and only two people had been arrested, both for public intoxication. Many of those in attendance had carried signs declaring their support for the loggers and condemning the judge's decision. A series of speakers, including Kevin McKinney, had denounced the "radical environmentalists" who were determined to wreak "economic havoc" on the people of the valley. They'd urged those in attendance to appeal to their state and national representatives for relief from the "tyranny" of "activist judges."

In a sidebar, the paper quoted a spokesman for the Northwestern Alliance who argued that Saturday's rally was "an insult to the memory of Creston native Toby Martin" and a challenge to all those in Montana and elsewhere who were determined to protect the national forests from exploitation by the "special interests who stand to profit from wholesale logging in them." The spokesman announced that the Alliance was sponsoring a rally of its own in Creston that afternoon to show support for the court's decision and to honor the memory of Toby Martin.

On the editorial page, in a much less neutral tone, the paper condemned both the court's decision and the Alliance's plans to rally in Creston. While granting that the environmentalists had a constitutional right to march and to speak in support of their views, the editor insisted that, in the most charitable analysis, the rally's organizers were "tone-deaf." Seen less charitably, their action was "deliberately provocative," and a "calculated slap in the face" of the loggers, mill workers and others who had been adversely affected by the court's decision.

The editorial predicted that the proposed rally would backfire on the environmentalists by alienating many of the moderates who favored a "sensible forest policy that recognizes the interests of both the environment and the people of northwestern Montana." The paper strongly encouraged those who opposed the court's decision to remain calm and to ignore the Alliance's rally, insisting that any attempt to disrupt it would simply play into the hands of the environmentalists.

***

I spent the morning debating whether or not to go over to Creston that afternoon. I had no interest in taking part in what I thought was an ill-advised march, but I was more than a little curious to see what sort of reception the marchers would receive. My alternative was to spend the afternoon clearing brush on the south side of my property, and in the end, I opted to throw on a pair of jeans and a tee shirt and drive over to Creston.

By the time I got there a little after one thirty, the small community was already throbbing with activity. The Northwestern Environmental Alliance had apparently chartered a couple of busses to bring supporters up from Missoula, and the vehicles were parked at the south end of town. A number of people were milling around the busses, getting organized for the march. In the middle of one group huddled in front of the lead bus, I saw Callie Buckner with a clipboard in her hand, apparently making last-minute preparations.

As I drove through town in the direction of the elementary school, I saw that maybe a couple hundred people had gathered along the road, holding signs protesting the decision to close the forest and condemning the "Enviros" in language that was often crude and to the point. I turned left onto Riverside Road and found a parking spot about a hundred yards south of the Volunteer Fire Department.

I walked back up the street and took a place on the route of the march behind a small boy who was holding a sign insisting that "My Daddy's job is more important than a bunch of stupid woodpeckers." A block farther north, I saw Kevin McKinney standing in the middle of a group of ten or twelve men, all of whom were wearing tee shirts with American flags on the fronts and screen-printed logos on the backs proclaiming their opposition to the "Eco-Fascists." Several of them also carried signs expressing their support for the logging interests and vilifying the NEA.

Chris's deputies were very much in evidence along the route and although I couldn't see Chris himself, I spotted his SUV parked in front of the Fire Department and wondered if he was perhaps inside the building, using it as his command post for the afternoon.

A little after two o'clock, I could hear people at the east end of town beginning to boo, and I assumed that the marchers had begun to work their way up the road toward the schoolyard. A few minutes later, the lead marchers came into view. As they did, the spectators around me also began to boo, and over the booing, a few people shouted obscenities at the marchers. I estimated that the Alliance had gathered about a hundred and fifty people to march in favor of the court's decision, and it appeared that they were outnumbered by the decision's opponents, roughly two to one.

As the parade reached my vantage point, I recognized Frank Kane, the NEA's president, at the head of the march. Callie Buckner walked a step or two behind and to his left, carrying a sign arguing that, "Public Forests Are Not for Private Profit." On the lower left corner of the sign, a circle with a slash drawn through it had been superimposed over a picture of a chain saw.

As the small knot of marchers worked their way toward the center of town, the pro-logging people they had left in their wake fell in behind them with their own signs, booing and jeering. Three sheriff's deputies had positioned themselves between the two groups and were attempting, without much success, to maintain some space between them. The marchers were about twenty-five yards short of the right turn that would take them into the school yard when, in an obviously orchestrated move, the men who had been standing with McKinney led ten or twelve members of the pro-logging group into the center of the road, blocking the progress of the march and leaving the environmentalists effectively surrounded by their opponents.

The volume of the pro-logging jeering and shouting seemed to increase dramatically, and the marchers huddled closer together, looking to each other in obvious confusion, trying to determine what they should do. Several more deputies pushed their way into the road, trying to open space between the opposing camps and attempting to move back the pro-logging people who were blocking the forward progress of the march. Around me, several people, including the young boy with the sign, had begun to chant, "Screw the enviros. Give us back our forests."

As others in the crowd picked up the chant, I saw Chris emerge from the Fire Department, dressed in his full Sheriff's uniform, with a bullhorn in his right hand. He pushed his way to the front of the march, raised the bullhorn to his mouth and ordered the crowd to disperse. He was answered with a chorus of boos, and from somewhere behind me, a man yelled, "Screw you too, Sheriff."

Chris turned to look in my direction and as he did, a beer bottle came flying from the back of the crowd and struck one of the marchers in the forehead. Two sheriff's deputies burst into the crowd attempting to find the person who had thrown the bottle and at that point, all hell broke loose.

Although Chris had assigned every deputy he could spare to police the march, his force was way too small to effectively keep a lid on the situation, which quickly degenerated into a brawl.

While many of the pro-logging people followed Chris's order and began pulling back away from the scene, several others, including McKinney's band, bulled their way into the street, swinging on the environmentalists and on Chris's deputies as well, in some cases with their fists, in others with the signs that they carried, and in a few cases with rocks and bottles.

The marchers tried to give as good as they were getting, but they were overmatched both individually and collectively. I pushed my way into the melee and saw a huge man, obviously drunk, swinging a beer bottle at the head of Tony Boyce, one of Chris's deputies, who was attempting to separate two of the combatants and who had his back turned to the man.

I hollered Tony's name and grabbed the guy's arm, causing him to drop the bottle. Cursing, he turned and took a wild swing at me. I ducked away, drove up and off my left foot, and threw a hard right into his solar plexus. The guy doubled over, fell to his knees, and lost his lunch, which appeared to have consisted mostly of barley malt and hops. Tony put a foot into the guy's back, pushed him down into the rancid vomit, grabbed his arms and handcuffed them behind his back. He shook his head, said, "Thanks, Dave," and headed back into the fray.

I turned toward the head of the march just in time to see a boy, maybe sixteen or seventeen years old, smack Callie Buckner in the side of the head with a sign that he was carrying. Buckner fell to the pavement, bleeding profusely. The kid dropped the sign, turned tail, and ran straight back in my direction. As he raced past me, I stuck out my foot and tripped him. He stumbled forward, and I jumped on his back, pushing him down hard to the concrete. I grabbed his right arm, bent it high up his back, and said, "On your feet, asshole. Make one move to get away from me and I'll snap your goddamn arm like a twig."

I yanked him to his feet and, maintaining the pressure on his arm, pushed him in the direction of one of the deputies. Over the

163

din of the mob scene, I shouted, "Hang onto this little bastard. He just seriously assaulted a woman with a sign he was carrying."

Leaving the kid with the deputy, I raced over to the spot where Buckner had fallen. By the time I reached her, a woman I recognized as one of her co-workers was sitting in the street, cradling Buckner protectively. Buckner appeared to be unconscious and was losing an alarming amount of blood. I knelt opposite the woman who was holding her and as I did, the woman stripped off her sweatshirt, and wrapped it around Buckner's head in an effort to staunch the bleeding.

A number of the other marchers formed a circle around us, hollering for help and offering a cacophony of advice. Over the din of noise, the woman across from me shouted, "We've got to her out of here and to a hospital"

Just then, we heard sirens screaming their approach from both ends of town, and I looked up to see the cavalry, in the form of several State Highway Patrol cars, riding to the rescue. One of the marchers broke away from the ring of people surrounding Buckner and raced over to an approaching patrol car. He leaned into the window, pointing in our direction and explaining the situation to the officer.

Beeping his siren to move people out of the way, the patrolman slowly eased his car through the crowd and stopped in front of our position. He jumped out of the vehicle, ran around to the trunk and grabbed a first aid kit. I moved aside, and he took my place next to Buckner. He gently drew the sweatshirt away from Callie's head and inspected the wound. Saying nothing, he shook his head and opened the first aid kit.

He removed a large bandage from the kit and asked the woman who was supporting Buckner's head to move as much of Callie's hair as possible away from the wound. Using her left hand, the woman gently parted the hair, and the patrolman applied some disinfectant to the wound. He then laid the bandage on the wound and asked the woman to hold it in place. While she did, he unrolled a length of gauze, wrapped it tightly over the bandage and secured it with adhesive tape. Then he looked to the woman and to me and said, "We've got to get her to a hospital, and we don't have time to wait for an ambulance. Help me get her into the back seat of my car."

Two of the men from the NEA office stepped over and the three of us lifted Buckner as gently as possible out of the lap of the woman who'd been holding her. The trooper opened the back door of his car and instructed the woman to get into the car so that she could continue to support Buckner's head on the way to the hospital.

The woman climbed into the back seat and we laid Buckner's head in her lap. The woman slowly slid across the seat, cradling Buckner's head and upper torso, as we gradually fed her into the vehicle. As the woman reached the far end of the seat, I gently folded Buckner's legs into the car and closed the door.

Another of Callie's co-workers jumped into the front seat of the car, and the trooper slammed his door and slowly backed up, beeping his siren to clear a path as he turned around. Once headed back in the direction from which he came, he hit the siren and raced off toward Kalispell and the nearest hospital.

***

In the face of the additional police presence, the noise level declined dramatically, and the crowd began to melt away. Perhaps fifteen people were in police custody, including the kid who struck Callie Buckner, the drunk who attempted to brain Tony Boyce with the beer bottle, and a disheveled Ed Ramsey.

Meanwhile, the marchers were regrouping in the middle of the highway, although their numbers too now seemed significantly depleted. Frank Kane picked up the sign that Callie Buckner had been carrying and began walking slowly toward the schoolyard followed by his remaining supporters and ringed by a contingent of sheriff's deputies and highway patrolmen. Once in the schoolyard, Kane climbed up on top of a picnic table and made a short speech insisting that the Kootenai Forest must remain closed to logging activity until the Forest Service could adequately document the remaining amount of old-growth forest and until it could determine the effect of the logging activity on the various species of wildlife that depended on the forest habitat.

On beginning the speech, he seemed flustered and somewhat disconcerted, but as he warmed to the topic, he grew increasingly animated. He insisted that the Northwestern Environmental Alliance and the "millions of others in this country who treasure the national forests" would neither be intimidated nor deterred by "a bunch of inebriated bullies and their self-serving, short-sighted, corporate masters." He closed with a moving eulogy of Toby Martin and vowed that he and the other members of NEA would continue to labor ceaselessly in an effort to ensure that Toby had not died in vain.

In the meantime, the NEA busses had pulled up to a spot on the highway opposite the schoolyard and waited, their engines idling. Kane finished his remarks to sustained cheering and applause from his supporters and to a stony silence from the few opponents who remained in attendance. He then hopped down from the table and watched as the marchers filed into the busses. The doors hissed closed behind them, and after another two or three minutes, the busses slowly pulled out onto the highway and headed back toward Missoula, escorted by a Highway Patrol car.

In the wake of their departure the center of the small town emptied quickly, and as I walked past the Fire Department to retrieve my car, I ran into Chris. He took off his hat, wiped his brow and said, "Jesus Christ, what an afternoon."

I nodded my agreement, and he said, "I understand that you not only saved Tony from a helluva headache but that you nailed the kid who hit Buckner."

"Well, in the first instance, I'm not sure. The dumb bastard was so drunk, I'm not sure he could've actually hit Tony. In the second, I saw the kid assault her very clearly and I'll be happy to sign a complaint and to testify against him if it comes to that. I saw that you had Ed Ramsey in cuffs. What did he do?"

"He was out there mixing it up in the thick of things, swinging randomly at any environmentalist he could find. We'll charge him with simple assault. Like most of the others it'll probably be bargained down to drunk and disorderly."

I nodded my understanding. "Not with the kid who hit Buckner, though, I hope. She was in pretty bad shape when they took her out of here."

"No, we won't let the little shit off that easily. And especially with the threat of your testimony, he'll do some jail time."

"Okay, let me know what you need. In the meantime, I'm going to head on home. I'll see you later in the week."

***

I started back down Riverside Road to the spot where I'd parked my car. Twenty-five yards before I reached it, I noticed that the car was listing badly toward the passenger's side which was away from the road. On reaching the car, I discovered that someone had slashed both of the tires on the passenger's side and had dragged a knife or some other sharp object along the full length of the car, badly gouging the finish. A piece of paper that looked like it had been torn from a child's school tablet was pinned under the windshield wiper.

I cursed, wishing like hell that I'd had the good sense to stay home and clear brush, and pulled the note from under the wiper blade. The paper was folded in quarters and I opened it to find a crudely printed message that asked: "What do you call one dead lawyer? A damn good start!"

Sighing, I turned and walked back up to the Fire Department. I described the damage and showed the note to Chris who arched his eyebrows and said, "Looks like you're making a whole pile of new friends today. I don't suppose you have any idea who might have left this little calling card?"

I shook my head. "Unfortunately, no, which is probably a good thing. If I had, he'd be on his way to the hospital with Buckner, and I'd be under arrest with those clowns you're hauling off to jail. But I'd appreciate it if you'd radio for a wrecker with a flatbed to haul me into Kalispell. The guy'll probably get here a lot faster if you call him than if I do."

Forty-five minutes later, the wrecker appeared, and the driver winched my car up onto the bed of his truck. I jumped in beside him and rode back to the garage where, thankfully, they had a couple of replacement tires in stock. I bought a Coke from the machine and watched as the mechanic unloaded the car. While he mounted and balanced the new tires, I speculated about the answer to Chris's question, wondering exactly who had left the warning for me and what he (or she?) expected me to do or to stop doing.

It was possible that the perpetrator was an environmentalist, enraged by the fact that I was defending the person accused of killing Toby Martin. Conversely, it might have been one of the pro-logging people, angered because I had come to Tony and Callie's defense. I wondered how many of the latter would have recognized my car. Not many, I concluded, except for Ed Ramsey and perhaps a handful of others that I didn't know.

26

I was still pondering all of this when the mechanic finished with my tires. I paid him, pocketed the receipt for my insurance agent, and drove out to the Kalispell Regional Medical Center. The receptionist in the Emergency Room informed me that Callie Buckner had been treated and moved to a private room on the second floor. I climbed the stairs, opened the door into the hallway, and saw Frank Kane and the woman who'd accompanied Buckner to the hospital walking down the corridor.

Kane was about my height, with dark brown eyes and a pale complexion. What little hair he had left was closely trimmed, as were his beard and mustache. A bit of a paunch hung over the belt of his trousers, and in truth, he looked much more like a settled, middle-aged college professor than a committed environmentalist who spent any significant amount of time outdoors. Both he and the woman appeared rumpled and exhausted. I walked down to meet them, introduced myself, and asked how Callie was doing.

"Better than I would have expected when we brought her in here," the woman said. "She lost a fair amount of blood and looked awfully scary by the time we got her to Emergency. But the doctor says that she has only a mild concussion. He's holding her overnight for observation, but I should be able to take her home to Missoula tomorrow."

"Well, I'm very glad to hear that," I said. "The way she looked at the scene, I feared it was going to be a lot worse. Is she awake?"

"No. The doctor gave her a sedative and said that she should sleep through the night." Nodding in Kane's direction, she continued, "Frank has to get back to Missoula, but I'm going to spend the night here with Callie and see what the doctor has to say in the morning."

I nodded. "In that case, is there anything I can get you? I'd be happy to run out and bring you back something for dinner that's certain to be more edible than anything you're likely to get here."

"No, thank you, Mr. Matthews. I'll be fine. To be honest, I'm not really all that hungry anyway. It's been a long and very draining day, and in spite of the fact that I'm drinking this coffee, I expect that I'll go back to Callie's room, collapse into the chair, and nap through most of the night myself."

"Okay," I smiled. I dug a card out of my wallet and wrote my cell phone number on the back. "If you change your mind, or if you should need anything, please call me. And don't worry about the hour — I'll be happy to come up."

She took the card and slipped it into her pocket. "Thanks very much, and thanks again for your help this afternoon. Things got pretty ugly out there for a while."

"You're welcome. Please tell Callie I stopped by."

The woman nodded, and Kane said, "There doesn't seem to be anything more that I can do here, Sarah, so I guess I'll say good night as well. You've got my cell number. Call me if Callie wakes up or if there's any change in her condition."

The woman assured him that she would, and Kane and I turned toward the stairs.

***

As we started down to the lobby, Kane said, "I want to thank you too, Dave, for your help this afternoon. Sarah's right. Things did get very ugly out there, and I really appreciate the fact that you came to the rescue."

I waved off his thanks. "I'm just glad that it didn't get any worse. In particular, I'm happy that Callie wasn't injured more seriously."

"Me too. She's had an awfully difficult couple of weeks. She didn't need this on top of it."

We stepped out into evening's fading light and I said, "Were she and Toby Martin particularly close?"

He hesitated for a moment, then shook his head. "If you're asking whether they were romantically involved, the answer is no. Callie obviously had very strong feelings for Toby that went beyond her appreciation of the fact that he was a good boss and that they were both strongly committed to the same cause. But Toby didn't have those kinds of feelings for her. He liked Callie a great deal. He valued the work that she did, and he certainly realized that she was a very attractive young woman. But for whatever reason, he wasn't attracted to her romantically or sexually. He kept their relationship strictly on a professional basis. Even so, as you can understand, Callie took his death very hard."

I nodded, and Kane gave me what appeared to be an apologetic smile. "Look, I know I'm probably not the most popular guy in Kalispell right at the moment, and I'd certainly understand if you didn't want to be seen in my company. But I haven't had anything to eat all day. Could I buy you dinner before I head back down to Missoula?"

"Sure, why don't I drive and then I can drop you back here at your car?"

"Fine. You doubtless know the city better than I. Why don't you pick the restaurant?"

I led Kane to my car and, after thinking about it for a couple of minutes, recommended that we eat at the Montana Club. It was fairly close; the food would be good, and I figured that at this time on a Sunday night, we weren't likely to encounter anyone who'd want to give Kane a hard time. The restaurant was about half full when we arrived, and on the sound system, Joe Nichols was quietly lamenting the fact that "She only smokes when she drinks." No one seemed to take any notice of us.

The hostess led us to a booth off to the side of the room and we each ordered a hamburger, fries and a beer for dinner. As the waitress went to place the order, Kane began toying with his fork. "Callie says you really believe that Steve Helstrom is not the person who murdered Toby."

I nodded, and he said, "If Helstrom didn't do it, who do you suppose did?"

I threw up my hands, "At this point, Frank, I haven't a clue. But as you saw this afternoon, and as you doubtless realized long before then, Toby's work had unfortunately made him a lot of enemies up here. It could have been any number of people, and it very well might have been a mill worker. But I'm pretty certain that it wasn't that particular mill worker."

Kane shook his head and said, "God what a mess this is."

The waitress returned with the beers and we each took a long and very welcome swallow. I put down my bottle and said, "So tell me, how did you get involved with the NEA?"

Smiling, he replied, "I was born and raised in a little town in Illinois. Before I went to college, I'd never even seen a mountain or a real forest. My girlfriend had decided that she wanted to get the hell out of Bethalto and being in love and having nothing better to do, I followed her out to Missoula to go to school. I lost the girlfriend shortly after we got there, but I fell in love with the country and I've never left. I became actively involved in environmental causes early on at the University, and the rest, as they say, is history. How about you — what's your story?"

I shrugged. "I took virtually the opposite path from yours. I was born and raised here in Kalispell, and rarely ever left the valley until I was out of high school. I grew up taking the beauty and the recreational opportunities of this region for granted.

"As is the case with a lot of the other natives, I suppose, those things were so much a part of my everyday existence that I never really thought much about them. In my youthful naiveté, I just more or less assumed that most people lived in places like this. It was only when I got older and had a chance to see some of the rest of the country that I began to realize how unique and special this valley is and how critically important it is to protect it."

Kane smiled. "I gather then that you're not entirely unsympathetic to our efforts?"

"No, not at all. As I told Callie the other day, I agree with most of your larger objectives. But, as I also told her, I thought that your march this afternoon was probably ill-advised for any number of reasons."

Kane waited while the waitress served our burgers and fries, and we ordered a couple more beers. He picked up a French fry and said, "I can understand that, and for what it's worth the decision to hold the rally was a close call. Also, for what it's worth, if I had it to do over again, I probably wouldn't. But for the pro-logging people to hold their march so soon after Toby's killing … Well, I don't know … it just seemed wrong to let it go without a response."

I nodded. "Certainly, you understand, though, that save for a handful of certifiable lunatics, nobody up here condones Toby's murder."

Kane smiled ruefully. "Yes, of course I understand that. Although judging by the crowd this afternoon, I'm not sure that there's only a 'handful' of those people around."

"I'm sure it seemed that way when you found yourself trapped in the middle of that mob, but I'd wager that even the majority of those people are more scared than they are angry. That's what brought them out today."

Kane put down his burger and nodded vigorously. "I understand that. I know these people are worried about their futures, and I certainly don't blame them for that — hell, anybody would be. But no matter how much they want to believe it, we're not the real cause of their problems. Like it or not, the economy of this region is in transition. And even without the efforts of groups like ours, the wholesale logging of the national forests that was allowed to go on virtually unchecked for so many years would be coming to an end. There are much larger economic forces at work here that have nothing to do with us."

Looking at me earnestly, he continued, "It takes seventy-five years to grow a tree to a profitable size in these mountains. On a tree farm in the south, it takes twenty-five years, and the trees down there are much easier to harvest. On top of that, there's a flood of cheap timber pouring into the United States from Canada. Unless the federal government basically gives away the trees in the national forests, there's simply no way the timber industry up here can continue to compete economically. And it's not like we need the timber from these forests. There's certainly no national shortage of lumber."

He paused for a moment, then said, "Certainly there is and always will be a need for people to work in the forests up here. If nothing else, there's a tremendous job to do just in repairing the damage that's already been done both by the logging activity and by the well-intentioned but misguided determination of the Forest Service over the last seventy years to extinguish every single forest fire that might otherwise have helped to naturally clean out the forests. But it simply makes no sense whatsoever to keep thoughtlessly logging these forests as a form of federal welfare to the people who live up here."

"All that may be true, but that doesn't make it any easier — or any more palatable — for the people who become the victims of those larger forces."

"Certainly not. But obviously Montanans aren't alone in having to confront wrenching economic change. And when you get right down to it, how are the loggers and mill workers up here any different from the steelworkers in Pennsylvania and Ohio, or the textile workers in the Carolinas who are losing jobs to factories overseas? How are our communities different than any others that are adversely affected by the loss of those jobs?

"Certainly, there ought to a safety net of some sort for these people while they retrain and look for other work. But I just can't buy the argument that, as a solution to the problem, we should allow them to continue logging the national forests indefinitely until there's no more trees left for them to cut. Whether they like it or not, this is a problem that Montanans are going to have to confront sooner or later, and I'm one of those people who believes that it ought to be sooner."

I said nothing, and he paused for a moment, collecting his thoughts and playing with his beer bottle. Then he said, "The other thing that really frustrates me about all of this is that when you listen to that crowd this afternoon and to the spokesmen for the timber interests, you'd think the economy up here was going to hell in a hand basket. But, as anyone with a set of eyes can see, just the opposite is true.

"The population of Flathead County has grown more than twenty-five percent in the last ten years. Despite the jobs that might have been lost in the timber industry, nearly sixteen thousand new jobs were created here in the last decade, and unemployment is at its lowest rate in over thirty years. The construction industry is booming, and so is tourism. Per capita income is rising faster up here than it is anywhere else in the state. The plain fact of the matter is that, in a lot of ways, the people up here are a lot luckier than the people in those other states I mentioned — and in other parts of Montana, for that matter."

I pushed away my plate, drained the last of my beer and said, "Well, Frank, I don't necessarily disagree with your argument, but unfortunately, we're probably not going to resolve these problems tonight."

"No, probably not. Although I sure as hell wish we could. It would make my life a lot easier."

"Yours and a lot of other people's as well."

***

I suggested that we split the check, but Kane insisted on getting it. The waitress returned with his change, he counted out a tip, and I drove him back to the hospital.

"I'm parked right by the entrance to the Emergency Room," he said. Why don't you drop me off there and before I go home? I'll slip up to see how Callie's doing and whether Sarah might need anything."

I pulled into the parking lot and braked to a stop at door to the E.R. Kane stuck out his hand and said, "Thanks again, Dave, both for dinner and for your help this afternoon."

We exchanged a firm handshake and I said, "You're welcome, Frank. Have a good evening."

He got out of the car and closed the door behind him. I shifted into first gear and reached over to crank the volume on an old Bob Seger album that had cycled into one of my Spotify playlists on the drive back from the restaurant. I'd just begun to pull away from the hospital when the sound of two shots exploded behind me. I slammed on the brakes and looked back over my right shoulder to see Kane falling to his knees a few feet short of the Emergency Room door. In the dim light of the parking lot, I saw the back of a shadowy figure running in the opposite direction.

I killed the engine, jumped out of the car, and raced over to Kane who was now lying still on his back. One of the shots appeared to have hit him just below the left shoulder and had opened a gaping wound in the upper left section of his chest. The other had caught him in the head, just above his left ear. As I knelt beside him, two nurses who'd apparently heard the shots and seen Kane fall, came running out the Emergency Room doors. I looked up and yelled, "Get a doctor — fast!"

The two nurses fell to their knees beside Kane and one of them said, "The receptionist is paging the doctor. He'll be here in a second."

There was obviously nothing I could do for Kane, so I jumped to my feet and sprinted off in the direction of the person who'd run from the scene. As I turned sideways to slip between two parked cars, it struck me that running off into the dark with no weapon, chasing an armed person who'd just attempted a cold-blooded murder, was perhaps not the brightest move I might have made. But the gallon and a half of adrenaline that was coursing through my system effectively overruled my saner instincts.

The east end of the complex was blocked by a row of buildings, and so near the end of the parking lot, I turned and raced south toward the Northwest Professional Center building, figuring that the shooter had to have gone that way. As I did, I heard the sound of an engine revving on the other side of the NPC building. Then tires squealed against the pavement, and a vehicle screamed away at high speed south down Claremont. By the time I managed to get around the corner of the building, gasping for breath, the vehicle was gone.

I turned and ran as fast as I could back to my own car. As I raced by the Emergency Room entrance, the two nurses and a man I presumed to be the doctor were frantically loading Frank Kane onto a stretcher. I grabbed my cell phone from the pocket in the driver's side door and punched in nine-one-one. When the operator answered, I said, "I'm reporting a shooting in front of the Kalispell Regional Medical Center. The shooter sped away down Claremont. I don't have a description of the vehicle he's driving, but doubtless he's already reached Highway 93."

The operator replied that the hospital's staff had just called in the shooting and that she would alert police patrols to be on the lookout for any vehicles speeding away from the general vicinity. Although the operator doubtless didn't need to be reminded, I asked her to advise the sheriff's office and the Highway Patrol as well, given that anyone fleeing the scene would no doubt very quickly leave the city limits. She told me that she would do so and asked me to remain on the line.

As the operator put me on hold, I heard the scream of approaching sirens, and a few moments later, a city squad car raced up the entrance road to the hospital, its Mars lights flashing red and blue. The car braked to a halt behind mine, and a patrolman jumped out. I quickly described what had happened and he returned to his car and got on the radio. As he did, a second squad roared up the entrance road.

***

Over the course of the next couple of hours, I repeated my story several times. I then made a formal statement, as did the nurse who witnessed the shooting from the hospital lobby. Regrettably, we had precious little information to give to the police detectives. Except for the brief glimpse I'd gotten, neither of us had seen the shooter, and although my impression was that the shooter was a male, I couldn't even be certain of that.

Neither the city police, the sheriff's department nor the Highway Patrol had stopped any speeding driver in the immediate aftermath of the incident, and so the shooter — whoever he (or she) might have been had gotten away cleanly.

And according to the physician on duty, Frank Kane had was dead even before his body hit the ground.

***

I was restlessly pacing the floor in my living room when the phone rang at eleven forty-five that night. I picked up the phone, noticing Chris's name and home phone number in the Caller ID screen, and punched the button to connect the call. "Any news?"

"No, unfortunately not. I've been on the phone with Ted Carlsen who's leading the investigation for the Kalispell PD, but they have virtually no leads. Several people heard the shots, but except for the brief glimpse that you got of the killer, no one saw anything. The police have canvassed the neighborhoods all around the hospital, hoping that someone saw the shooter fleeing the scene, but they haven't come up with squat."

"Oh, shit."

"My sentiments exactly."

"Are the people you arrested at the march today are still in custody?"

"No, except for the kid that attacked Buckner. The rest of them bonded out early this evening."

"Well, at least Steve Helstrom has an iron-clad alibi."

"Correct, although I don't know how much that helps your case."

"Well, it certainly opens a potential argument to the effect that somebody is angry enough at the Northwestern Environmental Alliance to have murdered its two most prominent spokesmen within the space of two weeks. And certainly, Steve can't be a suspect in the Kane shooting."

Chris exhaled at the other end of the line. "It's an argument all right, but you could just as plausibly argue that Steve killed Toby Martin and that a second person was thus inspired to go after Kane. I'm afraid that unless and until the K.P.D. finds the person or persons who killed Kane and can tie them to Toby's murder as well, Steve still looks pretty good for it."

27

A little after noon on Monday I was in my office, drinking a Coke for lunch and listening to the mid-day news on the radio. Kalispell police claimed to have no leads in the murder of Frank Kane. The newscaster also reported that overnight some unknown person or persons had vandalized five logging trucks belonging to the Simmons' Logging Transport Company in Kalispell. They'd drained the oil out of the crankcases and dumped sugar into the gas tanks. Drivers had come into work at seven o'clock this morning and started four of the trucks almost simultaneously. The engines had run for several minutes before freezing up solid. The transport company claimed that the engines were completely ruined.

The report continued, noting that someone had sent an e-mail to the offices of the Montana Logging Association at ten o'clock this morning, claiming responsibility for the sabotage on behalf of the Earth Liberation Front and announcing that the action was in response to the murder of Toby Martin and the attack on the NEA marchers yesterday. The message promised future retaliatory action for these "crimes" and for the murder of Frank Kane.

I was thinking that things were getting seriously out of hand when my reverie was interrupted by the sound of someone knocking at my outer door. I turned off the radio, walked through the receptionist's office and opened the door to find Mary Jo Watson standing in the hall looking even more emotionally bereft than she had when I'd talked to her five days earlier. I gave her a quick hug and said, "Hey, Mary Jo, how are you doing?"

In reply, she offered a sad attempt at a smile. "About as well as I look. Can you spare a few minutes?"

"Sure. Come on in."

I led her back into my office, sat down beside her on the couch, and said, "What's the problem?"

Starring at the floor, she shook her head, swallowed hard and said, "I'm really sorry."

I took her hand and said, "Sorry for what?"

Still starring at the floor, she replied, "This is so hard . . ." Then she raised her eyes to meet mine, squeezed my hand and said in a quiet voice, "I lied to you the other day."

"About what?"

"I told you that I hadn't seen Toby for three weeks . . . That wasn't true . . . I was with him the night he was killed."

A tear rolled out of her left eye and trailed slowly down her cheek. She wiped it away with the back of her hand and looked down at the floor again. "We were having an affair."

With that, she began sobbing in earnest. I put my arms around her, pulled her close and said, "I'm so sorry, Mary Jo."

Clinging to me, she buried her head in my shoulder and continued to cry for several minutes. Finally, she disengaged, and I handed her my handkerchief. She wiped her eyes, blew her nose, and said softly, "I'm sorry I lied to you."

"It's okay, Mary Jo. I understand. How long had you and Toby been seeing each other?"

"About eight months. We'd been running into each other periodically, of course, ever since he came back from California. Even though he was living and working in Missoula, he spent a lot of time up here, and Kalispell is still a pretty small town in some respects. Anyhow, last October, we bumped into each other one afternoon at an author's signing party at the Electric Avenue Bookstore in Bigfork. We went out for a cup of coffee after and wound up back at his family's old cabin. After that, we saw each other as often as we could, depending on what our respective circumstances would allow us."

"Did Don know?"

"He didn't at the time, but he does now. As you well know, he's always been extremely jealous of Toby, and he's been very upset about the fact that I've obviously been taking Toby's death so hard. We had a bitter fight about it last night, and I finally broke down and confessed. He stormed out of the house and didn't come back the whole night. I have no idea what he's thinking or what he expects to do about it, and at this point, I guess I really don't care."

"And you're sure he didn't know about it before?"

"No. If he had, he wouldn't have been able to contain himself. He would've exploded at me the moment he found out. He's been preoccupied with his own extramarital interests lately and hasn't paid that much attention to the way I've been spending my time. In addition to which, Toby and I were very careful. After that first afternoon, we never saw each other in public. We only ever met out at the cabin. It was our special place — the first place we ever made love together back when we were still in school."

"And you were there that Tuesday night?"

She nodded. "Tuesday night is almost always one of Don's 'nights out.' In the summer, he keeps the store open until nine on Tuesdays, and then always goes out somewhere after. He insists that he just goes out for a couple of drinks but given the way he acts and smells by the time he finally gets home, it's pretty obvious that he's been out with Carol."

Kneading my handkerchief in her lap, she took a deep breath, gave me a sheepish look and said, "Christ, what you must think of me? Last week, I'm the pathetic victim, crying on your shoulder because my husband's been whoring around on me, and now here I am confessing that I'm even worse than he is."

Shaking my head, I said, "I don't think that at all, Mary Jo."

"Well, it's true," she countered in a quiet voice. "When I agreed to marry Don, I thought I could lock my feelings for Toby tightly away in some small corner of my heart and still be a good wife to Don. I knew I didn't love him in the way that I'd loved Toby, but

I also knew that I'd never love anyone in that way again. And I did care for Don. I thought we could be good together — that we could make a life and be happy, even though life had disappointed each of us in some fundamental ways.

"I should have known better, of course, but at that age who knows anything at all? Maybe if I could've somehow exorcised Toby from my system, I would have been a better wife for Don and he wouldn't have felt the need to look elsewhere for the validation or whatever it is he thinks he's found with Carol."

I squeezed her hand again. "I think you're being pretty hard on yourself, Mary Jo. Certainly, you couldn't help the way you felt about Toby, and I can't imagine how you would have 'exorcised' him from your system. Unfortunately, life isn't nearly that convenient."

She smiled ruefully. "You'd know something about that, wouldn't you? But then you at least had the decency not to selfishly screw up somebody else's life while you were still trying to make sense of your own."

I waited a moment and then said in as gentle a tone as I could manage, "Tell me about that Tuesday night."

She took a minute to collect her thoughts, wiping her eyes again. "Toby'd spent the weekend in Missoula working. He came up late Monday afternoon, intending to drive back down to Missoula in time for work on Wednesday morning — something he did a couple of times a month.

"We'd agreed to meet at the cabin at seven thirty. I got there a little after seven and let myself in with a key that Toby gave me. He got there about fifteen minutes later in a furious mood. Mike had approached him that afternoon with his plans for the development he was proposing to build on the family property. They'd had a big row about it, and Toby was still fuming."

"What did he say about the argument?"

"He said that Mike saw the project as his ticket out of the used car business and into respectability as a local developer. Mike believed that he could leverage a successful project on part of the family land into other ventures around the valley, and he insisted that the family would see a significant profit out of the deal as well. He argued that it would be good for all three of them."

"How did Toby respond to that?"

"He said he told Mike that their father certainly didn't need the money and that he — Toby — would never need or want money badly enough to desecrate the land by developing it in that way. He said he'd starve first. He also told Mike that between them, he and Denny Graham didn't have brains enough to develop a lemonade stand, let alone a project of this magnitude.

"Mike responded by reminding Toby that he'd always been the favorite son, the one who'd had every advantage, while Mike was left to suck hind tit. He said he was sick and tired of taking a back seat to Toby and that he wasn't going to do it anymore. He told Toby that half of the family land would be his by inheritance before too long anyway and that he'd do what he damn well pleased with it, no matter what Toby thought.

"I asked Toby what he was going to do about it, and he told me that he was trying to convince his father to donate the land to the Flathead Land Trust as a means of preserving it perpetually."

"Did he tell Mike that?"

"Yeah. And Mike told him there was no fucking way that he'd be cheated out of what was rightfully his. Then he stormed out of the house. Toby went to the nursing home and warned his father about Mike's plans. Then he went to Moroldo's for dinner before meeting me at the cabin."

"Did he say what his father's reaction was?"

She nodded. "Yeah. As you can imagine, Robert was shocked. Despite his father's physical problems, Toby said that the old man is still sharp as a tack mentally, and he immediately dismissed the idea of developing the land. Toby said his father was intrigued by the idea of donating the land to the Flathead Land Trust with the provision that the family would retain the house itself and a few acres around it."

She wiped away a tear. "We talked about the idea for a while until Toby gradually calmed down, and then we made love. I left a little before ten. Toby said he was going to stay for a few minutes to straighten up before going home. He must have left a few minutes after I did, and then . . ."

She shook her head and began crying again. I gave her a moment and then asked, "What time did you get home?"

"About ten thirty."

"Was Don home by then?"

She shook her head and said, "No. He came in about an hour later."

"How did he seem when he came home — what was his mood like?"

She shrugged, looking down at the floor. "Like most other Tuesday nights, I guess. I was in bed by then, pretending to be asleep. Don snuck quietly into the house, the way he always does when he's feeling guilty. He undressed in the bathroom, crawled into bed and was snoring five minutes later."

Only then did she seem to realize the implication of my question. She jerked her head up and looked at me. "Oh God, Dave, you're not suggesting that Don might have killed Toby?"

"No, Mary Jo, I'm not — at least not at the moment. But certainly, you understand that in a situation like this he would have to be a logical suspect."

"But he didn't know about Toby and me — I'm sure of it. And even if he had, he wouldn't have killed Toby because of it — he couldn't have. Whatever else Don might be capable of doing, he couldn't kill a man in cold blood, let along come home and fall fast asleep less than an hour after doing so. He would've exploded at me and then used the affair as psychological leverage against me for the rest of our lives, assuming that he didn't divorce me because of it. But he wouldn't have gone after Toby."

With that, she started to cry again. I gathered her into my arms and tried to tell her that everything would be all right. But I knew full well that she didn't believe it any more than I did.

28

For an hour or so after Mary Jo left, I sat at my desk staring absent-mindedly out the window, thinking through our conversation. Regardless of the fact that she didn't think her husband knew of her affair with Toby and that she didn't believe he was the sort of person who could have committed a murder even if he had known about it, she'd still given me not one but two new suspects, both of whom would have had excellent motives for committing the crime. But had either one of them actually done so? More to the point, *could* either one of them have actually done so?

The problem, of course, was the damn ax handle. According to Mary Jo, the argument between Mike and Toby took place between four and four thirty, at which point Toby stormed out of the house. Mike's date had alibied him for the period from seven to ten. That meant that, in the two and a half hours between four thirty and seven, Mike would have had to decide to kill Toby and, for whatever reason, to pin the crime on Steve. Given that much time, he could have come up with the ax handle, assuming he didn't have one already. But how would he have gotten it into Steve's truck?

Certainly, he could not have done so in the short period between his brother's murder and the arrival of the first deputy to reach the scene. And given that the initial investigation at the scene had taken much of the night, it was hard to imagine how he would have had a chance to do so before Chris reached Steve's house and found the murder weapon. But that assumed, of course, that he would not have had an accomplice to assist him in the matter.

As for Don Watson, the case was almost as thin. One would have to argue that, contrary to Mary Jo's protestations, her husband *did* know about her affair with Toby and that he *was* capable of killing Toby because of it. You'd have to demonstrate that Watson learned of the fight between Toby and Steve and decided to make Steve the fall guy. You'd also have to break whatever alibi, if any, he had for the time of the murder.

Unless I was missing something, both scenarios seemed pretty improbable and unlikely to raise even a whisper of reasonable doubt in the minds of a jury. In truth, at this point I didn't even have evidence enough to take to Chris, and in good conscience, I couldn't destroy what little was left of Mary Jo's fragile world by running to him with insupportable suspicions.

***

Having no better idea, I decided to first try to discover how Don Watson had spent the night of Toby's murder. I was pretty sure that confronting Watson directly about the matter would be counterproductive and so decided to take an indirect approach.

Mary Jo said that Don's girlfriend was a young woman named Carol Norton who'd worked in Don's store for the last eighteen months or so. I googled her address and knocked on the door of her apartment a little after seven o'clock that evening. I could hear the thudding bass of a sound system with a good subwoofer coming from inside the apartment, but no one responded to my knock. I waited a couple of minutes, then banged on the door a bit louder. From inside, a woman shouted, "Hold your horses, for Christ's sake. I'm coming."

After another minute passed, a young woman jerked open the door and said, "Yeah?"

I recognized her immediately as the woman I'd seen having dinner with Watson several weeks earlier at the Beargrass Bistro. I guessed her to be somewhere in her middle twenties, but she had the hard, defiant look of a woman who'd seen a good deal of life and who hadn't been particularly well used by it. Tall and thin, she was mostly angles and lines, including a short blonde haircut that had been styled into a severe wedge. She was dressed in an abbreviated tee shirt and pair of tight, low-cut jeans that exposed her bare midriff and a small stone of some sort that adorned her pierced navel. The unmistakable aroma of good quality weed drifted around her and out into the hall. I handed her a card and said, "Carol Norton?"

She made a frank appraisal of me, then looked at the card. "I don't think I need a lawyer right at the moment, but thanks for stopping by."

She started to close the door again, but I blocked it with my foot. "Actually," I said, "I wasn't attempting to solicit new clients door to door, Ms. Norton. I was wondering if you could spare a couple of minutes to talk to me about a case I'm working on."

"And why should I?"

"Because you're a public-minded citizen who'd like to do her part to prevent a grave miscarriage of justice from occurring"

"And if I'm not?"

"Well, as much as it would pain me to do so, I'd have to subpoena you, drag you into court and ask you a lot of potentially embarrassing questions in public, rather than doing it quietly here."

She opened the door a bit wider and said, "Questions about what?"

I gave her what I hoped was a disarming smile. "Questions you'd probably rather not have me asking out here in the hall in front of your neighbors. May I please come in? I promise I won't take up too much of your time."

"Oh shit, what the hell?" she said, pulling the door open. "It's not like I was sitting here waiting for Brad Pitt to drop by."

She led me into the living room of a small apartment, which, though relatively cheap, was nonetheless clean and orderly. She picked up a remote control, clicked off a Luscious Jackson CD, and offered me a seat. I took a chair on one side of the coffee table and she settled onto the couch on the other side. "So, what sort of embarrassing questions did you want to ask me?"

"Well, Ms. Norton, this is a bit awkward, but I was wondering if you could tell me what you were doing two weeks ago tomorrow night — that would be Tuesday, the sixteenth?"

She leaned forward and spent a few seconds lining up the magazines on the coffee table while apparently thinking about the question. Continuing to look at the magazines rather than at me, she took a deep breath, exhaled slowly and said, "What the hell business is it of yours what I was doing two weeks ago tomorrow night?"

"Perhaps none, but why don't you humor me for a minute here?"

After another few seconds, she finally raised her eyes to meet mine and said, "Two weeks ago tomorrow was, as you said, a Tuesday. I worked until nine o'clock and then met a girlfriend at Rival's for a couple of drinks. I was home and in bed by eleven — alone, if it's any concern of yours."

"Work would be Watson's Menswear?"

"It would."

"You and Mr. Watson closed the store and went your separate ways?"

"I just told you we did."

I waited, holding her eyes with mine, until finally she said, "What, you don't believe me?"

"Ms. Norton, please forgive me for being intrusive here. I really have no interest in the details of your personal life except as they may affect the case I'm working on. But I'm given to understand that you and Don Watson don't always go your separate ways when you close the store together on Tuesday nights."

"And who the hell says that?"

"I'm sorry, Ms. Norton, but your relationship with Watson is hardly a closely guarded secret. In fact, I've seen the two of you out together myself."

She waited a couple of seconds, then shook her head and said, "So, that's your big case? His freakin' wife found out and is suing him for divorce, and now you're going to drag me through the muck?"

I shook my head. "Actually, no that's not my big case. Mrs. Watson does know about your relationship with her husband. In fact, she's known about it for some time. For the moment though, she has no plans to divorce him because of it — at least not as far as I know. To be perfectly candid, I'm simply trying to discover what Don Watson was doing last Tuesday night. His wife assumed that he was with you."

"Well," she said, rubbing a spot on her jeans, "his wife assumed wrong. I don't know where the hell he was. More than that, I really don't give a rat's ass. The dumb bastard's been feeding me a sorry, tired line for the last nine months. And being even dumber than dirt myself, I believed him, at least for a while. But it's pretty damn clear that I'm just his occasional piece on the side. He's not going to leave his wife — at least not for me. And at this point, I wouldn't want him if he did. He's a loser."

"And you have no idea where he might have been that night?"

"None." She ran a hand through her hair and said, "I expected that after we closed the store that night, we'd go out for a quick drink and then wind up back here — that was what we usually did on Tuesday nights. But earlier that evening, he begged off. He told me that he couldn't see me that night because his in-laws were going to be visiting and his wife insisted that he put in an appearance. He left the store a little after six, leaving me to close up by myself, so I called my girlfriend and met her for a drink."

I nodded, rose from the chair and said, "Okay, thank you Ms. Norton. I appreciate the information. I'll let you get back to your evening."

"And I suppose that by this time tomorrow, everyone in Kalispell who didn't know that I was fucking Don Watson will be reading about it in the morning paper?"

I shook my head. "Well if so, it won't be because they heard it from me. As far as I'm concerned, what you've told me won't go any farther — unless for some reason Watson tries to claim that he was with you that night."

"Yeah, right," she said, slowly shaking her head.

I left her sitting on the couch, reaching forward to rearrange her magazines again, as I closed the door behind me.

***

It was a little after eight when I drove back through Lakeside on the way home. I hadn't eaten anything since early in the afternoon, and my stomach was growling. I thought about having dinner at Alfredo's, but given the frustrations of the day, I wasn't in the proper mood even for the casual conversation that would be expected of me there. So instead, I drove a couple of blocks farther south down the highway and pulled into the graveled parking lot of the Avalanche Saloon.

As usual at this hour, there were only a handful of customers in the place. When I walked through the door, Patsy Cline was singing "Crazy" on the jukebox, and a couple I didn't recognize was slow dancing in the dim light on the small dance floor. I took a stool at the far end of the bar, leaving several empty places between me and a couple nursing beers while they watched some lame reality show on the muted television set. Randy walked over, dropped a napkin on the bar in front of me, and said, "How's things, Dave?"

I shrugged. "So-so. How about with you, Randy?"

"About the same, I guess. What can I get you?"

"A burger, medium-rare, fries, and a Trout Slayer Ale, please."

"You got it."

He turned and called the food order through the small window to the kitchen in back. He drew the beer, set it on the napkin in front of me, and then, realizing that I wasn't in the mood to talk, drifted down to the other end of the bar and began polishing glasses. I nursed the beer for the next fifteen minutes and then ordered another when Randy set the hamburger in front of me. As usual, the burger was excellent, but I ate it on automatic pilot, drinking the beer, and mulling over the events of the last couple of weeks.

Before I even realized it, the burger and fries were gone, and I drained the last of the beer as Randy cleared the plate. He stood there for a moment, holding the plate while I contemplated the empty glass in front of me. I set the glass down on the bar, looked up at him and said, "Jack straight up with water back, please, Randy."

He nodded, picked up the empty beer glass and dropped it into the bar sink. He set the plate on the ledge of the kitchen window, pulled a fifth of Jack Daniels from the shelf behind the bar, and poured a healthy shot into an Old-Fashioned glass. Then he set the whiskey and a glass of ice water in front of me and returned to the other end of the bar.

I picked up the whiskey and turned it slowly in my hands, the rich amber liquid glowing bright in the soft light of the barroom. I swirled it in the glass, brought the glass to my nose and inhaled deeply of the smoky vanilla scent that offered a tantalizing preview of a vague, less troubled place in my not-too-far-distant future. Then I closed my eyes and took a healthy first sip, savoring the smooth caramel and toasted oak comfort as it spread slowly through my system.

I thought of better days and happier times. I thought of Bill and of Alice, and I said a silent prayer, asking a god I no longer believed in to please keep her safe and warm, wherever she might be tonight.

And I thought of Sarah Parker, floating naked and dead in the chilly water off my dock on a beautiful summer morning ten months ago. I thought of the chaos her death had unleashed and took another sip of the whiskey, wishing fervently that I could somehow find my way into a deep, dark place where the world, past and present, could not intrude.

And then I thought of Mary Jo Watson, of Toby Martin, and of Steve Helstrom sitting in a jail cell in Kalispell. Shaking my head, I got up off the stool, dropped twenty-five dollars on the bar, and walked quickly out the door, leaving the whiskey unfinished behind me.

29

Sarah Parker was twenty-four years old on the morning I pulled her body from the lake — a beautiful young third grade teacher from Missoula who'd come up to the Flathead in an ill-fated effort to rekindle an affair with the married man who'd recently ended their relationship. She'd had sexual intercourse only minutes before dying from a single blow to the head with a heavy blunt instrument and was dead before she went into the water.

I found her body, floating off the edge of my dock, ten and a half hours later, setting into motion an investigation that stretched from Kalispell back to Missoula. Chris's small staff was already stretched thin by the everyday burden of policing a county larger than the state of Connecticut, and he urged me to return temporarily to the county payroll to assist with the investigation. He argued that my experience as the assistant county prosecutor equipped me with exactly the skills necessary for the task, and I ultimately agreed to assist him conduct a series of interviews with Parker's friends and acquaintances in Missoula.

As the case unfolded, it appeared that Parker might have simply been in the wrong place at the wrong time, murdered and dumped into the lake by a person or persons unknown to her. Otherwise, two principal suspects emerged.

The first was Parker's former fiancé, a law student named Martin Robertson. Sarah had broken their engagement a year and a half before her death, and Robertson was still carrying a torch for her eighteen months later. The investigation revealed that Robertson called Parker's phone number in the weeks before her death, and the alibi he provided for the night of the crime broke down almost immediately.

The other potential suspect was Sarah's mysterious married lover, Arthur. Parker confessed the relationship to a woman named Teresa Corpuz, her closest friend and one of her fellow teachers. But Sarah swore Corpuz to secrecy and steadfastly refused to tell her anything about "Arthur" other than his first name.

I was the one to whom Corpuz revealed her best friend's secret. I was the one who teased the details of the relationship out of the meager evidence that Sarah had left in her wake. And I was the one who had first reached the unthinkable but ultimately unmistakable conclusion that "Arthur" was, in fact, the husband of my own best friend.

30

Don Watson was steaming the wrinkles out of a suit coat when I walked into his shop just after nine thirty the next morning; Carol Norton was nowhere in sight. The business, on Main Street in downtown Kalispell, had clearly seen better days, and would have benefited immensely from a fresh coat of paint, inside and out. For that matter, the store would have been considerably more appealing if someone would have simply taken the time to vacuum the tired carpet, straighten the place up a bit, and at least make an effort to arrange the inventory in a more appealing manner.

As it was, suits, sport coats and slacks hung jammed together on crowded racks; dress and sport shirts lay piled haphazardly together on tables; and ties, belts, handkerchiefs and other accessories were randomly displayed in a similarly disordered manner. In a corner at the back of the store, two desks were cluttered with files, invoices, empty coffee cups, pop cans and the remains of what appeared to be someone's half-eaten cherry Danish.

When Watson's father owned the business, it was the premier men's clothing store in the Flathead Valley. The elder Watson stocked the store with goods from Hickey Freeman, Bill Blass, Hart Schaffner and Marx, and other top American labels of the day. He'd run the place with a firm hand, a considerable amount of spit and polish, and a strong emphasis on customer service. Today, though, the store was stocked principally with foreign-made goods from discount labels that were perpetually "on sale." Watson's was now *the* place to go if, for some reason, you needed two suits for $239.00, and if you didn't mind scaring up your own tailor to do the alterations.

I wondered what the senior Mr. Watson would have thought about the current state of the business he'd labored so diligently to build. In his son's defense, though, I also wondered what the senior Mr. Watson would have thought about a world in which growing numbers of American men seemed to believe that blue jeans, tennis shoes, a ratty old tee shirt, and a seed corn gimmie cap constituted perfectly acceptable attire in virtually any social setting.

Watson himself was dressed in an ill-fitting plaid sport coat, a blue shirt open at the collar, and a pair of dark gray slacks. In high school and college, he'd worked hard to maintain his weight and to stay in shape — at least until he'd failed to make the football team at MSU. In the years since, though, he'd gained a fair amount of weight and carried most of it around his waist. He looked like a heart attack begging to happen, and I was willing to bet that his blood pressure must have stretched about as high as Neptune.

I tried to imagine what Carol Norton could have possibly found attractive about the man, and the less charitable demons of my subconscious momentarily conjured up the image of the rail-thin Norton and her pear-shaped employer in bed together doing the horizontal bop. I suppressed the image as quickly as it surfaced; some things are better left unimagined.

As I reached the back of the store, Watson looked up from the coat he was steaming, grimaced, and then reached over and turned off the steamer. He laid the nozzle across the top of the machine, turned back and greeted me in a voice that suggested that he was not particularly thrilled by the fact that I'd dropped by. I returned the greeting and asked if he could spare me a couple of minutes.

"What for? I take it you're not in the market for a new suit."

"No, Don, not today. As you doubtless know, I'm defending Steve Helstrom. I wanted to talk to you about the night that Toby was murdered."

He folded his arms across his chest and looked beyond me, sweeping his eyes around the store that was, for the moment at least, empty save for the two of us. Looking back to me, he said, "What about it?"

"Well, to cut right to the chase, would you mind telling me what you were doing that evening?"

He shook his head. "Not gonna happen. What I was doing that night is none of your damn business."

I shrugged and said, "Well, Don, under normal circumstances, you'd be absolutely right. But I do have a good reason for asking."

"Ask all you fucking like. It's still none of your goddamn business."

Refusing to rise to the bait, I said in as moderate a tone as I could manage, "Look, Don, I have a client sitting in jail charged with first degree murder. He swears he didn't do it, and I believe him. Even if I didn't, I'd have to look closely at anybody else who might possibly have had a motive for committing the crime."

"And you think I did?"

"I think we both know that you had what a lot of people would consider an excellent motive."

Watson closed the space between us, his face reddening. "You are a miserable son of a bitch."

Giving no ground, I said, "Look, I have no interest in publicizing the details of your private life, although certainly not out of any concern for your feelings. But I'd rather not see Mary Jo publicly humiliated, which is why I'm coming to you personally — and quietly — rather than asking Chris to come talk to you officially. But I am going to protect my client's interests as best I can, and if you won't cooperate with me, then I'll have no choice other than to explain to Chris that you did have a reason to go after Toby and that you won't — or can't — account for yourself at the time of the murder."

Watson slammed a hand into the wall next to us. "You cocksucker. You have absolutely no reason to go poking around through the details of my private life. What I was doing that night

199

has absolutely nothing to do with Steve Helstrom or with that fucker Toby Martin. He was always so goddamn high and mighty, and he was damn well on the way to ruining the economy of this valley. I'm no hypocrite, and I'm not going to pretend that I'm sorry he's dead. Whether Helstrom hangs for it or not is no concern of mine."

Returning his stare, I said, "Well, Don, it is a concern of mine, and I don't intend to let it happen. The deeper I get into this case, the more apparent it becomes that there are any number of people who might have wished Toby dead, some for reasons perhaps totally unrelated to his work for the NEA. And I'm not at all reluctant to shine a spotlight on them if that what it takes to get to the truth in this matter."

Glaring at me, he shook his head. "Well, you go right ahead and do it. If you want to drag my wife through the mud, be my guest — it's not like the bitch doesn't deserve it. But you're not going to get to that stupid bastard off by suggesting that I killed Martin. If and when I have to, I can account for my time that night, and in the meantime, why don't you go fuck yourself?"

31

Chris was just getting off the phone with someone when I walked into his office and said, "So what's new?"

"Christ, you mean you haven't heard?"

"Heard what?"

Leaning back in his chair, he said, "Somebody firebombed the offices of the Northwestern Environmental Alliance in Missoula last night. The Missoula and Kalispell papers each received identical e-mails announcing that the action was in response to the vandalism of the logging trucks at Simmons' on Sunday night. The messages warn that if the 'tree-hugging, mother-fucking enviros' carry out their promise to attack additional logging targets, the arsonists will respond in kind — 'an eye for an eye' and all that shit."

"How much damage was there?"

"Too early to tell. The 'firebomb' was pretty low-tech, actually just your garden-variety Molotov cocktail — a whiskey bottle filled with gasoline and a rag fuse. Somebody lit it and then lobbed it through a first-floor window sometime around one a.m. A smoke detector went off and the fire department arrived on the scene almost immediately. The fire damage was pretty much confined to the room where the bottle landed, but I don't know how much smoke and water damage the rest of the place might have suffered."

"I assume that the two e-mails originated from the same computer?"

"Yeah. We're working with Missoula to track them back to the Internet service provider. Once we figure out where the service provider is located, either we or the Missoula P.D. will get a warrant for the originating machine."

"Are you getting anywhere on the vandalism to the logging trucks?"

"No. Whoever did it got in and out cleanly, leaving nothing behind them. We've canvassed the area thoroughly, but we can't find anyone who saw anything out of the ordinary that night. The people at the Northwestern Environmental Alliance claim to know nothing about it. Their official position is that they work within the law to achieve their objectives and believe that eco-sabotage is counterproductive. In that case too, we're tracing the e-mail that the vandals sent to the Montana Logging Association. We'll see where they lead us."

"What are you hearing from the police about the Kane murder?"

"Again, not much. Naturally, we're now coordinating our two investigations, and detectives are interviewing all the people we arrested at the march on Sunday. But I doubt that's going to get them anywhere. The only solid evidence they have is the two .38 caliber slugs they recovered. Fortunately, they're in good enough shape to be matched to the weapon that fired them. The only problem, of course, is finding the gun.

"But to answer the question you're really asking, aside from the fact that both of the victims were leaders of the Northwestern Environmental Alliance, nothing's surfaced yet to suggest that Kane's killing was somehow related to the murder of Toby Martin. I'm afraid that the case against Steve continues to look pretty solid."

"And you'd tell me the instant that anything happened to suggest that it wasn't?"

"Naturally."

"I know you impounded Steve's truck and confiscated the clothes he was wearing on the night of the murder. I assume you

202

must have the test results back from the lab by now. What are they telling you?"

Chris shook his head. "Nothing. As you already know, we couldn't get any vehicular tracks out of the ground at the Martin place and so aside from the ax handle in the bed of the truck, there was nothing to tie the truck to the scene. We also got nothing out of Steve's clothes. In particular, there were no traces of blood. But Toby's injuries were mostly internal, and he didn't bleed very much, so the killer may not have picked up any spattered blood. And, of course, we only have Steve's word for the fact that the clothes we confiscated were the ones he was actually wearing that night. It's entirely possible that he disposed of the ones he was wearing at the time of the murder and gave us another set."

"I gather that you've now interviewed everybody who was in the Crossroads the night of the fight between Toby and Steve?"

"Yeah. Or more accurately, we've interviewed everybody we know of that was in there around the time of the fight."

"Can I have a copy of the list of names?"

Chris shrugged, lifted his feet off the desk, and turned to a pile of folders on the credenza behind him. He shuffled through the pile for a moment, pulled out a file, opened it and leafed through the pages. He found the sheet he was looking for and said, "Hang on a minute."

He left the office, returned almost exactly a minute later, and handed me a photocopy of the list. "You're welcome to it," he said as he settled back into his chair, "but I'm not sure what you're looking for. Everybody on that list is going to tell you that Steve provoked the fight in the bar, and the ones who followed the action outside are all going to tell you that Steve definitely threatened to kill Toby. They're also going to tell you that he didn't sound like he was kidding."

"I know. And to tell you the truth, I don't know what I expect to learn by talking to them. For the moment, I'm just trying to cover all the bases."

I glanced down the list of names, looked up in surprise and said, "You didn't tell me that Denny Graham was in the Crossroads that night."

"You think it's significant?"

"Well, I certainly think it's interesting, given his business relationship with Mike Martin. What's his story?"

Chris went back to the file on his desk and flipped through it for a moment before stopping to scan a page. Reading down the page, he said, "Tom did the interview. According to the notes, Graham was in there with a client. They saw the pushing and shoving inside the bar but didn't go outside to watch the fight.

"Graham told Tom that Steve was drunk and belligerent and that he started ragging on Toby virtually the moment Toby walked into the place. The bartender told them to take it outside, and Graham knows nothing about what happened out there except what he heard second-hand from the folks who went out to watch. He saw them come back in and says that Steve went to the rest room while Toby went straight to the bar, paid for his drink and left. Steve came out of the men's room and went back to the bar. He was still sitting there when Graham and his client left about fifteen minutes later."

Chris closed the folder, leaned back in his chair again, and clasped his hands behind his head. "So how does that help you?"

"I don't know that it does. Again, I just find the whole situation awfully curious. Toby Martin is almost certainly the principal obstacle in the path of Denny and Mike's big plans. Denny sees the fight between Steve and Toby and before you know it, Toby winds up dead and Steve is charged with first-degree murder."

Chris arched his eyebrows, cocked his head to the left and said, "So now you're suggesting that Graham killed him?"

"No. But I am suggesting that he had a fairly strong motive, and he might have taken advantage of a golden opportunity that practically fell into his lap. He saw the fight. He could have waited until the next night and then killed Toby, setting Steve up to take the fall."

Chris leaned forward and propped his elbows on the desk. "Well, yeah, theoretically, he *could* have done that, but then so could half of the other people who witnessed the fight that night. And, yeah, perhaps he *might* have had a motive, but as I recall, you told me that Mike hadn't raised the issue with Toby yet. So, while Graham might have naturally suspected that Toby would be a hard sell, he didn't know for certain that he'd reject the idea. Moreover, assuming that Graham really is that much of a criminal mastermind, how does he know that Steve is going to be conveniently sleeping one off by the side of the road at exactly the time he chooses to kill Toby?"

"That I don't know," I said, throwing up my hands. "But I still think it's interesting."

32

I wasn't yet ready to break Mary Jo's confidence and tell Chris that, in fact, Mike Martin *had* discussed his development plans with Toby. As Mary Jo understood it, the conversation occurred only hours before Toby's murder, which meant that Denny Graham couldn't have known for certain the previous night that Toby would adamantly oppose the project. And if Graham were to be believed, he still hadn't known it when I'd first talked to him several days after the fight. But I decided to go have another chat with him anyway.

I found him at his desk again when I walked into his office thirty minutes later. "Hey, Dave," he said, pointing out the obvious, "you're back again."

"Yeah, sorry to interrupt you," I said, extending my hand. "I'm just doing the grunt work necessary to my preparation of Steve's defense and discovered that I needed to talk to you again. Can you spare me a couple of minutes?"

He shook my hand without much apparent enthusiasm and said, "I suppose so. Why don't you have a seat?"

I took a client's chair in front of the desk as he returned to his own chair and lit a cigarette. He exhaled a plume of smoke and said, "What can I do for you?"

I shrugged and said, "Well, I was reviewing the list of witnesses to the fight between Toby and Steve and only just now realized that you were in the Crossroads that night. I'm working my way through the list and was wondering if you could tell me what you saw."

"Not much," he said, leaning forward and balancing the cigarette on the lip of an ashtray. "I'd been out in that general direction with a client, Bruce Steiner, showing him a piece of property, and I offered to buy him a drink when we were finished looking at the place. We went to the Crossroads and took a table off away from the bar so that we could continue our discussion with a bit of privacy. Helstrom came in just after we got there. He sat down at the bar and ordered a beer.

"About fifteen minutes after that, Toby came in with a guy I didn't recognize. They sat down at the bar and right away, Steve said something to Toby, but we were far enough away that I didn't hear what he said. Toby said something back and pretty soon they were both off their stools, jawing at each other. Then the bartender came over and said something to them. They went out the back door and a few people followed them out. Bruce and I stayed at our table, and about ten minutes later, everybody filed back in with Steve looking a little worse for the wear. Steve went back to the head. Toby went to the bar and paid for his drinks, then he and his friend left. Steve came out of the john a few minutes later and sat down at the bar again. Bruce and I finished our drinks and left about ten or fifteen minutes after that."

"Okay," I said, nodding. "Just so I understand the situation, when Toby came in and sat down at the bar, how much distance was there between him and Steve?"

"They were three stools apart at the bar — maybe four. The guy Toby was with sat on Toby's left — the side away from Steve. There was a guy I didn't recognize sitting on one of the stools between Steve and Toby, and they were talking around this guy."

"And you didn't hear any of the exchange between Toby and Steve before they went outside?"

"No. But it was pretty clear from the tone of their voices that Steve was taunting him, and that Toby wasn't going to put up with it."

"Did you see who shoved who first?"

Graham screwed up his face in concentration, then looked at me and said, "As I recall, Steve was the first one up off his stool. He walked around the guy who was in between them and got right into Toby's face. Toby got up from his stool and kind of chest-butted Steve back away. Then Steve pushed back at him with his hands to Toby's shoulders. That's when the bartender came over and told them to knock it off."

I nodded my understanding. "I assume that when the fight was over and the people who'd gone out to watch had come back into the bar, they must have been talking about what they'd seen and heard outside?"

"Yeah, although I really wasn't paying much attention to it. To be honest, I was trying to keep Steiner focused on our discussion about the property I'd showed him. I was hoping to close the deal."

"So, you didn't overhear anything?"

"Not a lot. I gathered that Toby had clearly gotten the better of the fight, but that was about it."

"Did you overhear anything about Steve threatening to kill Toby?"

He pursed his lips and shook his head. "No, I sure didn't. But then, as I said, Steiner and I left only a few minutes after it was all over."

"Okay, shifting gears for just a minute, when we talked the other day, you said that as far as you knew, Mike hadn't raised the issue of your development plans with Toby before Toby was murdered?"

"Right." He nodded.

"And is that still the case?"

"What do you mean?"

"Well, have you talked to Mike about it since? Had they talked about it?"

Graham rescued his cigarette from the ashtray and took a long drag. Then, still contemplating the cigarette, he said, "Not as far as I know."

"Do you know if Mike has raised the issue with his father yet?"

He leaned forward and stubbed out the cigarette. "I'm sorry, Dave, but I don't see what that could possibly have to do with your defense of Steve Helstrom."

"Oh, sorry. It doesn't, of course. I was just curious to know how you were coming along with the project."

Graham nodded. "Is there anything else you wanted to ask me about the fight between Steve and Toby?"

"No, thanks Denny," I said, rising from the chair. "As I said when I came in, I'm just trying to cover all the bases here, and I have a number of other people I need to interview, so I'll get out of your hair."

He stood to see me out of the office, and I said, "One more thing, just for the record, of course. Do you mind telling me where you were on the night of the murder?"

He waited a long moment, then looked at me and said, "Yeah, in fact I do mind. What even makes you ask the question?"

I raised my hands and said, "No offense meant, Denny. I'm asking it of everyone I talk to. It's just a way of building as complete a picture as I possibly can about what was going on that night."

"Well, I'm sorry, but what I was doing that night has nothing at all to do with Toby's murder or with Steve's defense, so I hope you'll pardon me if I tell you that it's none of your business."

"No problem. Thanks for your time."

***

I went back to the office, grabbed a Coke from the mini fridge in the closet, and turned my attention to a number of relatively minor but pressing matters that I'd been ignoring while concentrating on Steve's case. I was working on some revisions to the will of a long-time client when the phone rang. I answered and found Denny Graham at the other end of the line. He identified himself, cleared his throat, and asked if I could spare a minute to talk. "Sure," I replied, "what's on your mind, Denny?"

"Well," he said in a tentative voice, "I just wanted to apologize about earlier today. You caught me a bit by surprise there and I wasn't prepared for your question about what I was doing the night of Toby's murder. I didn't mean to be rude about it, but to be honest, I'm in something of an awkward position here . . ."

The pause in the conversation lengthened, and so I finally broke it saying, "How's that, Denny?"

"Well, the truth is that the night of the murder I was with a friend. The problem is that my friend is married, and there's no way she can afford to have this kind of attention focused on her. The long and the short of it is that I just can't give you her name and have you interviewing her to check out my story. I can only promise you that on that night I was with her from a little before eight until just after eleven, and we were miles away from the Martin place. I assure you that I know absolutely nothing about what might have gone on out there that night. There's nothing I could testify to that would either help or hurt your defense of Steve. And again, I'm sorry that I was rude to you earlier."

I waited a moment and then said, "Well, Denny, I appreciate the call, and I'm sorry if I put you on the spot before. That wasn't my intention."

"No problem, Dave. I just wanted to clear the air. I'll see you around."

***

We both disconnected, and I sat back in my chair, wondering who Graham's "friend" might be, or if in fact she even existed. After thinking about it for a couple of minutes, I turned back to the project on my desk, but I couldn't force myself to concentrate on it.

For much of the afternoon I'd had the nagging sensation that I was overlooking something important. Ignoring the work that beckoned from the top of my desk, I settled onto the couch, propped my feet up on the coffee table, and began methodically reviewing the events of the day, trying to identify the connection I was failing to make. When it finally hit me a little after four o'clock, I locked the door, got into my car and drove over to the Justice Center.

I found Chris in his office, apparently just finishing a conversation with Jason Sloan, a local motel owner and one of the county commissioners. Chris was standing behind his desk while Sloan stood with one hand on the doorknob and the other on the head of the ornate walking stick that he always used while making his way around the city. I'd never been able to figure out if he actually needed the thing or if it was just a prop.

Sloan's usually florid complexion seemed a shade redder than usual and as I rounded the corner of the hallway, I heard him say, "I'm serious about this, Sheriff. You simply cannot allow this business to continue." With that, he stepped out into the hall, gave me a curt nod, and said, "Good afternoon, Dave." Without waiting for a response, he hurried on down the hall and disappeared around the corner.

I stepped into the office and dropped into the chair across from Chris. "What the hell was that all about?"

He collapsed back into his own chair and propped his feet up on the desk. "Oh hell, nothing new. Jason's just got a burr up his ass as usual. He's convinced that the county is dissolving into anarchy and that the streets of our cities will soon be running red with the blood of loggers, environmentalists, and the innocent bystanders who get caught in the middle of their epic battle. Mostly, of course, he's concerned that the negative publicity will drive the tourists away and that his dilapidated, bug-infested motel will be half-empty at the height of the summer season."

"And he expects you to do exactly what?"

"Basically, he'd like me to march out like Matt Dillon, U.S. Marshall, drive the killers, rustlers, outlaws, roughnecks and renegades out of town, and make the streets safe once again for our women, children and tourists. Short of that, he'd like to see the 'extremists' on both sides of the logging debate locked up and muzzled. And, naturally, he'd like to see your client speedily tried and convicted so that the unpleasantness of Toby Martin's murder could be put behind us."

I shook my head and he said, "Yeah, I know. Don't even say it.... Anyhow, what's up with you?"

"Maybe nothing, but something you said earlier this morning just finally registered in my pea-sized brain."

Chris arched his eyebrows and I continued. "This morning you were telling me about the e-mail that the newspapers received, apparently from the person or persons who firebombed the NEA offices. Do you have a copy of it?"

"Sure." He shuffled through some papers on his desk and handed me a photocopy. I nodded, quickly read through the message, and then handed it back to him. "Look at the second sentence — the reference to the 'tree-hugging, mother-fucking enviros.'"

He read the sentence and looked back at me. "Okay, I admit that it's not very polite, and I'm sure that Emily Post wouldn't approve. But in case you haven't noticed, unfortunately we do live in a society where standards of behavior appear to be sadly in decline."

"Admittedly so. But the combination of the derogatory references and the way they're strung together is fairly unique. Have you ever heard anyone refer to the environmentalists in exactly that way?"

Chris set the paper back on his desk and said, "No, have you?"

"Yeah, as a matter of fact I have. Ever since you told me this morning that the e-mail messages made reference to the 'tree-hugging, mother-fucking enviros,' something's been nagging at the back of my mind. It finally just struck me that when I interviewed Ed Ramsey a few nights after Toby's murder, he described the environmentalists using exactly the same words."

Chris leaned back in his chair and clasped his hands behind his neck. "Well, isn't that interesting? As it happens, Tom just told me not twenty minutes ago that, according to the Internet Service Provider, the computer from which the e-mails originated is located at the Union 76 truck stop at the intersection of 93 and I-90 outside of Missoula. Apparently, they have a couple of cubicles with computers for use by truckers who want to send and receive e-mail. There's no charge for the service. The company provides it as a convenience, and it's first-come, first-served. You don't even have to sign in, so unfortunately there's no way of knowing who might have been using the computer at the time the message was sent."

"Which was?"

"About one fifty this morning — a little less than an hour after the NEA offices were firebombed."

"So," I said, "just for the sake of argument, say someone had driven down from Kalispell, torched the building and wanted to send an anonymous e-mail on the way back home. A computer at that truck stop would be very conveniently located."

"That it would."

"Have you ever bought gas there?"

"Not lately."

"Well, I have. As a matter of fact, I stopped in there a couple of weeks ago, and while I was pumping the gas, I noticed that they have stickers on their pumps saying something to the effect of 'Warning! You have already been recorded on video and drive-offs will be prosecuted to the full extent of the law.' I wonder how long they keep those recordings and who might show up on them, say between one and two o'clock this morning?"

"An excellent thought," Chris said, reaching for the phone.

I waited while he explained the situation to a detective on the Missoula P.D. who indicated that he would go out and pick up the video. Then Chris hung up the phone and said, "Wanna take a ride?"

***

Twenty-five minutes later, Chris pulled his department SUV into the rutted gravel driveway that led to Ed Ramsey's garage on the outskirts of Creston. Ramsey's dilapidated Ford pickup was sitting in front of the garage with its hood up, looking rather more abandoned than simply parked. Somebody had punched a hole in the screen door leading into the house, and the house and garage were both badly in need of a fresh coat of paint. The lawn was thick with weeds and hadn't been mowed in a good long while, and the contrast between Ramsey's sad looking property and the beauty of the mountains beyond simply made you shake your head in wonder.

As Chris and I got out of the Explorer, Ramsey walked out of the garage, wiping his hands on a red shop rag, and sporting a tee shirt that said, "The Best Gun Control Is A Steady Hand." He nodded sheepishly and said, "Hey, Sheriff. Hi, Dave."

We acknowledged the greeting, and Chris said, "How you doing, Ed?"

Ramsey swallowed hard. "Okay, I guess. Again, I'm real sorry about Sunday afternoon, Sheriff. I shouldn't of gone anywhere that near friggin' march, especially with a load on. But I was just so pissed about the whole situation . . . and then, when the pushin' and shoving started I just waded right into it. Sorry."

Chris nodded without really acknowledging Ramsey's act of contrition. "You were released on your own recognizance about six o'clock that evening, is that right, Ed?"

"Yeah, about then, I guess."

"And what did you do then?"

214

Ramsey shrugged. "I came back home here, watched a little TV and then went to bed."

"And how'd you spend Monday?"

Another self-conscious shrug. "I went to work and then came straight home. I spent what was left of the day working out here in the garage."

"And Monday night?"

Ramsey hesitated for a moment and then, looking down at the gravel rather than at either of us, said, "Well, I ate some soup for dinner, watched a little TV, and went to bed early. Why're you askin'?"

Ignoring the question, Chris said, "Is there anyone who can verify that you spent the evening here?"

Ramsey shook his head. "No, I guess there isn't. I was home here alone all night. In fact, I didn't see or talk to anybody from the time I got home from work until the time I got back to work on Tuesday morning."

Chris nodded. "Do you own a computer, Ed?"

"No. . . . Well, that is, we have one, but it's my son's actually. He uses it for his schoolwork."

"Do you ever use it yourself?"

Ramsey colored. "Not really. I mean, I've looked at a few sites on the Internet, if you know what I mean . . ."

"Do you ever use it to exchange e-mail messages?"

"No. My kids and the wife send e-mail messages on it, but I've never used it for that. I don't really have need of it."

Chris nodded, acknowledging the answer and said, "Would you mind if I took a look at the computer?"

Ramsey dragged his foot through the loose gravel while looking off into the distance beyond us. Then he looked back to Chris. "Well now, I don't know about that, Sheriff. I'm sure Brian probably wouldn't want you pokin' through it." Turning to me, he asked, "Wouldn't he have to have a warrant for something like that, Dave?"

I raised my hands. "Sorry, Ed, but I've already got a client in this case. I'm not in a position to give you legal advice here."

Chris steeled his eyes on Ramsey. In a distinctly harder voice, he said "You're right, Ed. If you won't voluntarily give me your permission to look at the computer, I can't force you to do so without a warrant. Of course, then I've got to ask myself what you'd possibly have to hide here?"

Ramsey shook his head and scuffed at the gravel again. "Well, nothing," Sheriff. But I reckon' my kid's got a right to his privacy, don't he?"

Chris looked across the scruffy lawn to the neighboring yard where a middle-aged woman had apparently decided that this would be an opportune time to weed the small garden that marked the border between her property and Ramsey's. The woman returned his gaze with an undisguised interest in her neighbor's business. After a couple of moments passed, Chris turned back to Ramsey. "Just so I'm sure then. You came straight home after work on Monday evening. You did not leave the house after that until you went to work on Tuesday morning, but you have no one who can verify that?"

Ramsey swallowed hard again and said, "That's about it, Sheriff."

"Okay, Ed. I tell you what, we'll let the computer go for now, but I wonder if you'd mind if I took a picture of you standing there by your truck?"

Ramsey looked over toward his neighbor, who'd forgotten all about her weeding, and said in a strained voice, "Why would you want to do that?"

"Well, to be perfectly straight with you Ed, we've got a witness who claims to have seen a man in a truck a lot like yours in an incident we're investigating from last night. I'm putting together a photo array to show the witness, and I'd like to include your picture in it."

"To be honest, Sheriff, I really don't think I'd like to do that."

Chris walked the few steps back to the SUV and retrieved a digital camera from a kit in the back seat. Then closing the space between himself and Ramsey to well within the latter's comfort zone, he said, "Well, Ed. I guess I really don't understand your concern. You were here at home all last night, so there can't be any chance that this witness is going to identify you or your truck. What's the problem?"

Ramsey jammed his hands into the front pockets of his jeans. "Well, Jesus, Sheriff. What if your witness makes a damn mistake?"

Chris reached out with his left arm and guided the hapless Ramsey to a position near the driver's side door of the pickup. "Don't worry. That's highly unlikely, Ed," he said as he snapped a photo.

In quick succession, Chris shot several photos of Ramsey, his pickup and of Ramsey and the truck together. The three of us stood there, saying nothing, while Chris cycled through the photos. Then, apparently satisfied, he turned back to Ramsey. "Thanks for your time, Ed. I'm sure I'll be in touch."

Ramsey watched as we got into to the Explorer and backed out of his driveway. Then he turned slowly back in the direction of his garage. Chris settled into his seat and punched the accelerator. "There's definitely something hinky about that boy and it goes beyond mixing it up with the NEA marchers on Sunday."

"Yeah, he's seriously nervous about something. The question is, what?"

"I don't know, but I'll e-mail these pictures over to Missoula tonight so that they can check them against what they've got on the video from the truck stop. They can also show Ramsey's picture to the people who were working there last night Maybe we'll get lucky and somebody will recognize him. I think I'll probably come out here tomorrow while Ramsey's at work and talk to Mrs. Busybody next door to see if she knows whether or not he was home last night."

"Well, I'll be happy for you if it turns out that he's the guy who torched the NEA offices and you can tag him with it. But I'd feel a hell of a lot better about it if someone would identify him as the guy they saw driving out of Toby Martin's place about ten o'clock on the night of the murder."

"Yeah, I know you would, but my guess is you're not gonna get that lucky."

33

"Then again, maybe you are gonna get that lucky."

It was ten thirty the next morning, and I was sitting in my office trying to get a handle on Denny Graham's financial situation, when Chris walked through the door and dropped into a chair in front of my desk. I put down the credit report I was reading and said, "How so?"

"Your buddy Ed Ramsey is in the wind. Apparently, he loaded up his truck and cleared out for parts unknown about thirty minutes after we left him last night."

"You think he knew you were going to make him for the fire at the NEA offices?"

"I have no idea what the dumb shit was thinking, but we can't make him for the fire — at least not yet."

"What happened, then?"

"I sent the pictures I took to Don Chinski, the Missoula detective who's investigating the arson case. He reviewed the video from the truck stop cameras for Monday night, but saw no sign of Ramsey or his truck. He then took the photos out to the truck stop and interviewed the nightshift employees, one of whom did recognize Ramsey's picture. This woman says that she definitely saw Ramsey in the truck stop recently but can't remember precisely when it was."

"The woman is certain?"

"Absolutely. She pulled Ramsey's picture out of a six-pack that Chinski put together."

"What are you thinking?"

"Hell, I don't know what to think. But given the woman's identification, and given the way Ramsey acted last night, I decided I'd better have another chat with him. I sent Tom and a deputy out to the mill to bring him in, but the foreman told them that Ramsey didn't show up for work this morning. So, Tom and Pete went out to Ramsey's house but he wasn't there either. The woman next door said that he loaded some stuff into the back of his truck and left about seven thirty last night. We've got an APB out for him and the truck."

"I wonder how far he might have gotten?"

"Who knows? We're figuring that he could average a maximum of about sixty miles per hour in that truck, and that's probably generous. If he's been driving ever since seven thirty last night, that could put him as far as Seattle, Vegas, or Grand Forks, depending upon which direction he headed, and assuming that he didn't go north into Canada. That also assumes that he didn't just head off into the hills somewhere — apparently the guy's an expert woodsman.

"We're checking with the Canadian authorities in case he might have been dumb enough to cross legally through a border checkpoint. We've also contacted his credit card companies, and they'll alert us if he uses one of his cards for gas or some damned thing. Otherwise, there's not much we can do until we have some general idea of the direction in which he's running."

I digested that and said, "You don't suppose he's worried that you might be coming after him for something more serious than the fire at the NEA office?"

"Like what?"

"Like, I wonder what Ramsey was doing about nine thirty on Sunday night?"

"I wondered the same thing," Chris said. "So, before I came up here, I went out to talk to the nosey neighbor. She and her husband were over in Plains Sunday night at a birthday party for one of their grandchildren, so she has no way of knowing if Ramsey was home that night or not. As for Monday night, she says that Ramsey's truck was in his driveway when she last looked out the window about nine. She went to bed about nine thirty and can't say if he might have left after that or not."

"Well, needless to say, you've just brightened my day considerably."

Chris shook his head. "Maybe, maybe not. Even if Ramsey is the arsonist, and even if we could somehow make him for killing Frank Kane, we've still got nothing to tie him to Toby Martin's killing. Unless he was to confess to doing so, Steve's still on the hook. Obviously, this might help you raise reasonable doubt in the minds of jurors, but you know how your old boss will reply."

"Yeah, I know. He'll stand in front of the jury box, thrust out his chest, and go into hyper-bloviating mode, arguing that imitation is the sincerest form of flattery. He'll insist that Steve killed Toby Martin and that Ramsey was so inspired by what his friend had done that he killed Frank Kane to prove his own manhood or some damn thing."

"Exactly. So, what are you working on there?" he said, tilting his head at the papers strewn across the top of my desk.

"Denny Graham's financials. I was trying to figure out how desperately he might need this project with Mike Martin, apart from the ego issues that are obviously involved."

"And?"

"I'd say he needs it pretty badly. It looks like he's barely getting by, basically living hand-to-mouth and spending his money just a little faster than it's coming in. His mortgage payments and the lease payment on the Lincoln are eating up a good chunk of what he appears to be bringing in an average month. To make ends meet, he's gotten progressively deeper into the credit card companies and now he's turning to the local finance companies to stay afloat. Looks to me like he's about one or two bad months away from the bankruptcy court."

"You really think he's a possibility for Toby's murder?"

"Hell, I don't know. I'd argue that he did have a motive. Certainly, he had to realize that Toby would be a major obstacle in the path of the plans he'd hatched with Mike, and he knew about the fight between Steve and Toby. He claims that at the time Toby was killed, he was miles away in the arms of a married woman. But he also insists that the gentleman in him won't let him tell me who that woman is so that I can confirm his story."

"Well," Chris said, rising from his chair and heading toward the door, "I'd like to help you out, but unfortunately I have no legitimate reason to question him and make him account for his time that night. But if you can come up with one, I'll be happy to pursue it."

"Don't worry," I said, returning to the credit report. "You'll be the first to know."

***

I wasted another hour or so without learning much more about Denny Graham's financial situation and decided that it was time to pay him another visit. When I walked through his door about twelve thirty, he made no pretense of being glad to see me. He put down the sandwich he was eating and without rising from his desk said, "Dave?"

Standing in front of the desk, I held up my hands. "I understand that I'm probably the last guy in the world you want to see today, Denny. I can only ask you to understand that I have a job to do here, and that I'm trying to do it as well as I can. And, if it's any consolation, if you were my client, I'd doubtless be out annoying somebody on your behalf as well."

He showed a slight smile. "Well, if I ever need a lawyer, I'll be sure to keep that in mind. So, what do you need today?"

I returned the smile. "I'm really sorry to bug you about this again, but I'm hoping you'll change your mind and tell me who you were with the night Toby was murdered. I promise that I'll use the information discretely, but to be blunt about it, I need to check your story."

The smile disappeared, and he shook his head. "Not going to happen. And anyway, why do you need to check my story?"

"Because I have a witness — a credible witness — who tells me that Mike *did* tell Toby about your plans and that they had a huge fight about it only hours before Toby was killed."

Graham leaned forward, resting his elbows on the desk. "And you're suggesting what, exactly?"

"Well, to be blunt again, you've told me twice now that Mike had not raised the issue with Toby when in fact he had. I'm suggesting that it's not beyond the realm of possibility that Mike told you about the argument late that afternoon. Certainly, I'm not accusing you of anything, but as I'm sure you can understand, if I'm going to properly defend Steve, I've got to take a look at anyone else who might possibly have had a motive to wish Toby harm.

"You say that you were nowhere near the Martin place at the time of the murder, and if so, fine. But you have to understand that, given what I know, I just can't take your word for that. I'm asking you to give me the woman's name so that I can have a very quiet conversation with her to confirm your story."

"And if I don't?"

"Then I really don't have a choice. I have to take my suspicions to the sheriff and ask him to check your story officially. And obviously, you understand that under those circumstances your relationship with this woman is going to run a much greater risk of exposure than if I talk to her."

Graham angrily jammed what was left of his sandwich into a Subway bag and pitched it into the wastebasket next to the desk. "Shit, Dave, you're putting me in an impossible situation here. If I give you her name, I guarantee you that she'll never speak to me again. Hell, to protect herself, she might damn well refuse to admit that she even knows me let alone that we were together that night."

I gave him my best effort at a sympathetic nod. "Look, Denny, I understand your frustration. Again, I can only promise that I'll handle the interview as discretely as possible. I'm not out to embarrass anybody here. If your story checks out, that's the end of it. But I hope you can understand that I do have to verify it."

Shaking his head, he said, "Yeah, yeah, goddammit. You've got to do your duty and all that shit. Okay, but I'm going to talk to her myself first in order to explain things. Then you can talk to her. And if that's not good enough for you, you'll just have to go report me to the fucking sheriff."

I understood that, no matter what response I made, there was no way to prevent him from contacting the woman — or some woman — and convincing her to alibi him before either Chris or I could talk to her. And so, having nothing to lose, I said, "Okay Denny, that's fair enough."

Yielding with poor grace, he waved me out of his office saying, "I'll call her as soon as I can and set something up so you can talk to her."

34

Driven perhaps by the power of suggestion, I swung by the Subway sandwich shop two blocks north of Graham's office and picked up a turkey sub to go. I popped open a Coke and ate the sandwich at my desk, thinking about my conversation with Graham and wondering how long it would take Chris to run Ed Ramsey to ground. There wasn't much I could do on Steve's behalf while I waited for Graham to get back to me and for the authorities to catch up with Ramsey, so I spent the early the afternoon working through several minor matters that had piled up on my desk.

I was plodding through the revision of a real estate trust agreement when the phone rang a little after three o'clock. I picked it up to find Denny Graham on the other end of the line. He said that he'd contacted his married girlfriend and that he'd persuaded her to meet with me later in the afternoon. "She's pretty damned pissed off about it, and I don't mind telling you that I am too. You need to promise me that once you talk to her, no one else is going to find out about it."

"That's not a problem. If she can confirm that you were with her that night, that's good enough for me."

Graham told me that the woman's name was Rhonda and that she'd meet me at the City Brew coffee shop in Kalispell at four thirty. "I told her what you look like and what you were wearing this morning," he said. "She'll know how to find you."

***

I got to coffee shop at four fifteen and found that only a couple of tables were occupied. At a table next to the window in front of the shop, a guy sat by himself, drinking a cup of coffee and reading a newspaper. A couple of tables away, three women were carrying on an animated conversation over coffee and desserts. I bought a cup of coffee, took a table in the back of the shop away from the other customers, and settled in to wait.

At four thirty-five, a woman walked through the door and stood for a moment, scanning the room. She appeared to be somewhere in her mid-forties, a bottle blonde, thickening through the middle. She'd dressed in khaki shorts, tennis shoes, and a faded red tee shirt that hung out over the shorts. She glanced in the direction of the guy near the window who was engrossed in his paper and who appeared not to notice her. She looked quickly past the table of women and her eyes finally settled on me sitting in the back of the room. Looking for all the world like someone who was about to undergo root canal surgery without the benefit of any anesthesia, she slowly walked across the room and stood by the table. In a voice that seemed an octave or two high for a woman of her size, she asked, "Are you Mr. Matthews?"

I nodded, stood, and offered her a seat. She pulled out a chair on the opposite side of the table, and as we both sat down, I said, "I appreciate your taking the time to see me, Ms. ..."

"Just Rhonda," she said.

"Okay, Rhonda. I assume that Denny told you why I needed to talk to you."

She nodded, grimacing. Looking down at the table rather than at me, she said, "Yeah. He says you need to know that we were together the night that lawyer was killed. But Jesus, if my husband finds out, I swear, he'll kill the both of us."

Ignoring that unhappy prospect, I said, "Can I ask how long you've been seeing Denny?"

She shrugged and looked out the window. "I dunno. Three or four months, I guess. My husband ... Well, shit, you're not interested in my problems."

I waited until she finally turned back to meet my eyes. "Look, Rhonda, I know that this is very awkward for you, and I'm sorry to put you through it. But it's very important that I know the truth about what happened that night. A man's life literally depends on it. I'm certainly not asking for any intimate details, but can you tell me about that night? Did Denny pick you up, or did the two of you meet somewhere?"

She shook her head. After a moment, she said, "No. I went down to his place."

"What time did you get there?"

Again, she shrugged. "Seven, seven thirty. Sometime in there, I guess."

"And how long did you stay?"

"Ten thirty," she said, with no hesitation.

"You're sure about the time?"

Still looking at the table rather than at me, she said in a soft voice, "Yeah, I'm sure."

But she didn't sound all that sure to me.

"How do you remember the time?"

"I dunno, I just do."

"Do you remember what time you got home that night?"

"No, but it would've only been like fifteen minutes or so after I left his place."

"So maybe about ten forty-five?"

"Yeah, I guess."

"And how do you remember that it was that particular night?"

Sighing softly, she said, "My husband's a long-haul trucker. When I see Denny, it's on nights that Rick is out of town."

"And he — your husband — was on the road on Tuesday, the sixteenth?"

She simply nodded and began picking at a cuticle.

I waited a couple of moments, but she refused to meet my eyes. Finally, I leaned across the table. "Look, Rhonda, I really don't want to pressure you here, but are you absolutely sure about this? I wasn't kidding when I said that a man's life is on the line. My client's sitting in jail, charged with a crime that I don't think he committed. If he's convicted, he's probably going to go to prison for the rest of his life. Steve — my client — has a wife and kids. And not just his life, but all their lives will be ruined. If you're not absolutely sure about the date or the time, please tell me."

She looked out the window for a long minute and when she turned back, tears glistened in her eyes. I gave her a moment, then said softly, "What is it, Rhonda?"

Swiping at a tear with the back of her hand, she said, "Men are such shits. My goddamn husband is on the road half the time and I know the bastard's screwing every slut he runs into out there. When he's home, he's either drunk or beating on me — usually both. Then Denny comes along with his big plans. He's gonna make a fortune and take me away from all that. And being even dumber than I look, I fall into bed with him. But I know he's full of crap up to his ears. He's never going to make a fortune, and even if he did, he's sure as hell never gonna spend it on me."

"Meaning?"

"Meaning that I'm not gonna lie for him. We were at his place on Wednesday, not Tuesday that week. I have no damn idea what he was doing on Tuesday."

35.

I watched Ronda walk out of the coffee shop, looking totally defeated. I felt genuinely sorry for the woman; still, I couldn't help but be energized by what she told me. As a practical matter, she had just jumped Denny Graham to the top of my list of suspects. If he hadn't been the one who'd attacked Toby Martin, why would he have gone to such lengths to concoct an alibi for the evening in question?

There was, at least at the moment, no solid evidence to tie Graham to the killing, only the suspicions that I alone was harboring. Was it possible that there actually *was* some evidence that would come to the surface if Chris and his investigators started digging into Graham's whereabouts that night?

I knew that it was finally time to sit down with Chris and lay out everything I'd uncovered, beginning with my conversation with Mary Jo. But I also knew that he had taken the afternoon and evening off to go down to Polson to watch his son's baseball game. I didn't want to interrupt him and so sent him a text, telling him that I had news and suggesting that we should meet for breakfast in the morning.

There was nothing else I could do until I had a chance to talk to him and so I went home and vented my frustrations by mowing the lawn. That done, without a great deal of difficulty I persuaded myself that I'd earned a nice dinner. I showered, dressed, and drove into Lakeside. Johnnie gave me an awkward smile when I walked through the door of Alfredo's a little after eight and sat down at the empty bar. She grabbed a rag, wiped down the space in front of me and said, "Hey, Dave. How are you?"

I returned the smile, feeling a bit awkward myself. "Fine, Johnnie. And you?"

"Fine." She pitched the rag into a sink a few feet up the bar and then, continuing to look down at the bar rather than at me, she said, "Listen, Dave, I'm sorry about the other night. I really didn't intend to embarrass you or put you on the spot like that."

I covered her hand with mine and waited until she looked up to meet my eyes. "Believe me, Johnnie," I said softly, "the last thing I felt was embarrassed. That was the nicest thing anybody's said to me in the last ten months. And coming from you in particular, it was very special. I'm just sorry that . . . well, you know . . ."

She turned her hand up and squeezed mine for a moment. "Yeah, I do know. And thanks for not being upset with me about it. The last thing I would have wanted was to make you feel uncomfortable around me."

"That's one thing you don't ever have to worry about."

"Good."

She waited a couple of seconds, then squeezed my hand again and said, "What'll you have?"

I looked to the wines on the shelf behind her and said, "How about a glass of that Barolo you've got back there?"

"Great." She released my hand, poured the wine and then moved up the bar to fill an order for one of the waitresses. For twenty minutes or so, I drank the wine, chatting comfortably with Johnnie when she wasn't otherwise engaged. Then I moved over to the dining room, which was about a third full. I was just finishing my salad when Alfredo emerged from the kitchen, set my entree on the table in front of me, and said, "Mind if I join you for a drink?"

"Please."

He stepped over to the bar where Johnnie handed him a glass and the Barolo. He returned to the table, pulled out a chair, topped off my wine, and poured a glass for himself. He tasted the wine, nodded his approval, and said, "It's good to see you back in here on a more regular basis, Dave." Smiling, he continued, "It's even better to see you eating your dinner rather than drinking it. For a while there, I was beginning to think that I'd put you off my cooking for some reason."

I shook my head. "You know that's not true, and as a matter of fact, this Veal Marsala is especially good. So, how's the season going?"

He took a sip of the wine. "Well, it's still early of course, but so far, so good. The weekends since Memorial Day have been excellent. The rest of the week has been pretty good as well, so I really can't complain, except of course for the fact that it's now that time of the year when work interferes way too much with fishing."

"God forbid," I laughed.

Over the next hour we finished off the wine while I ate my dinner and we caught each other up on all the latest news from around the neighborhood. I finally made my farewells a little before ten, and twenty minutes later, pulled up to the head of my driveway. I pushed the button to open the gate, but it stubbornly refused to move. I punched the remote a couple more times with exactly the same result. Then, hoping that the batteries in the remote had died and that we were not having another power outage due to a downed line or some damn thing, I got out of the car to open the gate manually. I stepped up to the gate and was just reaching my hand around the post to release the lock when the back of my head exploded, and everything went black.

36

I was jolted awake, lying on my side with a splitting headache, and with no idea how long I might have been unconscious. My hands were bound behind me with some sort of tape while my legs were secured tightly together at the ankles and folded up into my chest. Another piece of tape had been placed across my mouth. Gradually coming to my senses, I realized that I was bound, gagged, and trapped in the trunk of a car that was being driven slowly over a very rough road.

I felt like I'd been blindsided by a truck. My legs were cramping, and I attempted to shift my position so that I could stretch them out a bit, but there was virtually no extra space in which to move. I managed to turn a little more onto my back and crabbed my way into a position along the diagonal of the darkened trunk, with my feet pressing up against the rear of the trunk on the driver's side and my head scrunched up in the general direction of the right tail light. Just then the car struck another bump in the road and my head bounced off the side of the trunk, sending another blinding shot of pain through my entire body.

I squeezed myself back into the center of the trunk in an effort to clear a little space around my head again, and as I did, the car made a sharp turn to the right and braked to a stop. The engine died, and I heard the driver's door open. Someone stepped out of the car and walked away from it, crunching gravel under his feet. A few seconds later, I heard the sound of wood splintering under the force of a heavy blow and the footsteps moved back toward the rear of the car. Then someone released the latch, and the trunk lid rose slowly into the night sky.

Before my eyes could adjust to what little light there was, someone flashed a bright light into my eyes. The light shifted away from my face and focused briefly on the tape that bound my hands and ankles. Then Denny Graham reached into the trunk, ripped the tape from my mouth, and said, "Comfortable, asshole?"

I shook my head, trying to clear out the cobwebs, and sucked in a few deep breaths of the cool fresh air. As my eyes gradually adjusted to the dark, I realized that we were parked in front of Phil Krause's office building at the Creston Mill.

Save for Graham's car, the parking area in front of the building was empty. A quarter moon and a few vapor lights mounted on poles weakly illuminated the mill yard and the exteriors of the buildings scattered around it. No light shone from the interiors of any of the buildings, and the night was eerily still.

The mill was a mile off the main highway, and even at the middle of the day, there was relatively little traffic on the road that ran from the highway past the mill. At this time of night, there would be virtually none at all. It thus appeared that Graham and I were completely isolated and alone and likely to be left that way. He backed a few steps away from the car, the flashlight in his left hand and what looked like a .38 caliber revolver in his right. I looked from the gun to him and said, "What the hell do you think you're doing, Denny?"

Shaking his head, he replied, "You'll find out soon enough. For the time being, just shut the hell up and listen carefully. I'm going to reach in there and pull your legs out of the trunk. While I'm doing so, this gun is going to be pointed right at your head. Make any stupid move and I'll blow your fuckin' brains out."

He stuck the flashlight into his coat pocket. Then, with the gun pointed steadily at my head, he reached into the trunk, put his left arm behind my knees, and pulled my legs slowly around and halfway out of the trunk. He reached into another pocket, came out with a large jackknife and pulled open the blade. Standing with the gun in his right hand and the knife in his left, he said, "Okay, I'm going to cut the tape around your ankles. Once I do, I'll pull you out of the car and onto your feet. Move slowly and remember, don't do anything stupid."

He jammed the gun into my chest and used the knife to cut through the tape. Then he closed the knife and returned it to his pocket. Transferring the gun to his left hand, he grabbed me by the collar with his right and pulled me slowly to my feet. Once I was standing, he backed away a couple of steps and motioned with the gun in the direction of the shattered office door. "Walk ahead of me into the building. And no quick moves."

I did as instructed, moving very deliberately up the steps and into the reception area. Graham retrieved the flashlight from his pocket, thumbed it on, and motioned me down the hall toward Phil Krause's office. I walked through the open door into the office, turned to Graham and said, "Now what?"

Graham flipped off the flashlight and set it on a table. Then he walked up behind me, pressed the gun into my back, and checked the tape that bound my wrists together. Apparently satisfied, he said, "Now you sit on the couch over there."

The vapor lights out in the main yard of the mill cast a soft half-light through the large window in the wall next to the couch, throwing Graham, me, and the office furniture into a shadowed relief. I made my way around the coffee table, turned and sank back into the couch. Graham produced a roll of duct tape from under his jacket and said, "Now put your feet up on the table. I'm going to tape your ankles together again, and then we'll have a quiet little chat."

Squeezing the gun between his arm and his side for a moment, he unwound about four feet of tape and stripped it from the roll. Then, pointing the gun at me with his right hand and holding the tape in his left, he moved around the table to my right side. He laid the strip of tape across my legs and pressed it firmly to my pants.

Keeping his eyes focused on mine, he reached under my legs, grabbed the far end of the tape and pulled it tightly up and over the top of my legs. Then he repeated the process, binding my legs tightly together again.

For the first time since he'd opened the trunk of his car, the tension went out of his face and he seemed to relax visibly. He grabbed a straight-backed chair from in front of Krause's desk and dragged it to a spot opposite me on the other side of the coffee table. He straddled the chair backwards, resting his arms on the back of the chair, the gun now hanging loosely in his right hand. "Well, now, isn't this a fine mess you've gotten yourself into?"

Glaring at him, I said, "What in the hell do you think you're doing? Are you out of your fucking mind?"

He waved the gun at me nonchalantly. "Considering the fact that you're the one who's trussed up like next Sunday's chicken, staring down the barrel of this revolver, you might want to be a bit politer."

"Well, excuse the hell out of me, but all things considered, I'm not feeling in a very polite mood right at the moment."

"Yeah, well, if you'd ever learned how to mind your own goddamned business, you wouldn't be sitting here. As it is, you've got no one to blame but yourself."

"What the hell is that supposed to mean?"

He exhaled heavily. "It means, shithead, that everybody but you was perfectly content to let Steve Helstrom take the fall for Toby Martin's murder. You shouldn't have gone digging into it, especially since it might threaten to screw up my deal with Mike."

"You son of a bitch," I said with as much contempt as I could muster. "Are you telling me that you *did* kill Toby?"

Graham nodded. "The guy came out of the womb an arrogant prick. He always thought that he was so much smarter — so much better — than anybody else. He should've just stayed in California. But no, he had to come back and throw in with those fucking environmental lunatics who're trying to cripple the economy of this valley. And if that wasn't bad enough, he was also standing directly in the way of the biggest deal of my life.

"I kept pestering his gutless brother to raise the issue with him sometime before the end of the next century, but Mike kept insisting that the time wasn't right — that he had to catch Toby when he was in the right mood.... Well, I was pretty sure all along that Toby was never going to be in the right mood."

"So why drag Steve into it?"

Graham turned, staring out the window for a moment, then looked back to me and shrugged. "He was convenient, and it was just his bad luck to be in the wrong place at the wrong time."

"How so?"

"Watching the two of them going at each other in the Crossroads the other night, I realized that Helstrom just might be the answer to my prayers. I figured that if Toby turned up dead after fighting with him, everybody would assume that Helstrom had killed him because he was pissed about the lawsuit — particularly if the murder weapon turned up in Helstrom's possession. With Toby dead and out of the way, I thought that Mike could probably handle his old man. If not, well, I figure that the old guy isn't going to be around all that much longer anyway...."

"So, you're telling me that you'd decided to kill Toby even before you knew that he and Mike had finally talked?"

"Yeah. I knew I'd have to act quickly if I was going to make Helstrom the logical suspect. I was trying to figure out how I might have an opportunity to get at Toby when Mike called me late Tuesday afternoon with the bad news. During the course of the conversation, he said that he was going out to dinner that night and that we should get together on Wednesday to figure out what we might do to try to change Toby's mind. I suggested that the two of us might talk to his brother together and asked when Toby was going back to Missoula.

Mike said he was leaving the first thing Wednesday morning, so I figured that Toby'd be home alone that night while Mike was out to dinner. I took a spare ax handle that I had in my garage and drove out to Martin's just after dark. I left my car in a cutout away from the road leading into the place, grabbed the ax handle and walked in. I went up to the door and rang the bell, but then of course, Toby wasn't there.

"I decided to wait, hoping that he'd show up before Mike got back, and hid in the trees off by the side of the porch. By ten fifteen, I was about to give it up for the night when I saw headlights coming up the road. I thought it might be Mike coming home from his date, in which case I would've just stayed hidden until he was inside. Then I would have slipped away and looked for another chance to get at Toby.

"But, of course, it turned out to be Toby who was driving in. He parked his truck in front of the house, and as he was getting out, I slipped out of the trees from behind him and hit him with the ax handle. He never even saw it coming. I hit him a few more times just to make sure, and then got the hell out of there. My plan was to drive by Helstrom's house in the middle of the night and pitch the ax handle into his truck."

I shot him a look of incredulity. "But what if Steve had an unbreakable alibi for the time of the killing? What would you have done then?"

Graham just shrugged. "I thought of that. But I figured that if Helstrom did have an alibi, the sheriff would just go looking for another mill worker, or for somebody else who was pissed off about the lawsuit. In that case, finding the ax handle in Helstrom's truck would have confused the situation, but there wasn't any way that the investigators could've tied it to me.

237

"But then, as I was driving home, I saw Helstrom's truck pulled off by the side of the road, not five miles from Martin's house. Christ, that was the most brilliant stroke of luck in the whole business! Helstrom was in the truck, sleeping one off. I carefully smudged any prints that might have been on the ax handle, laid it in the bed of Helstrom's truck, and drove off. The only way it could have been more perfect would've been if the deputies would've found him still there that night.

"Anyhow, the next morning, the sheriff arrested Helstrom, and everything was golden. Then you started screwing around, poking your nose into things that are none of your fucking business. I thought I could sweet talk Rhonda into covering for me, but then the dippy bitch has to go and tell you that she wasn't with me after all. She called me just after you left my office and told me that she wasn't going to lie for me and that she didn't want to see me anymore. Told me if I came sniffing around her again, she'd sic that Neanderthal husband of hers on me."

"At any rate, I figured that after talking to her, you'd be on your way to the sheriff with your suspicions. I don't think he could ever make a case against me, but even if he couldn't it would still probably poison my deal with Mike, and I can't afford to let that happen."

I gave a small laugh. "Well, I hate to disappoint you, but you're too late. I already called Chris Williamson and told him that you look like an excellent candidate for the killing and that you had tried to get your girlfriend to lie for you."

Graham stiffened for a moment, then smiled. "I don't believe you. If you had talked to the sheriff already, I'm sure I'd of heard from him by now. No, I'm sure he's still convinced that Martin's murder is a part of the uproar between the loggers and the tree huggers — especially what with poor Frank Kane getting shot and all."

Looking at the revolver he was holding and shaking my head in disbelief, I said, "Jesus Christ, Denny, you're not telling me that you killed Frank Kane too?"

He slowly shook his head. "No, I didn't. Somebody else had the great pleasure of shooting that bastard. But I will have to admit that his killing serves my purposes pretty well."

"And what the hell do you intend to do with me?"

"What do you suppose? I intend to get you off of my back permanently and fan the flames of the environmental battle a bit further, if you don't mind a bad pun."

His face hardened. "I'm going to torch this building and you along with it. Tomorrow the newspapers will get an e-mail from a radical environmental group whose name I haven't made up yet, taking credit for this fire as a response to the firebombing of the NEA offices in Missoula. The message will say that burning you up along with it is payback for the killing of Frank Kane and is also your punishment for agreeing to defend Toby Martin's killer."

"You're completely nuts. You'll never get away with it."

"Yeah, I expect that I will. With all the dust that's being kicked up between the loggers and the NEA, your pal Williamson will spend the rest of his fucking career trying fruitlessly to track down the nasty enviros who turned his best friend into a crispy critter."

With that, he pushed himself up off the chair. "Now, if you'll excuse me for a moment, I'll be right back."

He slipped the gun into his pocket and picked up the flashlight he'd left on the table. He turned on the flashlight as he headed down the hall in the direction of the reception area, leaving me alone in the office.

I dropped my feet off the table and began working my legs frantically in an effort to loosen the tape. I managed to stretch it a bit but didn't have enough leverage to break it. I scooted to the edge of the couch and heard Graham go through the door and down the steps outside.

I pushed up off the couch, almost losing my balance in the process. But I caught myself and stood up. Listening for the sound of Graham returning, I hopped around the table and across the room, hoping like hell that Krause had left his letter opener on top of the desk. Just as I made it to the desk, I heard the sound of a car door slamming outside.

In the dim illumination provided by the outdoor lights, it seemed like an eternity had elapsed before I finally spotted the letter opener on the opposite side of Krause's cluttered desk. I hopped around the desk, leaned back and snagged the letter opener in my right hand as I heard another car door slam.

Gripping the letter opener behind me, I hopped around the desk and back to the couch. Just as I dropped back onto the couch and swung my feet up onto the coffee table, Graham walked back into the room carrying two five-gallon gas cans. Trying to work quickly but unobtrusively, I began sawing at the tape that bound my wrists behind my back. But given my awkward position, the effort was painstakingly slow.

Now wearing gloves, Graham took the cap off the cans and began sloshing gas liberally around the room, starting behind the desk and working his way back toward the door. Trying to move the letter opener only with my hands and wrists, I said, "Denny, I really don't think that this is such a good idea."

He set the first can down and picked up the second. "And if you were me, you'd do what at this point?"

"I'd give myself up and confess to killing Toby, pleading temporary insanity because you saw your big business deal going down the drain and you desperately needed the money."

"Yeah, I'm sure that one of those famously liberal Flathead County juries would buy that. Maybe you could defend me."

Continuing to saw at the tape behind my back, I said, "Well, all things considered, I'd probably have to disqualify myself for having a conflict of interest. But I'd be happy to recommend someone."

He laughed. "I'm sure you would, especially at this point. Christ, Matthews, you're completely full of shit. Thanks for the offer, but I think I like my plan better than yours."

With that, he sloshed the last of the gas around the area immediately in front of the door. As he did, I felt the tape around my wrists start to give.

Graham pitched the gas can into the corner of the room and backed away toward the door. He took off the gloves, reached into his pocket and came out with a box of matches. Standing near the door at the far edge of the pool of gasoline, he said, "Well, don't think it hasn't been fun, Dave, but I think it's time for me to be on my way. When you get to hell, say hello to your buddy Martin for me."

He slid the box open, took out a match and struck it. Working frantically now, I finally managed to cut through the last of the tape just as the flame burst to life at the tip of the match. Graham watched as my hands came free, smiled, and said. "Too late, asshole."

Diving forward, I snatched a large ashtray from the coffee table and hurled it at his head. He ducked out of the way, moving into the room rather than out of it. The ashtray sailed by his head, flying harmlessly out into the hall behind him, and just as it did, the flame of the match reached his fingers. Swearing, he dropped the match into the pool of gasoline at his feet and the floor around him exploded into flame.

The next three or four seconds unfolded over an eternity as the sheet of flame flew across the room toward Krause's desk. Screaming, Graham slapped ineffectively at the flames that were shooting up the legs of his pants. But in his panic, he remained rooted to the floor, rather than trying to escape out into the hallway.

I knew that the fire would be upon me before I could free my legs, and I also realized that I had no chance to make it through the doorway, which was already burning fiercely. Moving desperately, I pushed myself up off the couch, hopped two steps to my right, and launched myself through the plate glass window.

I hit the ground five or six feet below the window, breaking the fall with my hands, but still landing hard on my left shoulder and banging my head again. A bolt of searing pain shot through my whole body, but I forced myself to concentrate on rolling away from the building until I finally came to rest against a forklift that had been left in the mill yard. I had one last blurry impression of the dry cedar office building bursting into flame before I lost consciousness for the second time that night.

37

It's just after ten o'clock on a chilly night late in August. For the last nine hours, I've known the identity of Sarah Parker's killer, but his secret remains safe with me. I'm sitting at the end of my dock, drinking Scotch and trying to decide how to proceed, when he walks out onto the dock, sits down next to me and says, "You know, don't you?"

"Yes, I do."

In the silence that follows, we watch the lights of a small boat, a few hundred yards out, working its way north up the lake. Without looking at me, he says softly, "So who did she tell?"

I explain that Parker had protected him to the end, and that it was only an unlikely and unlucky combination of circumstances that led me to his name. He sighs, nodding his understanding. Then, over the next several minutes, he explains as best he can the chain of events that led him first to betray his wife and then to impulsively kill his lover in a fit of rage when she threatened to expose their affair. He accepts his responsibility and makes no self-serving excuses for any of these incomprehensible and irredeemable actions. When he has finished, we sit quietly again for another several minutes, staring out into the blackness across the lake. Then I turn to him and say, "You know what you have to do."

"Yes, I do."

I hand him my cell phone and watch as he scrolls through the phone book, stopping at Chris Williamson's home number. He highlights the number, poises his finger over the 'Send' button and says, "Do you mind?"

Shaking my head, I rise to my feet and begin walking back up toward the foot of the dock.

The sound of a shot fractures the quiet stillness of the night and I turn to see him slowly teeter and slip into the lake, taking with him both the cell phone and the gun he'd apparently concealed under his sweatshirt.

I race to the end of the dock, dive into the water, and catch him by the collar about five feet below the surface. I pull him toward the shore and then drag him, obviously dead, onto the beach where scarcely two weeks earlier I had laid the body of Sarah Parker.

I stand there for several minutes unable to move, shaking and weeping over the body of the man who had once been my friend. Finally, I gather myself, go back up to the house and call Chris. And then, still dripping wet and in a state of shock, I walk slowly up the road to the West Shore Inn.

Alice answers the door and realizes immediately that something has gone terribly wrong. Shaking her head, she steps away, attempting to escape for a few precious seconds the unthinkable news that she knows instinctively must be coming. She begins sobbing even as I reach out my arms to gather her to me and tell her that Bill is dead.

38

"I'd say you don't look any worse for the wear," Chris said as he walked into my hospital room, "but that would be a total crock of shit. The fact of the matter is, you look like hell."

It was the middle of the afternoon, five days after my escape from the fire that had destroyed Phil Krause's office and roasted Denny Graham to a crisp. After taking two serious blows to the head within the span of a couple of hours, I'd been admitted to KRMC with a concussion, a dislocated shoulder, and a body full of cuts and stinging abrasions that had resulted from my dive through Krause's window and a slide across the hardened ground beneath it.

The shoulder injury was relatively minor, although the doctors insisted that I wouldn't be swinging a golf club comfortably for another month or so. They also promised that the ugly cuts and scrapes on the left side of my face would heal without leaving any permanent scars.

They were much more concerned about the fact that, for the first three days after my escape, I'd suffered from splitting headaches and extremely blurred vision. But a battery of tests had indicated no apparent brain damage and by Sunday morning my vision had returned to normal and the headaches had finally abated, for the most part at least.

The doctors insisted on holding me another thirty-six hours for observation, but they finally relented a little after noon on Monday and told me that I could go home after I promised that I'd continue to get a lot of bed rest and that I'd refrain from hurling myself through the windows of any more burning buildings for at least another week.

Chris had been in and out of my hospital room more often than any member of the medical staff, attempting to mask his concern for my well-being behind a thin facade of bullshit-as-usual. But his genuine relief at my recovery was written all over his face.

I'd finally been able to tell my story coherently around mid-day on Thursday. On Friday, the County Attorney dismissed all charges against Steve Helstrom, and Chris happily released Steve from jail. The doctors allowed Steve, Karen and Bob to visit briefly on Friday night so that they could express their gratitude.

To their credit, the editors of the local paper gave even more prominence to the coverage of Steve's release than they had to the stories surrounding his arrest. And in a front-page article in Sunday's edition, they also reported that, in memory of his son Toby, Robert Martin had donated the bulk of the family's Flathead Valley property to the Flathead Land Trust with the provision that the property remain in its natural state, undeveloped in perpetuity.

As a result of the fire that destroyed its main office as well as a lack of logs, the Krause Mill was now closed. Its eighty employees were laid off, and the economic effect of the closing was beginning to ripple through the valley. But a surprisingly upbeat Phil Krause was already working to rebuild the office and to reconstruct the files and other materials that had been lost in the fire. More important, he was reportedly close to signing a deal that would allow him to cut a new stand of timber that was located on private land.

Chris appeared with my car keys and a change of clothes just as I was signing the last of the forms that would finally allow me to get the hell out of the hospital. I handed the signed forms to the nurse who thanked me, smiled at Chris, and then left the room.

"Thanks for your support," I said. "I know that you'll take a great deal of comfort from the fact that I feel a lot better than I look."

"Christ, I hope so, because your left profile is not going to be getting you any hot dates for a while."

Ignoring that, I went into the bathroom and changed out of the hospital gown into the clothes that Chris had dug out of my closet. When I came out, zipping up my Dopp kit, he said, "You'll no doubt be interested to know that Ed Ramsey was arrested in Vegas this morning. A Nevada highway patrolman spotted his pickup outside a fleabag motel a couple of miles off the Strip. The Nevada cops searched the truck and found a .38 caliber revolver hidden up under the seat. Ramsey's lawyered up and insists that he'll fight extradition, but we'll get him and the gun back up here before long. I'll give long odds that a ballistics check will prove that the gun fired the bullets that killed Frank Kane."

I nodded my agreement, thinking sadly that the loss of Toby Martin and Frank Kane to two losers the likes of Denny Graham and Ed Ramsey was another of life's unfathomable tragedies. Just then the nurse returned with a wheelchair, insisting that hospital regulations required that I be wheeled at least as far as the front door. Taking the path of least resistance, I dropped into the chair.

Ever the gentleman, especially in the presence of an attractive young nurse, Chris volunteered to wheel me out of the room and down the hall. The three of us made our way to the front door where I got out of the chair, thanked the nurse for all her attention over the last several days, and then walked gratefully out into the warm sunny afternoon.

Chris walked me over to my car in the parking lot and handed me the keys. He stood there for a moment, looking at me and slowly shaking his head. Then he said, "Please tell me you were not stupid enough to deliberately bait that cretin into attacking you as a means saving Steve Helstrom."

"Sorry, I'm neither brave enough nor foolhardy enough, whichever the case would be, to have considered doing something like that. I fully intended to dump the whole mess into your lap at breakfast the next morning and it never occurred to me that Graham might decide to come after me before I could do so."

Chris nodded and looked away for a moment in the direction of the hospital behind me. Then he looked back and sighed. "Yeah, well, just don't think that you can use a lame-assed excuse like this to get out of tennis on Wednesday night."

"I wouldn't dream of it. I'm afraid that I'll probably have to ask Rusty to play for me this week, but I'll definitely be there for dinner and drinks after the match, so I'll see you then, if not before. And thanks, Chris."

"Yeah, whatever," he said, smiling. Then he gave me a small wave and walked off across the lot to the spot where a deputy had left his department SUV.

***

I opened the door of my Bimmer, pitched my Dopp kit onto the passenger's seat, and, still feeling stiff and sore all over, settled gingerly into the driver's seat. I fired up the engine, opened the sunroof, and cued up a Lucinda Williams playlist before pulling out of the lot.

Given that we were now well into peak season in the Flathead, it took me a good twenty minutes to make my way from the hospital at the north end of Kalispell to the four-lane highway at the south end of town. At that point most of the tourists pulled their motor homes, campers, boats and trailers into the right-hand lane, finally clearing the left lane for those of us who were anxious to drive somewhat faster than twenty-five miles per hour.

Another fifteen minutes later, I waited for a line of traffic in the northbound lane to clear and turned left off Highway 93. As I rolled down the hill onto Angel Point Road, the forest rose up to meet me, and the fresh clean scent of the pines flooded into the car. The sunlight out of a delft-blue sky filtered through the leaves of the trees, dappling the road in front of me, and in the woods off to my left, a doe and two fawns turned to watch me pass. All things considered, it was a great day to be alive and heading back home to the lake.

With no reason to hurry, I drove slowly along the narrow winding road, rolling up and down the hills, savoring the moment. Three hundred yards from my own driveway, I passed the West Shore Inn and started at the sight of the gates standing open, the "For Sale" sign nowhere in evidence.

My heart sinking, I pulled off to the side of the road and killed the engine. Then I dragged myself out of the car, closed the door behind me, and walked across the road to the head of the driveway. I stood there for the next several seconds and stared at the open gate, a flood of memories pouring through my mind, wondering to whom the realtor had finally sold the property.

I stepped through the gate and started slowly down the drive. As the road curved gently, the view unfolded, revealing a tan SUV with Flathead County plates parked in front of the house. And out on the kitchen deck, leaning against the rail in a pose so achingly familiar that it took my breath away, a tall thin woman with hair the color of late summer wheat stood looking out at the lake.

My heart pounding, I stopped dead in my tracks fifty feet short of the deck, afraid to move or even to breathe for fear that the sight before me would dissolve. Then a ground squirrel ran chattering across the road and Alice glanced up at the sound to see me standing there.

She stood still, watching as I moved slowly down the drive. I reached the house, stepped tentatively onto the deck and stopped, not knowing what to say or do next. For a long moment she continued to hold my gaze, her deep blue eyes steady and strong. Blinking back a tear, she flashed me the most tentative of smiles.

And then finally, after the longest ten months of my life, she closed the distance between us, pulled me gently into her arms, and laid her head on my shoulder. "Jesus, Dave," she whispered, "you look like hell."

Author's Note

In August of 1924, my grandfather, then a young man with a wife and two small boys, borrowed a car and drove 116 miles from Missoula to Kalispell, Montana. There he bought at a government auction three lots on the southwest shore of Flathead Lake. He paid one hundred dollars each for the lots, and the Government Land Office generously allowed him to pay twenty-five dollars down on each one and then to pay off the balance over three years at twenty-five dollars a year. He took final title to the properties on September 6, 1927.

His father-in-law (my great-grandfather) thought that my grandfather was crazy and demanded to know why in the hell he would buy property on the lake when he didn't even have a car which he could use to get there. But my grandfather had faith in his own future and in that of the Flathead. Shortly after buying the land, he acquired a car and began driving back and forth from Missoula to one of the lots he had purchased. He built a small cabin on the lot and over the years he expanded the cabin and added a boathouse and a dock. Over the next fifty years or so, through the spring, summer, and fall, and occasionally during the winter, he and his family drove up to the lake whenever they could, spending whatever time they could manage on one of the most beautiful spots in the country.

Initially, at least, it was no easy trip. The distance from their home in Missoula to the cabin at the lake was about seventy-five miles, and early on, the roads were bad and the tires fragile. Flat tires along the way were simply part of the experience, and my grandfather's record was thirteen flat tires on one trip alone. But still he persevered, and although I'm told that the air often turned blue on such occasions, the reward at the end of the journey was well worth the price of a few flat tires and over-heated radiators.

My Grandfather at the Lake, circa 1960

Growing up, and into his own adulthood, my father spent as much time as he possibly could at the lake and, if anything, came to love it even more than my grandfather. He ultimately wound up with one of the other two lots that my grandfather had originally purchased and, following in his father's footsteps, he built a small cabin on the lot, which he gradually expanded to accommodate his own growing family. As children, my brothers, sisters and I reveled in our time at the lake. We also carried about ten billion rocks of varying sizes to fill the cribs of the dock that my father built there. Unlike the rather flimsy dock that my grandfather had constructed, this one has stood the test of time and remains capable still of withstanding anything that an occasionally very violent lake can throw at it. Helping to build it remains one of the fondest memories of my childhood.

The cabin my father built at the lake, 1971

As my fictional character, Dave Matthews, suggests, for those people raised in the Flathead, the area and the lake in particular get into your blood. Everyone in my family still has a very strong attachment to Flathead Lake and the ten weeks I spend there every summer are the highlight of my year. I could never imagine spending a summer anywhere else and now, nearly a century after he made that long trip to Kalispell, I remain eternally grateful to my grandfather for ignoring the advice of his father-in-law. And, for what it's worth, those lots that my grandfather bought for one hundred dollars apiece in 1924 are now worth, with improvements, well over a million dollars each. If only he had bought a few more...

I'm extremely grateful to Wayne and Linda Muhlestein who have shared the most beautiful spot on the lake with my wife and me for the last twenty-five years. They are the best of friends, and I look forward to seeing them every year. Thanks again to Gene Robinson and the folks at Moonshine Cove for their efforts with this book.

Thanks to Leslie Budewitz who offered legal advice, and I'm especially grateful to Lisa and Kim, the Bling-Bling Sisters, who continue to do such an excellent job as co-presidents of the fan club.

Portions of this manuscript were written at the Stoner Creek Mercantile in Lakeside. Thanks to Randy Wienke for providing the space.

About the Author

James L. Thane was born and raised in western Montana. He has worked as a janitor, a dry cleaner, an auto parts salesman, a sawyer, an ambulance driver, and  a college professor. Always an avid reader, Thane was introduced to the world of crime fiction at a tender age by his father and mother who were fans of Erle Stanley Gardner and Agatha Christie, respectively. He began his own writing career by contributing articles on intramural basketball games to his high school newspaper. Jim is active on Goodreads, and you may also find him on Facebook, on Twitter, and at www.jameslthane.com. He divides his time between Scottsdale, Arizona and Lakeside, Montana.